Sherlock Holmes
Consulting Detective

Volume Nineteen

Airship 27 Productions

Sherlock Holmes Consulting Detective Volume 19

"The Lost Gospel" & "The Rhymes of Death" © 2023 Ray Lovato
"The Adventure of the Professor's Plummet" © 2023 Jonathan Casey
"The Quest for Guinevere" © 2023 I.A. Watson

Cover illustration ©2023 Howard Simpson
Interior illustrations © 2023 Rob Davis

Editor: Ron Fortier
Associate Editor: Jonathan Sweet
Production designer: Rob Davis
Promotion and marketing manager: Michael Vance

Published by
Airship 27 Productions
www.airship27.com
www.airship27hangar.com

ISBN: 978-1-953589-59-0

Printed in the United States of America

10 9 8 7 6 5 4 3 2 1

Sherlock Holmes
Consulting Detective

Volume XIX

TABLE OF CONTENTS

Sherlock Holmes

in

THE LOST GOSPEL

by
Ray Lovato

There were many cases that Sherlock Holmes and I were involved in that were of minor importance and some the outcome of which held the most major consequence. But little did I realize on that crisp March afternoon when we first met a member of the clergy that we were about to be thrust into an intrigue that would have the entire foundation of two religion's beliefs resting in the balance.

It was late one afternoon that I was sitting near the small fire in our study, a large copy of *Walsh's Retrospect Quarterly Compendium of Medicine and Surgery 1870* safely nestled in my lap, as Holmes was across the room hunched over his acid-scarred table with test tubes filled with a ghastly smelling liquid being slowly transported from one vial to the next. He had been at this task for well over three hours filling the place with a pungent stench.

"I say, Holmes, how long are you going to fill the room with that refulgent odor?"

"Sorry, old boy, I'm almost done with this rotting flesh," came the reply.

"Rotting flesh. Good lord, where did you get a handful of flesh from?"

My query was never answered as there was a gentle knock at our door.

"Come in, Mrs. Hudson," my companion said, knowing, I assume, from her footfalls and distinctive knock that it was our landlady.

""Mr. Holmes, you have a visitor," she announced in a hushed and almost reverent tone. "It's a man of the cloth to see you.""

"I wonder what charity that they are collecting for now," my companion said, placing the glass tube gently down into its holder.

"I don't think he's a parish priest," Mrs. Hudson said. "He's a right proper clergyman. A bishop or some such." She then made the sign of the cross over herself in a reverential display.

"A right bishop," said I, "then perhaps he's here to save your soul, Holmes," I ventured in jest.

"Dear Watson, I dare say that it would take more than a bishop to save my poor soul from eternal damnation."

"Sherlock Holmes," Mrs. Hudson exclaimed," don't you even jest about something like that."

"A thousand pardons, Mrs. Hudson. I meant no disrespect. By all means, let's not keep our guest waiting another second longer and please show him up."

With that, Mrs. Hudson started back down the stairs and brought the man of the cloth to our door.

In moments, there in our doorway stood a rather portly man of medium build with thick white eyebrows and a shock of receding white hair. He was dressed from head to toe in black and red. He wore red shoes, black trousers covered by a black cassock, a full length dress-like garment with reddish piping. He had a bright scarlet cape and a brilliant red ceremonial sash. On his head was a biretta, a four pointed square hat with a tassel on top, also red. He stood hunched in our entrance as bright as an ornament from a Christmas tree.

"I am Cardinal Alexander Higby of St. George's Church of York," he began, "I have come on a matter of great urgency."

I immediately stood up to greet our guest. Holmes followed suit.

"Can I trouble you for something to drink?" The clergyman immediately limped towards the settee across from the fireplace and gingerly set himself down.

"Your Eminence, I believe is the proper way to address a Cardinal," Holmes began, "please accept a glass of brandy from Dr. Watson there. I am Sherlock Holmes. But I assume that you know that, or else you would not have traveled so far and so quickly to come to us."

I had filled a glass with brandy and was handing it to the Cardinal when he said, "How did you know I have traveled a long distance and quickly? I have not told you anything about myself yet."

"It is obvious from the dust and dirt collected on your wrinkled vestments that you have been traveling a great distance and have not taken time to stop and refresh or stop for a night's rest. There is sweat collected on your white collar even though it is a brisk day showing that you have been cooped up inside your coach for quite some time. The apparent pain in your lower extremities shows the torment you have inflicted on your body by being jostled around in a carriage for many hours on end. The intense thirst was another sign of your long journey that wasn't to be interrupted for any purpose."

"Why that is remarkable. I have been traveling for two and one half days, making the usual five day trip to London from York in half the time. And time is truly of the essence, Mr. Holmes. And the fate of the Catholic Church hangs in the balance."

"That sounds rather ominous, your Eminence." Holmes said settling himself down in his chair and reaching for his long-stem cherry wood pipe and tobacco tin. "Do continue."

The clergyman gulped down the brandy and held the glass towards me. I dutifully took the tumbler and refilled it to the rim and presented it to him.

"You come well thought of in both Catholic and Anglican circles, Mr. Holmes. I have followed your exploits as chronicled by Dr. Watson in *The Strand*. And the Most Reverend Oliver Burton Armstrong, Archbishop of York, has firsthand knowledge of your skills and judicious practice. He is well aware of how you handled the affair with the First Anglican Church and the Naughton Preparatory School."

"Yes," said I, "I recall that. It involved Mrs. Hudson's young nephew Herbert. I believe I wrote it up as *The Most Unusual Dichotomy*." But I had cause to suddenly pause. "Did you say the Archbishop of York? Isn't he Anglican? Not Catholic like yourself?"

"Yes, Dr. Watson, he is. I come here on his behalf, as well as my own."

My confusion was immediate. Why would a Catholic Cardinal be entreating our aid on behalf of an Anglican Archbishop? The Anglican Church and the Catholic Church are in total opposition to one another. They have been since the time of Henry the VIII when the king formed the Church of England in 1534. What could the connection be between the Catholic Cardinal Higby and the Anglican Archbishop Armstrong of York?

"And what is of such great interest to you and this other Archbishop?" Holmes asked bringing a lit match up to the bowl of his pipe.

"It is a matter taking place in the Holy See in Rome, even as we speak. It concerns a lost gospel that was recently uncovered several years ago in Egypt during the excavation of a small temple near the city of Akhimen. This parchment codex is purported to be the Gospel of Simon Peter, the first pope of the Catholic Church. It had been lost to the ages; but had been referred to in the writings of Marcellus the Roman historian in 102 A.D., and Bishop Achanas of Nicene in 125 A.D., and the Bishop Eusebius of Alexandria in 217 A.D."

Cardinal Higby held his glass up for a refill which I promptly obliged him, then set myself down in my usual chair opposite my companion to discourage my role as servant to his grace.

"And what makes this gospel so important?" said Holmes.

"The parchment scroll has been kept in the Vatican Apostolic Library in secret for several years, untouched by the order of the popes. There are over one hundred and fifty thousand manuscripts there from the first century onwards, most of them yet to be translated. But our new pontiff, Pope Leo

XIII, has opened up the Apostolic Library for research and study of all the old texts that have been lying in state there. It has taken several years for the Gospel of Simon Peter to be translated, but it finally has. And it will be a disaster for the Catholic Church if its contents are revealed, as it will shake the very foundations of our religion." He took a big swallow of his brandy and gulped it down.

"And how would that be?" said I, now leaning forward in my chair.

"The gospel contradicts the teachings of the Gospels of Matthew, Mark, Luke, and John, the Holy Books that make up the canon of the New Testament, shattering the foundation of the church. It destroys the very template of the uninterrupted papal rule, stating that Judas was to be the first pope. The line of papal succession was to have started with Judas, not Simon Peter.

The Cardinal looked down at his half empty glass.

"It speaks of the '*Il Culto di Pietro L'empio*', the Cult of Peter the Unholy which vilified him as the betrayer of Christ. If the Holy Catholic Church isn't based on Peter being the original pope then our entire religion is false."

"The rift between the Anglican Church and the Roman Catholic Church is wide enough now after Pope Leo XIII recently issued his *Apostolicae Curae*, an encyclical, where in the pontiff claims to invalidates the Anglican Church's claim to being a recognized religion under God. It has only inflamed tensions between the two religions."

"Wouldn't this repudiation be a good thing for the Church of England?" Holmes said, raising an eyebrow and taking a long draw on his pipe.

"This would be a great boon for the Archbishop of Canterbury," Cardinal Higby said emphatically. "And it would cause another Holy War between the Church of England and the Holy Roman Catholic Church. The world seems to be inching toward great unrest as it is. Conflict on such a grand scale as this is unthinkable. That is why the Archbishop of York and I want to stop this before it comes to pass." He took a long swallow on the last of his drink.

"It takes a crisis for two great religions to come together," my friend said with a tinge of sarcasm.

"Yes, so it seems." Higby set his glass in his lap. "I'm sure that his Most Reverend Thomas Embury-Roberts Walker, the Archbishop of Canterbury, would relish this information with much passion. It would destroy the Holy See in Rome, making the Anglican Church the predominant religion in the empire.

"So I take it you are undertaking this mission without his approval?"

"Without his approval and certainly without his knowledge," the Cardinal replied. "The Archbishop of Canterbury is the supreme leader and shepherd of the Anglican Church. The Archbishop of York is second in the hierarchy of the Church of England. But my friend Armstrong is definitely the more level-headed. That is why he came to me."

"And you know of this plot how?" Holmes asked.

"The Archbishop Armstrong received the information from one of the acolytes in the service of Archbishop Walker of Canterbury. This acolyte has always been friendly with the Archbishop York. He relayed to him that Archbishop Walker of Canterbury has had an agent in the inner circle of the Vatican who is loyal to the Church of England for some time and he is willing to smuggle this newly translated document out of the Vatican to be delivered to Canterbury for presentation to the world. And it is slated to happen soon."

Holmes took another draw from his pipe, blowing a stream of smoke far into the room.

"And my part in all of this is to intercept this gospel and deliver it to you?"

"Yes, Mr. Holmes, that would be most ideal. I would then be able to return it to the Vatican so that the spy could be exposed and the gospel could be safely put back into the archives for all eternity." With that pronouncement, the Cardinal hoisted his glass once more in my direction. I decided quickly that his story did, indeed, deserve another drink.

"With so much at stake," Holmes said, "I don't know how I could refuse such a case. Dr. Watson and I will intercede on your behalf. If you would give me all the particulars on the matter, who to contact when we get to Rome, we shall be off as soon as we can pack and secure transportation to the coast."

"God be with you, my son," Higby said raising his glass in a salute to us. Then he swallowed half its contents.

We packed our luggage and in less than one hour we had made our way to Victoria Station and onto the Continental to the coast to catch the ferry at Dover to Calais. The Channel crossing was rather rough in the spring and we spent the entire trip inside the ship. At Calais we transferred to one of the newer French trains running through the eastern provinces all the way to northern Italy where the government had recently incorporated the railway lines to form the Rome Express, again making sure that all roads lead to Rome. The trip took less than three days in duration. My time was spent in reading the *Wound and Disease Care by the Royal College of Physicians* and Holmes buried himself in a score of newspapers that he replenished at every station along the way.

It was late in the evening when we disembarked from our train in the Eternal City. Holmes suggested that we seek out our lodgings and start fresh the next day. We secured an Italian version of a growler, a four-seater cab with ample luggage space on top, that was parked by the train station and made our way to *Locand di San Giuseppe*, the Inn of Saint Joseph, only about a ten minute walk to St. Peters Square and the Leonide Hill, the palace of the Holy Father. We experienced little trouble checking in as Holmes' was fluent in both Italian and Latin.

We bade each other good night and agreed to meet about eight the next morning and enjoy a breakfast at the inn. The evening passed uneventfully.

The next morning we were greeted by an ominous overcast sky. Storm clouds threatened the Seven Hills of Rome. We were pleasantly surprised by the size and the superb taste of the *gelatina e pane e caff'e e succo di frutt,* very strong coffee and jelly and pastry and fruit. A truly splendid way to start my day even under cloudy, threatening skies.

From there we went off to the Vatican Apostolic Library, which was slightly north of the famous Sistine Chapel, just east of the glorious St. Peter's Basilica. Once there we were to ask for Cardinal Raphael Dominic, Proctor of the Archives of the Apostolic Library. It was about a five minute cab ride in the brisk morning air when we approached the steps of the Library. It was a grand edifice in Roman classical-style, its pillars magnificent towers of strength supporting statues of saints.

We entered through the heavy brass doors to find ourselves in a large atrium with frescos on all of the walls and overhead on the vaulted ceilings. As we passed through the door, we realized that stationed behind us were four Swiss guards in their orange and blue striped uniforms and puffed pantaloons, lances in hand, standing at attention, guarding the entrance. A little way ahead of us we spotted a young priest with a pronounced limp carrying an armful of books crossing our path.

"Excuse me, Father," Holmes said. "Could you be so kind as to direct us to Cardinal Dominic?"

"Yes, of course," he nodded. "His office is the first door right down the hall to your left."

My companion thanked the priest and we made our way toward the opened door. There we found a priest seated behind an ornate walnut desk with a small stack of books on one end and several papers piled neatly on the other.

Holmes rapped lightly on the opened door. "Cardinal Dominic? I am Sherlock Holmes. This is Dr. Watson. I believe you're expecting us?"

A short, stocky man stood up. His face was a pleasant oval with brownish muttonchops dropping down from under his four-pointed red beretti. He was dressed similar to Cardinal Higby but his garb was much more ornate. The lace around his cassock was intricately embroidered. His scarlet watered-silk stole and sash seemed to sparkle with the candle light in his office space. It was obvious that he was a man of great importance. He stepped to the side of his desk and stretched out his hand.

Cardinal Dominic spoke. "Yes, Mr. Holmes, I'm so very glad to meet you and the doctor. I have a slight knowledge of your English language. I shall use it to the best of my ability. I am so very glad that you could make it here as quickly as you could. I would like to begin as soon as my—"

"A thousand pardons, Your Grace, I am late from morning prayers again." The interruption came from a priest in his forties standing in the doorway. He was as tall as Holmes himself, with a strong, handsome face. His dark, wavy hair curled back over his ears from a pronounced widow's peak.

"Ahh, gentlemen, let me introduce Monsignor Giuseppe Nicola, my assistant."

The priest, garbed in a black cassock with red piping, a short black cape, and black sash, extended his strong right hand to shake both mine and my companions and stepped back to the doorway unobtrusively.

"Good," the Cardinal said. "Now that we are all here, let us proceed to the vaults where the codex is stored. If you gentlemen will follow me." He gestured towards the door and we stepped back to follow him out into the grand vestibule.

I must admit that I was slightly awestruck by the sight of my present surroundings. Even in the dappled light of the overcast sky streaking in through the great windows on the massive alcoves of the vaulted ceilings, the great expanse shined in a soft golden glow. The pillars were gold embossed with blue jewel inlays. Every wall was covered with two-story frescos in the most vivid colors of Christian images, saints, apostles, and depictions of scenes from the Holy Scriptures. The floors were giant black and white squares of travertine tile that reflected the glory of the scenes above it. There was an unearthly majesty to the rows and rows of books beautifully preserved on marble shelves and intricately carved teakwood shelving.

The first floor stretched on for one hundred yards of the most ornate and dazzling masonry work and stained glass artistry I had ever seen. Half-way through the main aisle a priest who was as wide as he was tall waddled up to the Cardinal and whispered something in his ear.

"You will have to excuse me for a moment," he said stepping aside. "There is something that commands my immediate attention. But Monsignor Nicola will take you to the vaults. I will join you there as soon as possible."

We continued on with Monsignor Nicola taking the lead.

"Monsignor Nicola," the detective began.

"Please, Mr. Holmes, when it is just we three, call me John. I was raised in New York of Italian-American parents and I really don't like to stand on all this formality."

"Then I hope that you will call me Sherlock, John. Are you often late to your duties at the Library due to your pugilistic pursuits?"

John stopped and turned to face Holmes. "How could you possibly know that?"

"Elementary. Your knuckles are slightly purplish and your hands are both swollen. They show the unmistakable indentations of tape wrappings."

"Exodus 15, verse 6, 'Your right hand, oh Lord, is majestic.' I'm afraid you have found me out, Sherlock," Nicola said. "I had always wanted to be a fighter, but my father wanted me to follow my uncle into the service of the Lord. My uncle is the Archbishop of New York. That helped me in acquiring this post in the Vatican at my young age. But I still keep up with weight training and also target practice. It's in my blood as a New York juvenile," he chuckled.

"Your secret is safe with me," Holmes said.

Soon we approached a Swiss Guard standing at attention next to a slightly rusted iron gate at the far end of the immense hall. It was a small man gate, totally out of place in such splendid surroundings. The soft glow of several lanterns flickered from inside the enclosure. The guard stepped aside as the Monsignor stopped, reached down into the deep pocket of his cassock and withdrew a ring of keys. He flipped through them until he found the one he liked and then inserted it into the keyhole. He turned the key until the lock grudgingly gave way. He swung open the gate and we followed him into the narrow landing which immediately gave way to several steps that took us down to a large room that stretched out for what seemed like fifty square feet. It was ground level and was ringed with opaque windows with bars securely fastened. It was a plain, purely utilitarian room, stacked with tables and shelves holding reams of papyrus, parchment, rice

"Exodus 15, verse 6, 'Your right hand, oh Lord, is majestic.'"

paper, scrolls of every shape and size rolled up and fastened with string. On large tables lay ancient leather bound books open so that the hand drawn etchings, faded with time, could once again see the dim light of day.

"Gentlemen, I give you the secret archives."

"And aptly named," said I. "With all the dust down here you'd think you could afford a housekeeper."

"Dr. Watson, we don't wish to disturb the fragile parchments and codexes. The dust has been their companion since time immemorial. 'For dust thou art and dust thou shall return.' Genesis 3, verse19."

"Quite right," I agreed.

A few rows over I observed a thin priest of average height moving towards us in the dim light holding a lantern.

"Monsignor Nicola, *buongiorno*," the young man said.

"In English, please," the Monsignor said.

"How may I be of service to you?" the priest smiled.

"Good morning, Father Levitto," Nicola said. "We may have need of your lantern."

I cleared my throat with a slight cough. "And since this secret archive is under lock and key and guarded by the Swiss, where might this gospel safely be?"

"Come over here," Nicola motioned to follow him down a row of tables that stretched on for at least thirty paces. A ribbon of light shown down through the window onto the table. On the table sat three rolled parchment codexes, each one neatly tied with a brown string.

"And here they are. The three Gospels of Simon Peter," Nicola announced.

It seemed rather anti-climatic to me. Just these three fourteen inch wide rolls of parchment sitting in the dust on a dimly lit table.

"Three?" I inquired.

"Yes, Doctor. The first one speaks of the geography and tribal life of the Bedouin tribes. The everyday life. The second is the life and death of St. Peter and the Christ. The third scroll is a collection of psalms and prayers that closely resemble the Songs of David from the Old Testament."

"So it is the second scroll that is the most relevant and important of the three, I take it?" said Holmes.

"Yes," Nicola replied.

Holmes then asked if Father Levitto could bring the lantern closer to the table, took out his magnifying glass and bent down to inspect the parchments.

"Who inspected these scrolls last? And when?" he inquired.

"It was the Most Reverend Wilhelm Henkel, the foremost expert on Hebrew Aramaic languages. He finished them several weeks ago. That's when we discovered the, shall we say, true worth of these scriptures."

"Have they been moved since the Most Reverend Henkel sealed them up?" Holmes continued, his face now scant inches above the rolled papyrus.

"No," Nicola said. "No one except Cardinal Dominic, Father Levitto and I have been down here since he returned the scrolls. They have not been moved and are perfectly safe."

"Not exactly," Holmes snapped standing briskly up. "The second parchment, the one extolling the exploits of Simon Peter, has been stolen. The one before you is a fake."

As if the secret archive were not already as quiet as a tomb, it just became as silent as an entire graveyard.

"How in the deuce name would you know that, Holmes?" I asked.

"It's quite obvious, Watson. First, the dust pattern around the middle papyrus is different from the outline that is around the other two. When the middle one was picked up and replaced recently it wasn't put back precisely in the same spot. And the open edge of the rolled parchment is on the right side of the rolled paper. On the two outer scrolls it is facing the opposite direction of the middle tube."

Holmes dropped his small magnifier into the outer pocket of his jacket.

"Most importantly, the thief wanted to make sure that the fake scroll that replaced the real one had the same knot tied on it as the original three. Reverend Henkel used a simple noose knot to bind his papyrus rolls. But in his haste, he tied a knot identical to the slip knot, but instead inserted the bight from the long end of the string, not from the short end. The knot is not identical."

Holmes turned to face Father Levitto. "That was your mistake, wasn't it, Father?"

The detective reached out and grabbed the priest's arm to steady him as his pronouncement sank in. The lantern shook in his hand.

"If you would be so kind as to take hold of the lantern, Watson, and to bring it down to this level on Father Levitto's cassock," Holmes motioned to waist high on the still stunned man. "I believe that we will find a horizontal stripe of dust along the waistline of his black vestment where the dust from the papyrus that he rolled up has rubbed off on his garment. The detective then grasped the middle of Levitto's cassock and gave it a violent tear and split it apart.

"Mr. Holmes!" Nicola cried.

"Allow me to show you the vertical stripe left inside his vestment from the dust of the parchment being rolled up and smuggled out against his body past the guard at the gate."

And sure enough, there was the dusty imprint of a thin rolled impression inside of the priest's cassock.

"Since this is very fresh, it is not too late. You can still salvage some of your soul if you tell us what you did with the gospel of Simon Peter?" Nicola said. Holmes was now standing next to the quivering priest, the lantern casting an ominous shadow over the entire scene.

"I would suggest that you listen to the Monsignor and tell us where you delivered the gospel to while you still can." There was a fierce commanding tone in Holmes' voice. "Or these dead scrolls won't be the only things buried down here."

"It is God's will that the truth be revealed," Levitto protested. "I am doing His work. The lies about the Catholic Church will finally be told to all."

"So, you're the Anglican spy in the Vatican," I said.

"I am but God's messenger," he continued. "This false papacy must be destroyed."

"Father, please listen," Nicola said. "To tear down God's church is not God's work; it is the work of the Devil. You are committing blasphemy against the Lord Almighty. You must come to your senses."

"I am the only one who sees the one true path," he yelled.

"Then you must truly be blessed," Holmes said calmly. "Tell me, Father, are you the only one who God has spoken to with the truth of this revelation, or has he spoken to others here?"

"There is one more. Father DiPietro. He has seen the light also. We both know the truth uncovered by Reverend Henkel. I told him of what I found out while helping Henkel and he agreed to help me spread the word."

"Nothing like a zealot to tell you all you need to know," the detective said stepping back from Levitto. "Do you know where we can join DiPietro and help you spread this gospel to everyone who needs to see the light?"

"Yes, yes." There were tears in Levitto's eyes. "He is meeting with agents of the Archbishop of Canterbury tonight at the Colosseum to give them the divine proof." It was then that the realization of what he just revealed had come to him. "But you will never stop them. You are too late."

"Monsignor Nicola, do you know of this DiPietro?"

"Yes, I do," came his response.

"Good," said Holmes. "Then I suggest that we turn Levitto here over to the Swiss Guard and find DiPietro as soon as we can. Come, Watson, the game is afoot."

We rushed out of the archive as fast as our legs would carry us and reached the outside of the Apostolic Library just as the clouds continued to form heavily over the Leonid City.

"Come," Nicola said, "DiPietro works in the Chancery over on the far side of St. Peter's Square."

We ran across the square in front of St. Peter's Basilica, weaving through the throngs of devout Catholics there to take in the grandeur of the magnificent structure with its row of thirteen saints atop the far end of its wide parapet. It was no small feat bobbing around the crowd and the two fountains flanking the ancient Egyptian obelisk in the center of the piazza. The forecourt was designed to accommodate the greatest number of people as possible, it was said to hold about three hundred thousand pilgrims, to allow them to gather and receive the blessing from the pope from his window in the Vatican Palace. But this tradition had been discontinued by Pope Pius the IX when he withdrew into the Leonid City in protest of the Italian government annexing the Papal States in 1870. That would have made our dash nigh impossible. It was fortunate that the sky was overcast so that our sprint wasn't made in the heat of the midday sun.

We made it to the door of the Vatican Chancery Offices, a tall imposing classical structure supported by Doric columns. The Swiss Guards obviously recognized Monsignor Nicola and didn't move as we rushed past them and into the building. Its vestibule was imposing; its walls draped in medieval tapestries depicting Biblical scenes and representations of the sacraments. We continued past the score of priests in their daily routine of Vatican duties, following Nicola every step of the way.

He turned down a wide hallway, sliding on the polished marble floor, and continued straight ahead until he reached an open door. We followed him in, all of us now short of breath.

"*Dov'e padre DiPietro?*" Nicola huffed. The assembled throng all looked up, bewildered at the sudden interruption. Then a short proctor tilted his prince-nez and answered, "*Oggi non 'e entrato.*"

"He did not come in today," Nicola said between breaths.

"Damn," said Holmes, again apparently not appreciating the irony of swearing in the Vatican. "Do they know where he went?"

"*Sai dove potrebbe essere?*"

The proctor thought for a long second, then replied, "No."

"No need to translate," said I.

"Please thank them for us." He then turned to me. "Watson, I suggest that we get something to eat while we have some time as we have a date this late afternoon at the Colosseum. How far is that from here, John?"

Nicola, I assumed, had just got done thanking the priests for their indulgence. "It's about an hour on the other side of Rome from here. I should like to accompany you. I feel that I can be useful to you in navigating Rome."

"I would very much appreciate your participation. You look like a man who can take care of yourself in a skirmish." Holmes said. "Let's get lunch and prepare for the weather and our appointment tonight, shall we?"

And with that we were off.

Later that afternoon I placed my watch back in my vest pocket and moved over to my valise, took out my Webley service revolver and placed it on the end table. I still had the lingering taste of the superb pasta and bread that we had for lunch made by the inn-keeper's wife on my lips as I grabbed my ulster and placed my billycock on my head. I checked to see that the Webley was loaded and carefully slipped it into my outer coat pocket. Then I placed several spare cartridges into the other pocket, and left my room to join Holmes across the hall. Knocking twice, I was bade entrance. There was my friend pulling on his familiar Inverness and deer-stalker hat. He moved over to his valise and to locate his .45 short-barreled Webley and several spare cartridges. Finding it, he stood up and faced me once again.

"Well, all we need is for Monsignor Nicola to join us and we shall be on our way." He barely finished his sentence when there came a knock on his door. "It's me. John," the voice announced.

"Come in," my companion said.

John Nicola entered the room, dressed in a long black over coat, which was open, revealing a smart black suit and a vest with gold piping. His head was bare.

"Is this casual wear for a Monsignor?" I inquired.

"Easier to move around in than my cassock and robes," he smiled back.

"Pardon the weapon," Holmes said. "But I'm afraid it might be necessary tonight."

"No need to apologize," said Nicola. He patted the outside of his suit pocket. "I have my own Adams revolver here. It is Jeremiah 22, verse 7, that admonishes, 'I will prepare destroyers against thee. Everyone with his weapons.' So I thought I'd come prepared."

"A truly wise man that Jeremiah," said Holmes.

"I also have a clarence waiting outside. It will bring the four of us comfortably to the Colosseum." Nicola smiled. "The driver, Alberto, is a friend of the Church. He will take us there with all haste."

We stepped outside to a distant thunder clap and the beginning of a slight drizzle. Alberto urged his team of horses on and we started our trek east across Rome in the afternoon gloom. It was less than forty-five minutes when we were deposited at the north entrance to the magnificent structure, the Colosseum. The overcast skies could not diminish the golden tone of this five story travertine, limestone, and ancient concrete architectural wonder. The north side with its breathtaking arched entrance was still standing tall after all the centuries, a testament to its Roman builders.

Monsignor Nicola graciously paid the driver and we stepped out into the breezy drizzle, finding that we were going the opposite way against the crowd of tourists who were flocking out of the Colosseum due to the approaching inclement weather.

As we pushed through the crowd, Nicola stopped and pointed out, shouting in his husky voice, "*Guarda la*. Look there. It's a minor miracle. It's DiPietro."

I just caught a glimpse of a priest in a short black cape over his cassock darting into the entrance to the Colosseum. He was carrying a long tube wrapped in a canvas cloth, similar to a map case that a ship's captain would have.

We began to sprint forward, shoving the people out of our way to reach the front of the Colosseum. As we entered the magnificent arena, we spotted DiPietro standing at the top of the long stairway leading down to the subterranean area that was the floor of the mighty ancient oval. He was flanked by four thugs, all of medium build, with shocks of dark hair, three with wool caps, two in heavy short wool coats, one in an ankle length wide lapel long coat, and the third in a wool sweater. The thug in the sweater and one of his compatriots pulled pistols from their pockets and began firing at us, heedless of the crowd around us that was trying to make its way to the exit.

Screams filled the area as bullets ricocheted off the ancient stones. We all drew our weapons simultaneously and returned fire. The five villains immediately began to weave and duck. They then bolted back, pulling their bandanas, over their noses and ran down the stairway to the ruins below them.

Quickly, the three of us charged down the steps in front of us, arriving at the platform that the attackers had just vacated, crouched down, and returned fire. Several of our shots chipped away at the stones surrounding the quartet. Two of them paused to reload their revolvers before they turned and scampered down the remaining steps and reached the now damp Colosseum floor, taking cover behind the twenty-four foot pillars that once formed the perfect rows on the subterranean supports for the stone floor of the great arena. From their position of cover they sent a spray of bullets once more our way.

One bullet passed through the fold of the short cape of Holmes' Inverness, narrowly missing his shoulder by scant inches. As the other two of the thugs ducked behind the pillars to load their spent pistols, Holmes and Nicola did the same as I carefully spaced out my remaining shots to keep the villains at bay. Once reloaded, the detective carefully peered out from our vantage point at the thugs while I pulled several rounds from my pocket to fill the chambers of my trusty Webley.

The crooks took this pause in the volley on our side to turn and scamper along the row of the mossy floor of the great arena where mighty gladiators once strode into battle against each other or ferocious beasts. With their backs turned towards us, we immediately moved forward, reaching the safely of the first columns before they had the chance to turn and send a short barrage of shots our way.

Nicola popped out to send two shots towards the thieves, and then withdrew.

"Be judicious with your shots, John," Holmes admonished him. "We only have so many bullets left."

"*Si*," the Monsignor replied.

There was a short pause in the action.

"Holmes, I do believe that they have made a break for it into the rows behind them," said I.

"I agree, Watson."

The stones were arranged in vertical rows from where we stood, forming perfect rows to separate the floor of the Colosseum into a maze of rooms and alcoves, some that must have been closed off as compartments for the gladiators, some as pens and cages for the wild beasts to be released to the arena above and some as makeshift hospitals to mend the wounded or to store the more unfortunate combatants who did not survive the trial by combat.

We darted across to our right and carefully made our way from row to row using the mighty pillars as cover. I was in front of our line when I looked out to check that the row was clear and a shot rang out. The bullet flew past my shoulder and continued down the corridor.

"I think I've found them," I said.

"Be careful, old friend," Holmes replied.

The sky had opened up and it was now a steady drizzle descending around us on the basement of this grand Roman monument. As I gingerly poked my head out from the safety of my position, I saw one of the short jacketed villains making a dash for the stairway at the far south end of the mossy floor. I steadied my arm against the pillar, took careful aim, and fired off two shots. Both found their target squarely in the back as the crook immediately lurched forward and dove head first to the ground. I could see no map case in his hands.

"I do believe I got one, Holmes," I said.

"Good shot, Watson," said my companion." Let's move on carefully."

Holmes and I moved across the corridor. Nicola hesitated. "I'm going to move up this row and see if I can outflank them.

"A good plan," the detective said. "Use caution."

With that, Nicola began to creep up the row towards where the body lay lifeless.

"I think they are all going to make break for the stairway at the opposite end," Holmes said.

"Then perhaps I should follow the Monsignor's lead and travel up a separate corridor to gain on them," said I, pausing to fill the empty chambers of my revolver.

"A capital idea," the detective replied, "that way we can cover all three rows that they might choose to use."

Saying that, we split up, Holmes taking the next row over and we proceeded toward the south end of the Colosseum. It was my companion who encountered the first thug as he was making a mad dash up his aisle in an attempt to escape.

Through the opening between the rows I could see the thug attempt to run.

"Halt," the detective shouted, but to no avail.

The fleeing thief turned and fired three shots in Holmes' direction, all going wide. The detective held his ground, carefully took aim and fired off two shots. The crook twisted violently, slamming into the limestone column, and then slid down to the mossy earth. His hands, too, were empty.

I quickly turned my attention back to my own row ahead of me, quickening my pace to make up for the time that I had just spent watching Holmes dispatch the thug. The rain had now increased slightly, causing a small rivulet of water to cascade down the brim of my billycock obscuring my eyesight and obfuscating my hearing with its pitter patter sound. As I briskly passed an opening between rows, I obviously didn't see or hear DiPietro step out behind me and level his pistol at my back.

Suddenly, I heard a loud report from behind that startled me greatly. I turned just in time to see the rogue priest crumple, clutching his chest, and sink to the muddy ground. Slowly, Nicola stepped out from behind the stone pillar, gun still extended.

"Thank you, Monsignor. You surely saved my life."

"You would have done the same, Doctor." I looked down, still a tad bit shaken from my close brush with death, and saw that DiPietro was empty handed. It was now obvious that the fourth thief had the gospel.

"Look," Nicola said, turning around. "There is the other *'teppista'*—thug—getting away up the stairs at the end of the Colosseum."

I could see that the thief, his identity hidden by his bandana, was, indeed, carrying the gospel. The rain was still steady in its intensity.

"Hurry, we may still catch up to him," said Holmes.

Quickly we scrambled up the steps at the end of the Amphitheater and reached the entrance. Looking down we spotted the thief. He had stopped and was talking rather animatedly with another man in a black sweater sporting a beret. We ran as fast as we could to close the gap between us, dodging the people who were crossing the plaza trying to outrun the raindrops. Soon we found ourselves about thirty yards behind them when the thug wearing the bandana and holding the map case spotted us and set the pair in motion.

They bolted around the outer circle of the Colosseum and veered off to a large iron gate that separated the city by a stone wall from the other side of the rather tawdry appearing side of the town.

"This is the Jewish ghetto," Nicola huffed out as we passed through the gate which was protected by two Swiss guards huddled together under a small sycamore tree for protection from the rain. Once inside the ramshackle interior, the buildings seemed to lean on each other for support. Balconies were seemingly tied together by long lengths of rope with rows of laundry swaying in the rain. The streets, long and twisted, were cluttered with fruit carts and rugs. Old men in black suits and yarmulkes were departing their rickety chairs on either side of overturned barrels where they had been playing checkers. The place smelled of desperation and poverty.

Holmes used his height to our advantage and spotted the two slightly

Slowly, Nicola stepped out from behind the stone pillar..."

ahead of us.

"I'll follow them. Watson, you and John see if you can find a way to cut them off."

Holmes continued to push himself through the crowd. Nicola and I ran to the side of the throng and eventually made our way to a side street that turned to the right. It was a narrow thoroughfare, cluttered with large wicker baskets filled with damp hay. Carefully we wound our way through the maze of puddles and obstacles. When we reached the end of the street, we saw Holmes run past at the far end chasing the crooks ahead of him.

With that we sloshed off down the street. At the next intersection we spotted Holmes take another right down an alley. Sliding to a halt as we almost passed up the entrance to the small opening to the alley, the two of us splashed our way to come only a few yards behind the detective.

"Holmes, this is impossible," I shouted.

"Remember, they don't know where they are running to either, Watson. Sooner or later they will run out of options. Then they will be ours."

The two thugs reached the end of another street and at that intersection, they split up. The rogue with the map case went to the left. Holmes shouted above the storm that he would take him. The other one bolted to the right, so Nicola and I slid around the corner and gave pursuit. Running as fast as we could through the now flooded streets, we came to another intersection. We spied the thug running away about ten yards to the left of us.

Suddenly, a broom handle came swinging out from the corner of a building, catching him squarely in the chest, stopping him in his tracks, and knocking him back to a great puddle below. Out stepped Holmes standing over the thug with the beret now floating in the muddy water.

"We caught one," the detective said, "but not the one we wanted." There was no map case.

Nicola looked down the alley across from the one that Holmes had just stepped out from.

"I believe we might have lost him for good," Nicola said. "Down this street is the gate that we came in. We have circled back on ourselves. And since he is from Rome, he will surely know that's the only way in or out of this ghetto. And the guards close and lock the gate at sundown, which will be at any moment now that the rain has all but concealed the sun."

"It's bad enough that these people have to live like this, but they lock them in every night?" I said incredulously.

"The authorities say it is for their own good, Doctor." Nicola said.

"Hogwash," I said as the rain pelted the three of us.

"Well at least we know where the gospel is headed. We will return to the inn," Holmes said, "and check out and catch the first train to begin out journey back to Calais and England. We must get back to Canterbury before they do."

"I would like to accompany you," Nicola said. "I wish to see this carried out to its conclusion. I owe it to the Papacy and to myself."

"I would be honored to have you by our side, John," Holmes said.

And so would I, I said to myself.

It was half past ten after we had paid our bill at the inn and arrived at the train station and boarded the first train out to begin our journey home. There we secured a compartment for the three of us and hung up our coats. Holmes and Nicola had purchased several newspapers before we disembarked and I had removed from my valise *The Practical Guide to Emergency Field Surgical Techniques in Military Situations* by Colonel *Joseph Barrington Whimple, M. D.* A book I hadn't reread in many years.

After about some thirty minutes, Holmes stood up and moved toward the compartment door.

"If you'll excuse me, I'd like to check the passenger cars to get a look at the occupants on this train."

"Why, do you think that the thief is aboard this train?" said I.

"If we made this train to Calais, then we must assume that the thief also made the train," Holmes pronounced as he stood next to the door open.

"But how would you recognize him, Sherlock?" Nicola asked. "He was too far away from us at the Colosseum and he wore a bandana over his face."

"It would be rather presumptuous of me to think that I could recognize him now, as the rain would have washed away any clues as to his being in the Colosseum or ghetto. And I would assume that he wouldn't be so careless as to keep the gospel in his hands; but rather, he might have it secured under his seat or safely hidden up in the upper shelf above his head in his compartment."

"Then what purpose will it serve to check every compartment on this train?" I asked as Holmes began loosening his four square, rolled up one sleeve of his jacket, and disheveled his hair.

"Elementary, my dear Watson, I will eliminate all the passengers who do not fit the height and weight of our thief and then have a clear identification of the possible perpetrator so that when we see him again at Canterbury I will be able to pick him out as one of the gentlemen that I observed on this train." He gave his hair a final tousling. "Now, do I look sufficiently inebriated to pass as one who has spent the early evening in revelry?"

"Wait, Holmes," I said. "I might have something in my bag that should help you sell your ruse."

As I stood up the train rocked suddenly, throwing me off balance causing me to throw my hand out to steady myself against the window.

"Perhaps you should play the part of the drunken scoundrel," Holmes smiled.

I took my medical bag down from its perch above us, undid its latch and pulled out a small bottle of brandy. "Here, I keep this in my case if I need to sterilize a wound in an emergency. Taking a swig and holding it in your hand might further your act."

"Excellent, as usual, Doctor. I don't know what I'd do without your aid."

"You are a very formidable team," Nicola said.

"Thank you, Monsignor," I said graciously.

"Now to stumble into every compartment and take stock of their occupants." With that Holmes was off.

Settling into my seat across from Nicola, I began a conversation with him. "Tell me more about the contents of this gospel and what makes it so valuable to the Catholic Church."

"Simon Peter was a fisherman on the Sea of Galilee and one of the first disciples of Christ," Nicola began. "He became the unofficial leader of the twelve apostles as Christ favored him over all the others. Jesus announced that Peter was the rock upon which His church would be built, making Simon Peter the first pope. He is referred to as the Vicar of Christ. All the popes that followed are successors of St. Peter."

"So why is this new gospel so dangerous," I asked. "Wasn't the Bible written in stone since the time of Jesus?"

"No, my friend, the books of the Bible were a loose gathering of ancient texts in the early centuries after Christ's death. It wasn't until 382 A.D. that the Holy Roman Catholic Church convened the Council of Rome to formalize which texts would make up the books of the Bible. Those books that were included were the various books of the Old Testament plus Matthew, Mark, Luke and John, and Revelations which make up the bulk of the New Testament."

"So, Monsignor, where does this Gospel of Simon Peter come in?"

"It was only recently discovered in 1891 in the ruins of a temple in Akhimen in Egypt and just recently translated. And what it reveals will shake the very foundations and destroy the Catholic Church."

"How can this be?" I was now totally engrossed in Nicola's tale. I slipped my hand into my coat pocket, retrieved my pipe and my elaborately etched tin of Turkish tobacco. I carefully opened the case.

"The gospel significantly changes Peter's role in the Bible story and his importance to the Church. Especially concerning the last days of Christ's life. It gives a more detailed account of the Last Supper and Christ's crucifixion. Even Peter's life is changed."

"How so?" I placing a pinch of tobacco in the bowl.

"Well," Nicola continued, "there are twenty-seven canonical differences from the Holy Bible to this new account. Peter was married to Mary Magdalene according to this gospel. It was Herod who condemned Christ, not Pilate. Pilate tried to save Jesus."

Nicola paused. "It was Peter who betrayed Christ for thirty pieces of silver, not Judas. Peter was the traitor."

Lowering his eyes, Nicola then he gazed up slowly. "This gospel purports that it was Judas who Christ actually said that He wanted to be the rock upon which He wished to build his Church. Not Peter. The story that it was Peter was a conspiracy perpetrated by the four gospel writers for some unknown reason. The gospels of Matthew, Mark, Luke, and John would then be false."

You could have knocked me over with a feather. My faith had always leaned towards Protestant; but the Bible stories were well known to me. If this was in fact true, then the unbroken chain that the Catholic Church had based the power and authority of the pope on was indeed false. And the belief of the Church of England that the pope had no earthly sway over penitents and believers was the truth, and then religious belief in the Papacy would be turned upside down.

"But this is only one lost gospel. It can't be taken as fact," I said striking a match.

"Belief is a strong thing, Doctor. Men have gone to war for ages based on their beliefs, as you well know. Both sides will endorse either the veracity or the spurious nature of this claim. As usual, both will believe that God is on their side."

I cleared my throat, realizing that Nicola's supposition was all too true. This would make the Anglican Church's assertion more credible. There were several international skirmishes looming on the horizon. What we didn't need was a Holy War.

"Sorry," I apologized.

"No need for an apology. I get choked up when I contemplate the horrors that this gospel could bring about."

He obviously mistook my choking as a symptom of the gravity of his tale, not as a result of the pipe. But I saw no reason to correct him. We sat in silence for a while until Holmes entered the compartment, looking more disheveled then when he had left.

"Well that was fairly informative," the detective said brushing back his black hair with his hand.

"Any luck?" I asked.

Holmes bent forward and handed me my flask of brandy. Not a drop more had been drunk since he had left us many minutes ago.

"There were three distinct groups that lent themselves to suspicion of being the culprit we are after. All three wore short black coats, like the one our thief was wearing when we last saw him. None wore a bandana, but that was probably disposed of before he boarded this train."

"How did you sort them out?" Nicola inquired.

"Well, I naturally dismissed the ones who were either too young or too old. Ones that were too fat or too thin or too infirm or were obviously traveling with families. But one" he continued, "was seated in a group with three other men, all similarly dressed in black short coats, which is the current fashion in Italy today. If they were startled by the appearance of a drunken visitor to their compartment, they didn't show it."

Holmes began to tie his foursquare carefully folding it around his collar to start.

"The second was seated with a matronly grandmother who was knitting. The man looked startled upon my entrance to their compartment. But the old, Italian lady kept her head down and didn't miss a stitch."

My companion swayed slightly with the motion of the railway car and continued on with his tie.

"And the last?" I asked.

"The last was sitting alone in a compartment, his head tilted to one side, napping like a baby. Not a care in the world."

"Then your mission was a failure," said Nicola.

"On the contrary," Holmes replied. "I got a good look at all of their faces and committed them to memory. When we arrive at Canterbury Cathedral, I will be able to pick out our thief as one of the men I saw on this train and we shall then apprehend him and the gospel," he said, finishing his foursquare and taking his seat next to me.

"And if our thief didn't make this train, then we shall have plenty of time to stake out the Cathedral and look for a man with a map case."

He reached into his jacket pocket and retrieved his long-stemmed cherry wood pipe, followed by a sterling silver tobacco tin and began to pack the bowl. "I think I'll start with one of those papers, if you don't mind, John." He gestured with his pipe to the stack on the seat next to the Monsignor. "We will have plenty of time to relax for the next two days."

و

It was quite fortuitous that at the next station there was a peddler selling newspapers. Both Nicola and Holmes snatched up as many different editions that they could and were well fortified for the next part of the trip. We continued on through northern Italy and then the long trek through eastern France where Holmes and the Monsignor switched to French newspapers.

I, on the other hand, spent the beginning of the trip sleeping to ease the discomfort to my leg caused by the dampness of the continuous rain and all the recent running that we had experienced. I finished Colonel Whimple's tome and went back to *Wound and Disease Care by the Royal College of Physicians*, which I had read on the trip down through France. I thought that I couldn't be too familiar with the information on the human anatomy. A second review of the contents of the book would only make me a better surgeon. We also passed the time in both idle and sometimes interesting conversation.

It is one of these conversations that was most memorable when the topic of religion came up and Nicola asked Holmes what faith that he might be.

My companion who was smoking his favorite pipe at the time lowered it and paused, staring off out the window where he was now seated, and appeared to be either contemplating or ignoring the question.

After about a minute, the Monsignor leaned forward and said, "I didn't mean to offend you. I was merely making conversation."

"No offence taken, John. I was just collecting my thoughts on the issue. Religion is one of the few major subjects that demands much reasoning and careful deliberation. One must choose their words carefully when expressing their views. I am not sure that a single word can sum up my religious belief on the subject; neither Roman Catholic, Anglican, Protestant, Lutheran, atheist, nor agnostic. I suppose that I can't classify my religious beliefs into one convenient category. A system of devotion and dedication is certainly most helpful in making sense of the everyday turmoil and tribulations of life. A belief system gives one faith and hope in an eventual reward for living a good life. It also keeps the fragile bonds of civilization intact."

Holmes brought his pipe to his lips and took a languorous drag on it.

"Then you see religion as only a social construct?" Nicola inquired.

"Its rituals do most surely give comfort to those who have need of comforting at times in their life. It allows one to have a formalized structure to express their joy or grief with their community and circle of friends. But ritual and tradition are merely human inventions," said Holmes.

"But ritual," Nicola replied, "isn't the only means of worship or solace. There is private prayer and solicitation. There is the belief that there is a reward waiting for you in heaven."

"I see its value as a great communal system that promises rewards for good behavior and a life well-lived," he expelled the smoke towards the window. "But as a firm, verifiable set of specifics, I believe it is rather lacking in provable evidence."

"But that is where faith comes in," the Monsignor said. "That is where the promise of salvation fills that void, that emptiness that is left when that faith in civilization lets you down."

"I approach religion from facts, not faith," Holmes said.

"But you do have faith that we will catch up to the thief and regain the gospel, don't you?"

My companion didn't reply immediately. He drew in another long drag on his pipe and let the smoke swirl from his pursed lips.

"Yes, I do have faith in that," Holmes said.

"Hebrews, Chapter 11, verse 1," Nicola said. "'Faith is the assurance of things hoped for, the conviction of things not seen.'"

My companion smiled. Both parties were satisfied.

Eventually, we found ourselves at the ferry after what seemed to be a never-ending trip by train. The more I thought about the importance of the lost gospel and its ramifications on two sets of religious beliefs, the graver our quest became. As we stepped off the train, we were greeted by a sweeping mist at the port of Calais to begin our crossing from France to the welcome shores of England. We turned our collars to face the north wind and began our journey homeward. The boat trip across was rather choppy, but the ship made decent time.

It was nightfall when we set foot on English soil and secured a brougham, stored our luggage, and were off with great haste to the station in Dover proper to catch the train for the half hour trip directly to Canterbury.

We arrived early in the morning and had no problem in arranging another groaner to take us and our luggage to the nearest inn and, after rousing the innkeeper from his morning chores, we secured two rooms. Our luggage was promptly stored in our rooms and we had the driver take us immediately to Canterbury Cathedral. Holmes requested that the driver get us there as quickly as possible and we then set off with great haste, making good progress in the early morning. Holmes was generous with a shilling for the grateful driver who wanted to know if there was anything else he could do for us. I thanked him and sent him on his way.

We stood across the square from the great Cathedral. It had been exactly eight years since we had last set foot in Canterbury, and then we had not had time to visit the famous Cathedral. And now we had to view it from afar. We took up a position across the street from the House of Worship behind a cluster of trees and shrubs, out of sight from the main entrance to the church. Once safely ensconced there, it was Monsignor Nicola who volunteered to go in search of a local pub and procure a few pints of ale to slake our thirst and several biscuits after the end of our journey. I was much appreciative of his gesture.

We settled in across the square from the architectural splendor that was one of the most impressive churches in all of England. The morning sun cast long, deep shadows on its four magnificent spires that reached up to heaven and its five massive towers ringing the Cathedral, standing like enormous parapets on one of the most imposing structures I have ever witnessed. The vast square in front of the Cathedral began to fill up with scores of parishioners and supplicants as they filed out of the church as the holy mass had ended. Gradually, the square emptied to what must have been the usual traffic of a typical morning.

It was then that Nicola rejoined us with three pints of stout and several slices of bread. The brisk morning breeze and the shade of the trees had cooled us down and we settled in to start our vigil. We kept our eyes on the worshippers who streamed in and out through the large wooden doors of the Cathedral.

"Gentlemen, I believe we should widen our view of the entry points to the Cathedral. I've noticed a side door on the back entrance to the church on the right side. It could be used to gain entry to the sanctuary and, possibly, be a meeting place for our thief and a cleric. I suggest that we reposition ourselves so that we have both doors under observation."

He motioned to the both of us. With that he bolted with his long strides across the edge of the square and ran parallel to the Cathedral to get into

Nicola rejoined us with three pints of stout and several slices of bread.

position to observe both the main entrance and the door on the side of the church. In order to not be too obvious as to having three men standing around staring at the Cathedral, we had to move a ways back to use the corner of a small apothecary shop as cover.

I was glad that Monsignor Nicola had switched his priestly robes for his current black suit and trousers and vest. It helped us blend in with the crowd so much better. From our new vantage point we could still make out the figures coming and going, but it might be slightly more difficult to identify them if not for the keen eyes of Sherlock Holmes.

For several hours we took turns sitting on the bench in front of the shop and traveling down the street to the pub that Nicola had located to procure sandwiches and ale and use the loo out back. It was more than once that the thought crossed my mind that somehow the rogues had made it here before we did and the deed was done already. I only asked Holmes once.

"Do you think that they have already handed off the gospel?"

"It would be a miracle, in the parlance of the Monsignor. But anything is possible. If we do not catch sight of them by nightfall, then I think it best that we take shifts watching the church to observe the comings and goings of the priests and intercept anyone who looks like they might have a rolled up gospel in their possession. Otherwise, we wait until tomorrow noon and then make our move on the Cathedral proper."

That was assurance enough for me.

As the sun began to set on the western side of the massive Cathedral, the golden stones positively lit up proclaiming God's glory. It was truly an awe inspiring sight. All three of us were standing guard when Holmes spotted four men making their way to the back of the church.

"Halloo, what do we have here?" he said. "See the second man in that procession; he is burdened with an armful of long palm fronds."

"Yes, that is for the upcoming Palm Sunday mass, "Nicola said."It is the celebration of Christ's triumphant entrance into Jerusalem. The palms are blessed and given out to the congregation to commemorate that event at mass this coming Sunday."

"And," Holmes said, "It is a clever way to walk through the streets of Canterbury with a map case hidden within the thick stems of the palms."

"Good Lord," I exclaimed, "what a clever ruse. If they were worried that somehow they were followed, they have covered their tracks and their mission quite well."

"Precisely, Watson. And with the afternoon sun illuminating his face, I recognize him as the gentleman seated with the three other men on the train. I believe we should make our way to apprehend them as surreptitiously as possible. But keep your revolvers at the ready. Let's split up, gentlemen."

Holmes walked to the left of the church trying to get to a spot ahead of the four thieves so that he might attack them from the front. Nicola and I began to stroll towards the front of the Cathedral where the thugs had just come from; hoping that they would not turn around to check behind themselves to see if anyone was approaching them from the rear. As careful as they were with their plan to disguise their transporting of the gospel, they were as careless with their trek to the back door of the house of worship. They never looked back.

But the distance was too great between us and them, so we could not close the gap unless we broke into a full gallop that would alert them to our presence, and they reached the small wooden door and slipped into the church before any of us could reach them. Once they were inside the Cathedral, we ran to the side door and pulled it open. Holmes was the first to step in. It took several seconds for our eyes to adjust to the dim light inside the small vestibule which led to a darken hallway.

"Watson," the detective reached into his coat and withdrew his revolver. "We can only assume that they are armed."

Nicola and I both drew our weapons and followed Holmes down the corridor.

Several seconds later we saw an illumination at the end of our hallway, a soft light that became brighter as we approached the arched opening. Hugging the wall, we spied the altar in front of the nave of the great Cathedral. We realized that we were in the sanctuary of the grand church, the holy of holies that surrounded the altar and the tabernacle that was neatly delineated and separated from the rest of the Cathedral by the railing made of Carrara marble with a solid gold top rail. From there back was the one-hundred-foot-long by one-hundred and fifty-foot-wide nave of the church filled with rows and rows of pews.

The brilliant white marble altar was in the center of a raised platform in the middle of the upper quarter of the front of the church, being at least ten foot long by four foot wide. It was draped in the finest white linen cloth with a purple runner down the center. It held the customary six tall candles on either side of its ends, fully ablaze. A brilliant scarlet carpet led down the nine steps to the railing, stopping at the solid brass gates in the center. Off to our right was the lectern, its several steps leading to the pulpit raised above the congregation, so that the minister could preach down to the assembled flock. The lectern's sides were ringed with intricate wood carvings depicting Biblical scenes and angels.

The remainder of the magnificent Cathedral spread out before us with all of the grandeur of a Michelangelo painting. Massive pillars, giant arches and gloriously painted frescos larger than life filled the alcoves and complimented the towering stained glass windows that let the dappled afternoon light stream in with all the colors of God's rainbow.

Slowly we made our way down the sixty-foot hallway and stopped at the end of the narrow opening. There we spied the group of thieves and a deacon in his white and long black cassock standing by the railing next to the one crook holding the palm fronds securely under his arm. Holmes stepped out of the hallway first and shouted, "Halt. Drop the gospel right there and surrender."

We three had our revolvers pointed at the quartet.

It was then that the villains turned and two of them withdrew their weapons from the waistbands of their trousers and fired off two shots in our direction. We immediately dropped back into the safety of the opening of the archway as the two farthest scoundrels dashed to the first two pews. The thief with the armful of bulky palm fronds and the gospel, along with the deacon, scampered up to the altar. The closest scalawag to us bolted forward to the lectern.

The duo by the first row of pews fired two more shots our way. The first one went wide and off into the hallway causing us to flatten ourselves further against the wall. But the second shot hit Nicola in his right arm. He gave out a cry and grabbed his arm where the bullet had struck him. I turned and placed my revolver on the floor and using both hands I tore his black jacket away from the bullet hole. There was a nasty red line that was bleeding slightly.

"It appears to be only a flesh wound," said I. "Here," I pulled a clean handkerchief from my suit coat pocket, "place this on it for a minute or two to stop the bleeding. You should be fine."

"Thank you," he said. "It's nice to go into a battle with a doctor on your side."

The words echoed slightly in my mind, bringing up memories better left unremembered.

It was then that the crook by the lectern crawled up the several steps to the top level of the lectern.

Nicola leaned out and fired a shot in the direction of the pair of thugs hiding by the pews.

"Be judicious with your bullets." Holmes said, "We only have so many rounds available to us."

The Monsignor nodded in agreement.

It was then that the man at the top of the lectern eased his head and his gun over the top of the rail, took aim, and squeezed off a shot at us. The bullet hit the wall at chest height only a foot from Holmes sending plaster flying in all directions.

"He has the advantage of the higher ground," said I, as I picked up my Webley.

"Most assuredly," Holmes replied.

It was then that the crook up at the altar dropped the long stemmed palms, revealing not only the gospel in the map case, but also a Vetterli single shot rifle, the weapon of choice of the Italian military. It had the advantage over conventional rifles in that it used a four bullet clip with a pull string on top of its wooden frame for quick ejection of its magazine clip. He handed the map case with the gospel inside to the cowering deacon and took aim at us.

His first shot echoed throughout the Cathedral. It tore out the plaster about waist high far to the side of the detective, causing us all to recoil.

"That gives them a further advantage," I said stating the obvious.

Suddenly the thug atop the lectern popped up and fired wildly at us again, his bullet skipping off the floor harmlessly down the corridor.

"We must do something about him," Holmes said.

Holmes aimed his revolver carefully at the top of the lectern and waited. The pair by the pews sent another two shots our way, this time hitting the archway above our head.

With that the assassin above in the lectern stood up to take aim at us and was greeted by two shots from Holmes. The first bullet hit him in the shoulder and the second caught him in the side of his head, sending a torrent of blood pouring out. He recoiled and then dropped forward, slumping over the top rail, dropping his pistol over the edge.

"Well done, Holmes," I said.

"Thank you, Watson."

"Might I make a suggestion?"

"By all means," said Holmes.

"I suggest we all fire at once and move forward," I offered, experiencing a flash of my military training and service.

There was a quick nod of agreement of all. A flash of memory of Maiwand now settling heavily in the back of my mind.

"Ready. Now."

With that we all moved out from our cover, each firing off one shot as Holmes and I rushed to the lectern while Nicola ran the furthest to the front pew across from the pair of crooks. Our sudden charge either caught them by surprise or else they were reloading as no shots were fired back at us. The lull was quickly broken as several shots by the pair in front of the church were directed at the Monsignor who was now the closest to them.

Holmes was on the outer edge of the lectern closest to the altar and the rifle man. "I don't think I can get a clear shot at him from here, Watson. The angle is too steep." With that, the detective poked his head out a little to take a clearer assessment of his position. The Cathedral again echoed with the sound of the bullet ripping into the wooden face of Christ the Redeemer above the head of Holmes.

"A little too close for comfort," he said.

I spied the pistol next to me dropped by the gunman from the top of the lectern. I bent forward and picked it up. There were still bullets left in the cylinder.

"Here, Monsignor," I yelled. "Take this." I quickly summoned all my strength and slid the pistol across the platform. It skidded along the marble floor, down the steps, and came to rest by Nicola's feet.

"Wait one moment," I yelled again, "I'll cover you."

I fired off two shots at the first pew across from Nicola as the Monsignor hooked the revolver with his foot and drew it into his body.

"Now we must take care of the chap with the rifle," said Holmes.

"I think that the rifle man only has one shot left in his magazine. If I counted correctly and he didn't already stop and reload after three shots then we might have an advantage here."

"And what is your plan, dear fellow?"

"Well," I said. "I suggest that I draw his attention and entice him to take his last shot, forcing him to take time to reload. That would give you a short gap to make it to the other side of the altar. The lectern is at such an angle that you will be partially shielded from the two pesky buggers in the front pews."

"That is, of course," said Holmes. "If he has only one shot left and didn't reload."

"Yes, quite right," I replied, suddenly doubting the chances that my plan might succeed.

"Well, you were always one to count correctly for as long as I have known you." He smiled. "So I will take that chance. Ready when you are, Watson."

I took my billycock off my head, a hat that I had grown rather fond of over the years, and placed it on the end of the barrel of my service revolver. Then I hunched over above the detective.

"Ready?" I balanced my chapeau precariously. "Steady." I stood up further and drew in a deep breath. "Go," I shouted and poked the hat out from the side of the lectern.

Immediately the shot tore through the billycock, sending it spinning like a whirling dervish. I stepped out from the safety of my perch and took aim and slowly squeezed off a series of shots at the rifle man.

Holmes, like a jungle cat, sprang out and flew up the two steps and across the platform, sliding to a halt at the side of the altar opposite the gunman and the deacon. I ducked back behind the lectern, as several shots from the pair of scoundrels hiding behind the front pews tore into the wooden figures of Gabriel the Archangel in the front of the pulpit which afforded me the protection that I had anticipated.

Nicola took advantage of the carelessness of one of the crooks who had stood up to get a clearer shot at me. The Monsignor stood up quickly, fired the last two shots from his own revolver and struck down the rogue. He fell backwards, crashing into the seat of the pew along side of him. I took the respite in the action to check the remaining rounds in my Webley.

I had only one unfired cartridge left.

Out in the knave, Nicola had switched to the spare gun that I had tossed him and took careful aim at the crook crouched behind the front pew. He squeezed off a shot that tore into the top of the wooden seat back sending the crook ducking for cover. Nicola thought he had the thug in his sights and squeezed of another shot. Unfortunately, the thief had just that very second crouched down even further. The bullet slammed into the pew inches above his head. Nicola leveled the revolver and had the thug in his sights and pulled the trigger

Nothing. The spare gun that he was using was now out of ammunition. He pulled the trigger again. The result was the same.

Nicola stood there and pulled the trigger continuously, but to no avail. Hearing the sound of the hammer hitting the empty chamber, the thug stood up, an evil grin snaking across his lips.

The villain stepped out of the front pew and took three steps down the aisle to come into a direct line of sight with Nicola. The ruffian slowly raised his revolver, stretched out his arm, and took aim. In seconds the Cathedral was filed with the sound of a gunshot echoing through the dimming light, but it wasn't from the thug's weapon. It was from mine.

The ruffian grabbed his chest, twisted violently and fell to the floor.

I lowered my revolver and nodded to Nicola. He, still stunned, slowly returned the nod.

While atop the sanctuary, Holmes fired a shot across the marble top of the altar, missing the thief and the deacon who were crouched at the other end across from him. I could see that the thief was trying to tug the pull string to free the spent magazine from its holder atop the rifle, but was having no luck, as it was jammed. The clip was not coming out of the rifle. The thug yanked on the string, but to no avail. Holmes gingerly peeked around the side of the altar.

"Now, Holmes," I shouted. "His rifle is jammed."

Upon hearing my words, the detective sprang forward and rushed the kneeling gunman. As he approached the thug, the thief thrust his rifle up and used it as a club, striking Holmes in the forearm, knocking his revolver out of his hand.

Before the rogue could draw the rifle back, the detective grabbed the end of the barrel and ripped it away from the hooligan flinging it across the marble floor. Holmes then threw a right cross solidly into the jaw of the thief. But the thug was much bigger and stronger than the detective and shrugged it off. He pushed Holmes back and scrambled up to his knees, then threw a devastating left hook to the detective's stomach.

Homes recoiled into the now standing deacon. The cleric took advantage of this to clasp his arms around my companion's neck, using the map case as a sort of bar to choke him. Standing up, Holmes used his height advantage to grab the deacon's arms and flip him over his side onto the altar, knocking the row of candles over.

Holmes was immediately set upon by the large thug who shoved the detective away to create some space to deliver an overhand punch. But Holmes quickly lashed out with a powerful kick to the solar plexus causing the man to double over. Holmes then unleashed a powerful right uppercut to the man's jaw, toppling him and sending him crashing to the floor with his head taking the full brunt of the fall.

The deacon was trying to roll off the now flaming altar, the linen having burst into flames. The canvas wrapped map case was engulfed in fire, as was the cleric. His screams filled the Cathedral. Holmes grabbed the deacon's leg and began to pull the screaming man off of the altar top; but the cleric, his arms flailing about, grabbed the cloth, tangling him and the gospel further into the inferno.

Holmes was forced to release his grasp as the cassock burst into flames, increasing the screams to a fever pitch. Then all was silent, except for the crackling of the fire. I stood there and watched the lost gospel of Simon Peter being consumed as if by the fires of Hell.

ﻋﻠﻲ

After a rather long explanation to the local constabulary and the religious hierarchy as to the nature of what had caused the unfortunate and destructive fire, Holmes, Monsignor Nicola and I were able to make a discreet departure. Most fortuitously, the stone walls of the structure remained intact, and the blaze had been contained by a brigade of bucket-bearers from the town. Since we hadn't had a bite to eat since late mid-day, we decided to stop at the small inn that had been the location of our sustenance the entire day. Finding a booth along the wall by one of its only two windows, we settled down for kidney pie and ale.

Naturally, the conversation turned to the events of our day.

"I'm sorry about the fate of your gospel, Monsignor," said I. "We almost recovered it."

"We all did our best. No one should be ashamed of the effort that we put forth," came his reply.

"Perhaps it is better that it ended this way," my companion said. "Now its words shall not perplex anyone any longer. Whether it was the truth or not, it wasn't worth starting a religious war over. Either way, it would have truly tested people's faith."

"Speaking of people's faith," Nicola said, "I have something for you both." He unbuttoned his jacket and dug into his vest pocket producing a small cloth bag and began to untie its draw string.

"I was given this by Archbishop Dominic before we left Rome to be given to you upon the successful completion of this mission." He dropped two shiny gold coins on the table, then picked them up one at a time and placed them in each of our hands.

"And what might this be?" said I, turning the coin over and over. One side had the impression of Pope Leo XIII on it. The other side had the papal crest and a Latin inscription.

"The inscription says, 'The nation and kingdom that will not serve me will perish.'" Holmes said.

"A rather harsh and bold statement," I said.

"This pope is a rather bold man," Nicola replied.

"And how did Archbishop Dominic know that we would succeed in our mission?" I asked.

"Elementary, my dear Watson," said Holmes, "he had faith."

THE END

THE STORY BEHIND THE STORY

A great author, and my best friend, Michael A. Black, has always said that research is one of the most enjoyable parts of writing. It opens up whole new worlds to you and can take your story in unexpected directions never dreamed of.

I have always been fascinated by the ancient scrolls and texts that were deemed not worthy to be included in the Holy Bible by the Council of Rome in 382 A.D.; gospels that were worshiped by early Christians as, well, the gospel truth. So, I decided to put my two loves together: Holmes and the Lost Gospel. Here, in chronological order, is some of what the research revealed.

The story had to start out in March, preferably mid-March, as I had to end prior to Palm Sunday, April 3rd, if I placed the story in the year 1898.

The reference to Watson's tale of *The Unusual Dichotomy* and the First Anglican Church's involvement is a fortunate happenstance as it a reference to Michael A. Black's Sherlock Holmes' story in *Sherlock Holmes, Consulting Detective, Volume 6*. A wonderful read and gripping Holmes' mystery.

The *Apostolicae Curae* of Pope Leo XIII stating the invalidity of the Anglican Order was written in 1896; right in time to add to the conflict between the Roman Catholic Church and the Anglican Church on England. More fuel to my fire.

Pope Leo the XIII was the first Pope to open up the Vatican Secret Archives to allow scholars to come in and translate many of the ancient texts and scrolls stored in the Vatican for centuries. In many ways he was a progressive pope at the turn of the century. Luckily for my story.

The train route from Calais in France to Rome, Italy was officially opened in 1896, again just in time for Holmes and Watson to make the trip in less than three days by rail. It was christened the Rome Express. Again, as Watson commented, assuring that all roads lead to Rome.

The Jewish ghetto in Rome was of considerable size and was, in fact, walled off from the rest of the city with iron gates that were locked at sunset. Not a very enlightened or Christian attitude by the Italian government.

Lastly, the gold coin with the image of Pope Leo XIII was real along with its inscription. He was rather fond of minting coins to commemorate any events that he partook in during his reign as pontiff. Pope Leo XIII was a powerful political figure in international affairs and was considered a great diplomat by improving church relations with Germany, Russia, France, and Britain.

Those are some of the research facts that constricted me to 1898 for the timeframe of my story. But happily added to the verisimilitude of my story: all unknown to me until I started to research my tale.

I will always be grateful to Ron Fortier for allowing me to explore the world of Sherlock Holmes, consulting detective, and all the wonders of the Victorian world.

My sincerest gratitude goes out to my Victorian historian, Carl Wayne Ensminger, for his unwavering service above and beyond the call of duty.

To my best friend, Michael A. Black, who has guided me throughout our entire life together, always encouraging me to do my best and never letting me fail.

To my saintly mother, Elaine, who still guides me to this very day.

To my lovely wife Susan, the gentlest soul God has ever created.

This story is dedicated to Susan.

RAYMOND L. LOVATO - was born on the south side of Chicago, Illinois, the oldest of eleven children. He wrote his first play in eighth grade grammar school. He has a Bachelors of Arts degree from St. Xavier University in Chicago where he was editor and wrote a monthly column for the university newspaper and had several poems published in the university's literary magazine. His varied careers included: English teacher, designing a college credit course in Popular Culture, the study of the Twentieth century through Music, literature and movies; a hospital administrator; a resort owner in Palm Springs, CA.; wrote a monthly column for an Antiquing magazine; advertising and marketing; and newspaper columnist. His tourism articles have appeared in prestigious magazines in Australia, England, Germany, as well as the U.S. While in Palm Springs, he helped establish and was president of the Desert Screenwriters Guild.

Ray has written several short stories for independent publishers and authored an e-book, DARK HAVEN. As creator of Doc Atlas, Ray has collaborated on and written parts of various Doc Atlas stories with his life-long friend, Michael A. Black. He has contributed to a number of the

Doc Atlas series produced by Michael A. Black and wrote HIS MASTER'S VOICE and THE GREEN DEATH. He co-authored THE INCREDIBLE ADVENTURES OF DOC ATLAS, a full length novel with his best friend. For Airship 27, Ray and Michael have collected several Doc Atlas stories and reissued them as DOC ATLAS VOLUME 1.

Also for Airship 27, Ray has had the privilege of writing the adventures of the Great Detective, Sherlock Holmes. He has authored five short stories, one novella: THE CHARWICK GHOST, THE SINGULAR TRAGEDY, THE LOST GOSPEL, THE INDEFATIGABLE SPIES, THE QUEEN'S TIARA, and THE RHYMES OF DEATH. He has also co-authored a full length novel with Michael Black, SHERLOCK HOLMES AND THE ADVENTURE OF THE IRON CROWN.

Ray's long-time hobbies include photography and collecting old books. His real passion is traveling the world with his inspiration, his lovely wife, Susan.

Sherlock Holmes

in

The Adventure of the Professor's Plummet

by
Jonathan Casey

"**D**o you suppose, Watson, that were you to fall from this window to the unyielding pavement of Baker Street below that you would meet your ultimate demise?"

As I sit here at my desk listening to the soothing crackling sounds of the fire on this frigid winter evening and review at random pages from the countless notebooks in which I have documented my participation in those singular adventures that comprised the unmatched career of my dear friend Mr. Sherlock Holmes, it is the sight of those words above which has quickly caught my attention and has gotten my mind working. In reflecting on the biographical writings which document the years of my partnership with Holmes, I realize that I have more often than not chosen to set down in print those events and crimes which are of a more sensational nature. This realization on my part is not without a tinge of regret, as I find that in so doing, I have often neglected to share some of those instances of pure, undiluted deduction that my friend would undoubtedly agree are more indicative of his true investigative talents. To be sure, all of the cases that have been published for the public's perusal are legitimate demonstrations of Holmes ascertaining the answers to what would be, to most others, truly unfathomable questions. But, in some ways, I am surprised to find that I have failed to recall some of these other cases over the years, and it appears that on many occasions I have turned past their pages in search of something more dramatic and thrilling.

So worn are these notebooks by the time of this writing that many of the pages have broken loose of their binding and have been held in place either by rudimentary means or by simply being wedged between the more stable pages. Not being able to fully redirect my thoughts from the seeking of the fantastic, I should not be surprised that I have first glimpsed before me pages documenting numerous strange and fascinating untold tales, including the tale of the Malicious Miner, a dark tale with a history spanning two continents; the tale of the Buttermilk Barrel, an adventure noteworthy from its very origin, it having been brought to the attention of Holmes by a girl named Lily, one of his Irregulars and a girl whom Holmes helped on the path to becoming a truly remarkable young lady; the tale of the Murder Boxes, a series of chilling events that found Holmes participating in a deadly game of wits at the behest of a madman; the tale of the Sorcerer's Sigil, a case late in Holmes's career with a title that my readers will certainly recognize, it having been the impetus for a train ride which was to ultimately be diverted so that Holmes could address the horror of the Necrotic Needle; and, of course, the tale of the Headless Pedestrian, in which a man wandered into traffic one fine summer day without the company of his head.

With all of that being said, I cannot now help my gaze from falling to those pages containing the facts of these other, neglected adventures with my friend that were in no way of any less interest to me—and certainly not to Holmes. In fact, if one were to mention to Holmes the curious affair of the Twofold Farewell, a captivating set of circumstances in which a man disappeared from his home one Sunday evening, leaving nothing more than two goodbye letters to his wife written in different languages, he would surely greet such a question with a grin of fond remembrance and would regale one and all with the details of one of his favorite cases from the early days of our partnership. In fact, as I sit here this evening with a broken page in my hands, I resolve to set forth the facts of that case in the future. It is my hope that my readers will forgive my temporary detour into the past and will be pleased with the narrative that is soon to follow.

Long before I became acquainted with the name and deeds of the dreaded Professor Moriarty, that criminal mastermind whose remains lie in state at the bottom of the Reichenbach Falls, Holmes and I found ourselves dealing with the death of a far less infamous professor who too had fallen to his death. For anyone in academia who may be reading this, I can assure you that there is no scientific correlation between professorship and death by great fall. Nevertheless, as a medical man, I would be remiss if I did not note that it would be unwise for a person of any given profession to take lightly the danger of falling. To me, the events surrounding the professor's death were fascinating in several respects from a medical point of view. To Holmes, the events of this intriguing puzzle provided the mental stimulation he so craved and a solution that truly showcased his extraordinary and marvelous powers of deduction. And so it is with a smile at the fortune of my having seen scrawled on the page my recollection of Holmes's words, that I begin my tale of the professor's plummet.

I remember that it was a particularly damp morning at the beginning of the summer in the early days of my residence at Baker Street, and I was sitting in my favorite armchair reading the newspaper. The weather during that week and the week prior had been unpredictable and had fluctuated from patches of sun to periods of downpours that had lasted for days on end. Perhaps it was a response to the dreariness of the weather or simply just the toll of the very uneven and irregular hours that I had been keeping as a result of my involvement in the seemingly unending flood of cases that had been brought before Holmes in the preceding months, but I found myself feeling rather fatigued and without motivation to do more than sit down and try to recoup some of my energy. Thus, after breakfast, I had found myself enjoying the comfort of an adventure novel before Mrs. Hudson had been so kind as to bring up newspapers for us.

For his part, Holmes had not spoken so much as a few words in at least two days, but it is a testament to our friendship even then to note that it was a rather companionable silence. As he was wont to do, Holmes had fallen into one of those periods of intense melancholy and unrest resulting from lack of sufficient input for the deductive factory that was his mind, episodes with which I was to become much more familiar as the years marched on. The day before had found Holmes dressed in his smoking jacket hard at work on a monograph on some obscure topic of criminal investigation that must have included some element of laboratory science, as he alternated from concentrated writing to extended experimentation with his numerous chemical apparatuses. As I look back on that day, I am glad that 221B—and Holmes and I for that matter—remained intact, as it seemed as though one of Holmes's concoctions had come close to exploding more than once. To his credit, Holmes was never rattled and expertly worked the problem to his satisfaction.

Though I had eaten up the trays of bacon and eggs that Mrs. Hudson had been gracious enough to prepare for us, Holmes had neglected his repast entirely, instead choosing to voraciously review the contents of one of the newspapers. As I grinned to myself in between bites of my breakfast, I tried to apply my friend's methods to determine his interest in the newspaper. I knew that he was not embroiled in any present case, so he had not been checking to see if a false advertisement he had placed was accurate. Judging by the rather mundane nature of the headlines, I could not imagine Holmes having been captured by any particular article. And knowing my friend well, he would be completely uninterested in the results of any of the local horseraces. Ultimately, I felt satisfied with my reasoning and decided that he was in search of a new case. It could be said that I was correct in the end, but I was soon to learn that his attention had been captured by what I had found to be the most common and uninteresting of articles.

The morning wore on, and I made significant progress in my novel and had returned to the newspaper. After sitting in his chair in a state of intense thought, Holmes had risen and had extricated from his Persian slipper a heaping clump of that cheap shag tobacco he seemed to prefer, despite his good taste in most other things. Before long, he lit his pipe and was lost in a fog of smoke that seemed to swirl unpredictably as he began to pace with ever increasing frequency in front of the fireplace. The first pipe carried him through his preliminary thoughts, and he was soon at work filling yet another pipe for assistance with his continued contemplation of whatever problem had taken hold of his mind.

Holmes stopped at the window overlooking Baker Street not long after his second pipe was finished and stood with his hands clasped behind his back. Then, turning to me, he uttered the words that began this narrative.

I must admit that after not having heard him so much as make a few sounds for the last few days, I was quite startled at his question. I lowered the newspaper and looked at him with what must have been a rather profound look of confusion and concern, as he produced a small chuckle.

"No, no, Watson," said Holmes, lightheartedly, "I have not gone mad. You can rest assured that I do not intend for you to now be the test subject in some violent experiment in criminological science."

"I am certainly glad to hear it, Holmes," I said with a laugh. "I am starting to notice in even your day-to-day behaviors a flair for the dramatic. What a bizarre question for you to ask after not having even uttered one word in days!"

"I assure you that the question is not at all bizarre and is instead quite pertinent to the matter at hand."

"What matter? You have no cases to speak of at the moment," I replied.

Palms upturned, Holmes shrugged his shoulders in apparent agreement.

"Officially, no," he said, "but after what I have just read in the newspaper this morning, I have no doubt that my prospects are definitely much improved."

"I have been through most of the articles already, Holmes, and I have not seen one thing that could possibly have piqued your interest."

"Clearly you were not reading carefully," he replied smugly.

Not wanting to fall into the trap of increasing his ego even further, I said nothing and began to browse each of the articles again in hopes of finding whatever it was that had interested Holmes. Holmes returned to the Persian slipper once more and filled his third pipe, no doubt trying to give me time to catch up to him. Several minutes passed, and I continued to be at a loss.

"Now, now. Don't be so hard on yourself, Watson. I would wager that most who read the newspaper today did not give so much as a passing thought to the article which has so consumed my thoughts over the last hour."

"Perhaps you would like to enlighten me, Holmes," I said curtly.

Holmes grinned and said, "There is no need to become irritable, Watson. After all, I have no doubt that even Scotland Yard is most likely without much suspicion either."

"If I am to understand this, Holmes—a crime has been committed, the results of this crime have been published in the newspaper, and the only person in London who cares about it is you?"

"Precisely, my dear fellow," said Holmes. "You have certainly provided an accurate summation of events."

I could do little more than shake my head and hand him the newspaper so that he could show me the article to which he had been alluding.

"Read it aloud, Watson. That's a good fellow."

"A NASTY FALL," the headline read. "Professor Roderick Norton, a notable literary academic, was killed by a fall after walking off of his bedroom balcony."

The article ended there, and I looked up from the paper to see Holmes sitting back down in his chair with his fingers steepled before him.

"You cannot be serious, Holmes?" I asked incredulously. "This is what has had the wheels of your mind turning?"

"It is incredible, is it not, Watson?" asked Holmes in a serious tone.

"I am not sure we are referring to the same story, Holmes," was my reply.

"Come now, Watson. You have not answered the question that I posed to you earlier. Your thoughts as a medical doctor are of extreme interest to me."

Gathering my thoughts and flattered by the importance he had placed on my judgment, I said, "I suggest that it would be quite possible that I would perish if I were to fall out of the window to the street below us. At the very least, I would be severely injured. Much of this would be dependent upon how I landed, particularly since many who fall to their deaths experience some sort of head injury, the results of which—a broken skull, internal hemorrhaging, and the like—can be almost instantly fatal given the right circumstances."

"Capital!" exclaimed Holmes. "Now, if you were unconscious, would you expect the probability of your death to be increased?"

"Absolutely, Holmes," I answered with conviction. "You must consider that an unconscious man involved in a fall might very well suffer far worse injuries than a conscious man, as the unconscious man will not have the awareness and wherewithal to brace for impact and will instead be at the mercy of physics."

"Very well put, Watson," said Holmes. "I would tend to agree with everything that you have just said."

"So, if I am following your thoughts, Holmes, you believe that this professor did not simply fall but was somehow murdered either by force or by other means?"

"I submit, Watson, that your deductive faculties are certainly improving by the minute. Now, be a good fellow and continue to ponder over these ideas while I deliver a message to the telegraph office to be sent to our old friend Lestrade."

So saying, Holmes proceeded to remove his smoking jacket and put on his Inverness, and before I knew it, he was hurrying down the stairs and out into the rain, sending us on a collision course with yet another adventure.

⁂

As Holmes had requested, I spent much of my time in the early part of the afternoon mulling over the questions surrounding the circumstances that he had presented to me, limited as they were at that particular moment in time. After having read the brief newspaper article several times, I started to conjure up ideas of the numerous scenarios which could have resulted in the professor's death. As random thoughts and musings started to consume me, I attempted to mimic the deductive processes of Holmes, and I eventually found myself pacing about the room, stopping abruptly at those times when I thought that I had finally hit on the crux of the matter. Yet with all of that, something continued to linger at the very edge of my thoughts, but for the life of me, I could not get that notion to manifest itself—that is until I looked out the window and observed some tradesmen at work down at the far end of the street.

The hour had just tolled three o'clock when the door to our rooms was thrown open by none other than the thin figure of Holmes himself, who was carrying in both arms stacks of what appeared to be newspapers, books, and a variety of academic journals. I quickly made my way to the door to help him, and we soon had all of the documents spread out across our table.

"You certainly have been busy this afternoon," I said. "But a few moments ago, I realized what has been troubling me about this entire situation."

Holmes, who had been starting to sort and organize all of the documents chronologically, stopped and turned to me with a curious look on his face.

"Whatever do you mean, my dear fellow? Now is not the time to be troubled. We have only just begun."

"That is just it, Holmes. I still do not grasp why you feel that this is something worthy of your attention. Frankly, I fear that you are breaking one of the foundational tenets of your deductive method. You seem to be deducing a crime out of the ether, making bricks without clay as it were."

This last statement earned a grin from Holmes, and then he shook his head in obvious frustration with what he must have perceived as my lack of imagination.

"While I am happy to know that you are integrating my remarks into your criminological thoughts, I fear that it is you who have erred in your reasoning, Watson. You see, I have not yet elaborated on any specific means by which a crime may have been accomplished, nor have I stated anything about a motive. After having read the same article that you have and then having weighed the probabilities, I find it more likely than not that this unfortunate professor has met his untimely death at the hands of man, not by the fickle hands of chance. Beyond that, I have drawn no further conclusions."

"If I am being honest, it still does not hold much water to me, Holmes," I said.

"Then let us be glad that you rely on buckets and bottles rather than thoughts," said Holmes abruptly.

He stopped for a moment, shook his head again, and continued on in a more conciliatory tone, "Nevertheless, I have never claimed infallibility, my dear fellow, and I would argue that our time would be better served determining the truth of the matter, whatever that may be, than in debating the merits of the investigation itself. Perhaps you will be correct in the end, after all."

That there was some hint of sarcasm attached to that last statement, I was sure, but I decided to forego any further verbal repartee so that I could see if Holmes's methods would prove out in the end.

"What do you have here, anyway?" I asked.

"These, Watson, are all of the reviews and critical essays that Professor Norton has published over the last thirty or so years of his professorship.

In addition, there are also a few original works scattered within the dusty covers of some of these journals—poems, short stories, and the like. However, original works from him were quite rare, as he seems to have been an extremely private individual. Being the literary academic that he was, he would surely know that one cannot write something meaningful without a small part of oneself ultimately being revealed in the end. While we wait for Lestrade to arrive, let us just get acquainted with the workings of the mind of our deceased client."

After a few moments, Holmes had finished his arranging of the documents into stacks sorted by the decade of publication, and it would have been clear to anyone that there had been quite a considerable decline in the professor's once-prolific writing career. I remarked as much to Holmes.

"Yes, I had thought as much myself, particularly in the last five years," he agreed. "My contact at the library, who was gracious enough to gather all of these materials for us, did not seem to have much of an explanation for that."

"If there is a mystery surrounding this man's death, then maybe you will find out what led to his decreased writing production as well."

"Good old Watson. Now, be a good fellow, and take up those stacks there. I would wager that we will not hear from Lestrade until after dinnertime."

Not surprisingly, Holmes was correct, and it was at about a quarter past six when we heard the familiar sound of Inspector Lestrade ascending the stairs to our quarters. Shortly before his arrival, I had just managed to finish reviewing my portion of the professor's writings. I have never been one to engage in the explication of poems or novels, my belief being that many people are simply determined to either find some meaning where there is none or to apply their own personal interpretations rather than read works as they were written and intended; however, I found the literary criticisms and analyses put forth by Professor Norton to be truly exceptional and well-nuanced. There was no doubt that the professor was a man who truly loved the written word and who put all of his energy into immersing himself in the space between the lines of the printed page. Even Holmes, who I had not known to have any interest in literature, seemed to respect the man's work, as he was most complimentary of both his analytical structure and his thoroughly reasoned and evidence-based arguments. I assumed that Holmes's views on the matter were such as they were because he attacked his cases in much the same way, with his enlightening those in the dark by striking down with alacrity those hypotheses which were not based in logic and factual statements. After all, he would be the first to contend that a hypothesis without a foundation in fact is little more than fiction.

Norton's original works were certainly solid pieces of poetry and prose, and it struck me that many of them were quite tragic and dealt with ghosts, hauntings, loneliness, and the search for the ethereal woman of his dreams. The content of the last couple of these original pieces differed considerably from the rest though, as they seemed to focus on a radiant young woman whose beauty and passion were undeniable. After reading several of the pieces, Holmes made a passing comment in jest about another great mind having been corrupted by the allure of romance, and I could not help but laugh heartily, knowing that my friend no doubt subscribed to that notion on some level.

There were two knocks on the door, and after Holmes bade him to enter, Inspector Lestrade opened the door and stood in the entranceway, a frustrated sneer reflecting upon his rat-like face. The rain had picked up in the late-afternoon hours, resulting in the inspector's shoes squishing as he walked forward and his hair dripping water onto the shoulders of his thoroughly saturated black overcoat. I noticed that he was also without his hat, and I wondered what had led to him ending up in this condition.

"How good of you to drop by, Inspector," said Holmes jovially. "To what do we owe the pleasure this evening?"

"Seeing as how I received a telegram from you requesting that I call to discuss some urgent matter, I would say that you already know that, Mr. Holmes."

"Of course, Lestrade. Forgive me for my little foray into dry humor. It was good of you to accommodate my request. Have you brought the information with you?"

Lestrade patted his chest with his hand, saying, "I have, and it's probably the only part of me that is dry."

"Watson, be a good fellow and get a chair and a glass of brandy for the inspector while I get an item to exchange with him for his troubles."

I directed Lestrade to a chair near the window and quickly poured him a second glass after he very nearly inhaled the contents of the first.

"What is Holmes supposed to be exchanging with you, Inspector?" I asked.

"The devil if I know, Dr. Watson," was his reply.

As he was ever on cue, Holmes immediately stepped back into the sitting room with a bowler hat in his hands and handed it to the inspector, whose face showed a look of bewilderment that was rather typical of him.

"How good of you to drop by, Inspector," said Holmes.

"Where did you get this, Mr. Holmes?" Lestrade barked. "I demand to know at once."

"Now, now, Lestrade, settle yourself," said Holmes calmly. "There is no need for you to become upset."

"That is easy for you to say, considering I was the one walking around in the rain for the better part of the day without a hat."

"Fair enough, Lestrade. I shall tell you the facts of how I came to be in possession of your hat, but it is with the understanding that you will go easy on those parties involved in its theft."

"That all depends, now, doesn't it?"

"Very well. You will recall that Watson and I, along with my Irregulars, assisted you in clearing up that little matter of the kicking terrier about a fortnight ago."

"Yes, I remember it."

"Then you will also recall that after leaving here, you went to dispatch a telegram at the telegraph office."

"Of course. I wanted to ensure that the prison released the man that I had arrested for arson."

"Yes, well, be that as it may, in so doing, you set your hat down on the desk. Because they felt that you were—how shall we put it?—impolite to them, the boys decided to play a little game with you. They brought it here directly afterward, and here it has remained in my possession until this moment."

Lestrade's face had contorted into an expression of that anger that follows from those instances of extreme embarrassment, and he slammed the hat down on the table.

"I will have all their heads for this!"

I attempted to hold in my laughter as best as I could, but a small chuckle slipped out; this did not escape the inspector's attention.

"You may laugh, Dr. Watson, but those urchins better hope that I do not find them."

Holmes patted Lestrade on the shoulder, "They best be on their guard then. At least take comfort in the fact that I was sure to reprimand them myself."

"Very good, Mr. Holmes. That will suffice for the time being. Do not think me above fun and amusement, but it has been a long day. A difficult few weeks for that matter, if I am being honest. That is why I had not even noticed or cared about my missing hat until the last few days."

Holmes seated himself in his usual armchair and rested his head against the back of the chair, his eyes closed and his hands steepled in front of him.

"What have you learned about the death of Professor Norton?"

"I'll tell you that coming by any information at all was like having a rotten tooth removed. Those country constables don't always appreciate Scotland Yard inserting themselves into their affairs. I was lucky to get what information I did."

Lestrade removed from his jacket a thin file containing a packet of no more than five pages of handwritten notes. Holmes opened his eyes when he heard the shuffling of the pages, and Lestrade tossed the file over to him. Holmes studied its insubstantial contents for several minutes, and he nodded his head a few times as he went through the pages.

"It looks like the matter was examined by a Constable Geoffrey Taylor—I have not heard of him. Nothing in his notes seems to suggest that anything is amiss. I am pleased to see that the coroner's report was included at least. Have a look at this, Watson."

Holmes handed me the coroner's report, and I took the necessary time to thoroughly review my colleague's findings. The main findings were that Norton was found to have fractured his neck and cracked several bones in his face and skull. All of these findings were consistent with injuries sustained in an accidental fall. The coroner also noted that while there was essentially no injury to Norton's arms, slight bruising was present on his right shin, though there was nothing to suggest that this was suspicious in any way. Overall, there was no evidence of foul play, and the ruling was that the professor's death was accidental.

"This report is fairly standard, Holmes," I said. "There is nothing here that would immediately suggest anything nefarious."

"You are correct to a point, Watson, though I would remind you to review the details of our conversation earlier." said Holmes. "Regardless, I would like to see the body and visit the professor's home if it can be arranged. What do you say, Lestrade?"

Lestrade shook his head, "I believe that Constable Taylor would be rather unwilling to waste time on a matter that has already been closed."

"Perhaps you could persuade him for us, Lestrade. The incident is only two days old. Please send him a telegram and inform him that Watson and I will be in the area tomorrow and that we would like to have a conversation with him. That is, Watson, if you are up for the trip."

Despite my reservations, I was reluctant to doubt the sharp mind of my friend, and I readily agreed to accompany him in his travels.

"Excellent, Watson!" said Holmes. "I only hope that we are not disappointed in the end."

Out of respect for Holmes, Lestrade agreed to correspond with his fellow policeman, and he stood up and prepared to leave so that he could dispatch the telegram before he finally went home for the night.

"Thank you again, Inspector. And do keep watch of your hat this time. I noticed the boys about earlier, and children do like to test their limits."

Lestrade smirked and said, "I would like to see them try it."

With that remark, Lestrade exited our rooms, and Holmes and I quickly began to pack our things so that we could make sure that we were aboard the next train.

Our passage to the countryside proved to be rather uneventful, with Holmes staring vacantly into the deductive abyss for the majority of the journey. I occupied my time by reading over the professor's writings from the primitive stages of his career in academia, and I must admit that I found the earliest of them to be rather stuffy and almost impenetrably dense. Clearly the professor had carried quite a bit of that arrogance which comes sometimes with the maturing of intelligent youths.

As we disembarked from the train and made our way towards the awaiting carriage, my attention fell upon one of the most beautiful women on which I had ever laid my eyes. She was a petite woman adorned in a ruffled black dress and black hat, both of which were accentuated by scarlet red roses. I estimated that she could not have been more than thirty years old. She had lustrous, flowing hair that was as black as the night sky, dark brown eyes which captivated all around her with just a batting of her full eyelashes, and a way of moving which was not quite graceful but instead paradoxically rough and yet delicate. I must have been far too distracted, as I found myself being jolted from my reverie after slamming my shoulder into a rough-looking man who was aiming to board the train.

"Did you catch a glimpse of that woman back there, Holmes?" I asked, finally catching up to my friend.

"Indeed, I did, Watson," he said. "She would certainly be difficult to miss."

Having finally navigated our way through the crowd, we reached our carriage and were off to the coroner's office, which proved to be a relatively short distance away from the train station. Still, in the time that I had available to me, I gazed out the window and took in the incredible sights of the endless sea of green, rolling pastures and hills, which is in some ways so

unique to England. We had caught a stroke of luck with the weather, the
rainclouds of London seemingly having been swept away by the speed of
the train and replaced with a bright summer sun and a sky mixed with
varying shades of blue.

Within about ten minutes' time, we had reached a grey brick building
with a rusting sign that read simply: EDWARD BURNSIDE, M.D.

"I would say that this is our destination, Watson," said Holmes, his step
quickening at the proximity to the next stage of his investigation.

Before we reached the front door, it was opened by a burly, bearded
fellow who stepped out into the summer sunlight, his hat pulled down
slightly over his eyes and his hand resting on his holstered pistol. Despite
his menacing silhouette in the frame of the doorway, the young man did
not seem to be the least bit upset by our presence, as he stepped forward
and displayed a wide, welcoming smile to my friend and I.

"Mr. Sherlock Holmes, I presume," said the man good-naturedly. "It is
an absolute honor to meet such an esteemed investigator as yourself."

"You are far too kind, I am sure," said Holmes humbly.

"Nonsense, Mr. Holmes. I have been keeping tabs on some of your little
adventures and must say that I have learned a considerable amount from
you. But I think that I have foregone the appropriate manners for which
this situation calls. I am Constable Geoffrey Taylor, and I am at your dis-
posal."

Constable Taylor turned to me and said, "And of course, Dr. Watson. It
is a pleasure to meet you as well. While I would certainly enjoy being documented in the annals of crime and detection, let us hope that this situation
is simply as it appears to be and not anything more serious."

The constable shook our hands in turn, and never one to be anything
less than direct with his thoughts, Holmes said, "It is interesting to me,
Constable, that you are so accepting of our presence here. My colleague
and I, along with Inspector Lestrade of Scotland Yard, felt that my request
would be—let us say—ill-received."

Shaking his head, the constable replied, "Perhaps there are those police-
men who would prefer not to interact with amateur detectives, but I do
not subscribe to that notion. I have remarked to my wife on many occasions that my duty is to get the heart of the matter and determine the facts,
whatever they may be—even if they are in complete opposition with my
proposed line of thinking. However we get there is of no importance to me
as long as we do get there."

"An admirable view, I would say, Mr. Taylor," I put in.

He paused, looking out at the quiet landscape. There were sounds of birds in the distance, and after their singing subsided, he said, "Besides, I have never been to London, but it seems to be a land of strange and fascinating happenings, unlike here."

Constable Taylor emphasized the last two words with a flick of his hand toward the pastureland.

"I would really caution you against that sort of thinking, constable," said Holmes sternly. "It is with great certainty that I say that there are far more bizarre and wicked events going on in the immediate area than you have even conceived possible. Perhaps another reading of one of Watson's tales would be in order."

The look of consternation and anxiety displayed on the constable's face was one that was rather humorous; as it appeared that the foundation of his entire world-view had been shaken by that single comment made by my friend. Suddenly, the quiet, boring area that he patrolled had been transformed into a dark, nightmarish land filled with swindlers, thieves, and murderers at every bend in the road. In some ways, I felt pity for the constable's naivety, and so I decided it was necessary to lighten the mood.

"Do not be troubled, constable," I said, laughing. "He surely has made such remarks to me as well, and I do not enjoy my trips to the countryside any less than I ever have."

"Nor do I, Watson," said Holmes. "I am never disappointed with what I find in these environs. If you will pardon me, Constable, I think that we have spent more than enough time with pleasantries. Show us to the body."

"Very...very well, Mr. Holmes," said the constable, trying to regain his composure. "Dr. Burnside is right this way. Though, I must warn you, despite my approving your presence here, you will find Dr. Burnside to be a tad inhospitable."

"That is of no concern to me, Constable," said Holmes as he strode unceremoniously into the office leading to the examination room.

Holmes rapped on the open door twice as he passed through the entranceway, and the old coroner was obviously startled and demonstrated his unease by jumping halfway out of his seat.

"You must be the ones from London," grumbled Dr. Burnside as he stood up from his desk.

The coroner was at least seventy-five years of age, with rough, wavy white hair, and glasses that seemed to be perpetually perched on the edge of his sharp nose. He was dressed impeccably in a custom black suit and vest, and when he spoke, his voice was tinged with a light Scottish accent.

"Correct you are, doctor," said Holmes. "We would appreciate your assistance in the matter of Professor Roderick Norton."

Dr. Burnside harrumphed and said, "Waste of time if you ask me my opinion. I was not aware that the police were in the business of whiling away their days examining closed cases."

"I am not the police, Dr. Burnside."

"But he is," Burnside said, pointing at Constable Taylor. "And he should be out there investigating all of the other business that remains unsolved in these parts."

"He is just upset because he thinks that someone stole some paint and wood from the old barn on the edge of his property. Probably just some children causing a little bit of mischief."

"Well, we would know more than 'probably' if you were doing your job, wouldn't we?"

Holmes was clearly impatient and said, "The body, if you would be so kind, Doctor."

Burnside produced some more of his typical grumbles but did as Holmes requested, and soon we were examining the remains of Professor Roderick Norton.

"Please conduct your examination, Watson. I would very much like to see if the results of your inquiry match those documented on the report that we read."

Ignoring the further remonstrations of the obviously disgruntled medical man, I began my examination. There could be no doubt that Professor Norton had died as a result of a combination of a severe skull fracture and break of his neck. A large portion of jagged bone protruded from the top of his head, and his neck bent sharply to the right, leaving him in a rather unnatural position. His eyes seemed cloudy and appeared to have minor abrasions that had most likely been caused by the shattering of his glasses when he fell. There was no evidence of any fractures in his hands or arms, though I did note the same minor contusion on the front of his right shin that Dr. Burnside had mentioned in his report. Overall, I could not fault any of the conclusions that Dr. Burnside had reached, and I said as much to the other parties in the room.

"And there is no evidence of any intentionally inflicted trauma of any kind, Watson?" asked Holmes.

I lifted the mangled head off of the table and tried my best to examine the back portion of his skull.

"Honestly, Holmes, it is difficult to say with certainty, him being in this condition and all. But, if you forced my hand, I would say no—there is no evidence of any sort to support the idea that he was struck in the head prior to his fall."

"Very good, Watson," said Holmes with a nod of his head. "I shall take your word for it. Now, Dr. Burnside, please show me the clothes that Norton was wearing when he was brought in."

"Perhaps, Mr. Holmes, I could retrieve those for the doctor and meet you outside on the veranda. The sunlight may help you to see more detail," said Constable Taylor, trying to prevent another outburst from Burnside.

"Very well, Constable. Watson and I shall wait outside."

As we departed, Holmes added, "Thank you for your time, Dr. Burnside. It was not my intention to trouble you, but it troubles me when conclusions are so quickly drawn."

With that, we were once again out in the warm summer air, and after having examined yet another corpse, it was nice to feel the breeze and smell the freshness of the air. Holmes, on the other hand, filled his pipe and began smoking and sending smoke rings out into the summer wind.

"I thought that you were a bit harsh on Dr. Burnside," I remarked while we waited for the constable.

"Really? I thought that I was not as harsh as I could have been. He is the type of man who is out to do the bare minimum in order to collect his pay, and in a field like this, that is dangerous indeed."

"You forget that the conclusions from my examination are not so different from his, Holmes."

"Not different in medical terms, no. But different in the sense that I do not believe that you are yet willing to come definitively to the same final conclusion of Norton's death as Burnside."

"You mean that it was the result of an accident? Well, I expressed my reservations to you before we left Baker Street, and I have not seen anything that would indicate criminal acts as of yet. It is strange that his arms are completely intact though."

Holmes removed his pipe from his mouth and grinned, "You are hedging your bets, Watson. Still, influenced as you may be by my continued interest in this little problem, it is important to note that you still wonder about the possibilities—and that imagination is what sets you apart from the likes of Burnside, my dear fellow."

"So you are still convinced that he was murdered, then?" I asked.

"I am convinced of no particular theory," he replied, "though I firmly believe that the probabilities are still very much in my favor."

"If that turns out to be true, I shall never believe it," I said with a laugh.

"There you are wrong, my dear fellow. With the proper evidence before you, granting that such evidence exists, you would certainly believe even the most outlandish chain of events to be entirely plausible."

The door opened behind us, and we turned to see Constable Taylor walking over to us with the belongings of Professor Norton.

"I apologize for the delay, Mr. Holmes," said Constable Taylor. "Dr. Burnside can be…"

"Difficult, yes. I gathered as much."

Holmes held what were seemingly Norton's pajamas before him and then first took the shirt over to a nearby workbench to examine it with his magnifying glass. He repeated this process with all of the possessions that were on Professor Norton's person when he died, and he finished the process with an examination of the professor's trousers. That he had found something of interest was apparent, as he smacked his hands together and turned to me with a satisfied expression on his face.

"Take a look, Watson. What do you see?"

I took Holmes's magnifying glass and began my own minute examination of the trousers, but I saw little more than mud and grass stains and told my friend as much.

"I would draw your attention to the right leg if I were you, my dear fellow," said Holmes with the air of a professor teaching a struggling student.

With a grunt of displeasure, I examined the right leg again and noticed a faint, white streak about one-third of the way up from the bottom, but I was not quite sure what it could be. Constable Taylor also proceeded to examine the trousers as well.

"Constable," Holmes began, "I would ask that you keep these items in a safe place. They may become important should my hypothesis be proven correct."

"Absolutely, Mr. Holmes. Is there anything else that I can do for you at this time? Would you and Dr. Watson like something to eat? I am sure that we can find you an adequate establishment, and you are both welcome to come and dine at my home. It would be no trouble at all, and my wife would be delighted I am sure."

While I had certainly worked up an appetite during the course of our travels, I knew very well that there was no way at all that Holmes would be diverted from his investigation now. Holmes was confident that he was fresh on the scent of something, and he would not want the trail to grow cold.

"We are much obliged to you, Constable, but I shall have to decline your offer. If you can direct me to the home of Professor Norton, I would very much appreciate it."

"Of course, Mr. Holmes. I can actually take you there if you would like. The staff is most likely not there—or should not be at any rate—as I had requested that the house be cleared once I heard of your imminent arrival."

"A wise decision, Constable. I would very much like to conduct my examination unencumbered by the prying eyes of the household."

"Of course."

"Tell me. How large is the staff that keeps up the professor's home?"

"I had not really had much interaction with the professor or the area of his small estate, but then, I am relatively new in my position and know very little about him. In fact, not many do—even old Dr. Burnside who has been here forever. The professor was a rather private person and retired here after leaving his post at his university. I believe that he kept four or five on, a groundskeeper, a tradesman, a housekeeper, and a butler. Forgive me if it turns out that I missed anyone."

"What had they to say about the death of Professor Norton?"

The constable's face turned red, and I knew that the answer that he was about to give would embarrass him greatly. To his credit, he soldiered on.

"I have not spoken with them. I really only spoke with Mr. Peters, the groundskeeper, as he was the one who had found the professor lying broken in the front yard."

Holmes was frustrated but not as much as I had expected. He stood silent for a moment, scratched his chin, and then turned to speak to the constable.

"That is a rather poor error on your part, Constable. However, your mistake may, in fact, have its advantages."

"I do not understand, Mr. Holmes."

"No, but you may once this is all over with. You may even learn some invaluable lessons in the art of detection."

Having made his point, Holmes made his way to the Constable's carriage, and I soon joined him.

"Well that is not very good police work, is it Holmes?"

"No, and let that serve as a lesson to him. Regardless of how this all turns out, I can assure you that Constable Taylor will not only look the part of a constable but will also act the part too."

Holmes relit his pipe and steepled his fingers before him, and I rested my head back and closed my eyes, just listening to the hooves of the horses

"We are much obliged to you, Constable, but I shall have to decline your offer."

as they clipped and clopped down the road toward the spot where the professor had literally come face to face with death.

$$\wr$$

If it were not for the fact that we were investigating a death and possible murder, I would have said that the trip itself was quite pleasant, and I could not help but marvel at the natural beauty and privacy that the land encompassing the professor's small estate provided. We passed no one along the way; save for an older gentleman who seemed delighted to be out walking in the fresh air. The constable confirmed as much when he told us that the man lived many miles away and quite lived for his country strolls. So patterned was he that he became rather enraged when the inclement weather prevented him from engaging in his favorite pastime. Holmes nodded and noted the man's name before leaning his head back and continuing to puff on his pipe.

The professor's home was set back amongst a splendid grove of trees whose long branches were packed with bright green leaves which were positively flourishing in the heavenly rays of the glowing summer sun. The driveway led up to a front lawn that was comprised of grass that was so well kept that I had a difficult time believing that it was not some luxurious carpet that had been left outdoors to dry. The house itself was two-stories and was made of white stone that had begun to age, its once bright sheen having been replaced by a natural greying. While I am not an expert on architectural design, I thought that the building in some ways exuded an almost gothic quality, with its two chimneys set atop it like spires and its sides flanked by stone balconies. The windows on the building's face were curious in the sense that they were set back behind exquisitely carved white wooden balconies—not stone like the others—which were supported by braces set into the stone of the home proper. Considering that the professor had been found in the front yard, I assumed that one of those second-floor windows belonged to the professor's bedroom.

"Constable, have you any objection to Dr. Watson and I conducting our examination of the premises ourselves while you gather the remaining members of the household?" Holmes asked.

If the young constable was disappointed at his exclusion, he did not show it. Instead, he produced a key from his pocket and handed it directly to Holmes.

"Not at all, Mr. Holmes. This is the key to the front door. You are certainly friends and agents of the law, and I have no issue with your being allowed the opportunity to examine the scene at your leisure."

"Thank you, Constable. I would ask that you at least allow us three to four hours before returning with the others. That should be ample enough a period for me to produce a preliminary analysis."

"Very good, Mr. Holmes. Dr. Watson. I shall see you both later this afternoon. I would mention that the professor's body was discovered right over there below that window."

The constable, facing the home, pointed his finger at a window on the right and a patch of ground below the balcony.

"Good day, Constable," said Holmes. "I hope to be able to provide a satisfactory update upon your return."

Holmes and I watched the constable's carriage disappear into the depths of the grove, and once he was out of sight, Holmes immediately snapped into action.

"Come, Watson. The game is afoot! Before we begin our search of the house itself, let us first see what the ground can tell us. I can only hope that the rains and the trampling of the lawn by the feet of the curious has not damaged or eliminated any possible evidence."

"Let us hope that is not the case, Holmes," I said in agreement.

Holmes walked directly over to the spot that the constable had indicated and immediately began to employ those unique methods of examination that I had come to recognize as a crucial part of his investigative process. After standing back a ways in the lawn and peering up at the window and balcony itself, he dropped to the ground and crawled slowly through the grass, his keen eyes transfixed on the ground below. The grass was still wet from the rains of the previous days and the dew of the morning, and I could see the water and grass stains soaking into the fabric of Holmes's trousers. Holmes himself did not care in the slightest, and he seemed to be as happy as a child who had just been given a new toy.

"See here, Watson," he said, motioning me over with a wave of his hand, "you can still make out the outline of where Norton was found lying. Despite the ground moisture and condensation, it is still possible to see some of the blood comingled with the grass here."

"Yes, you are certainly correct, Holmes. In fact, I would say that the fact that the ground was saturated has actually helped to outline the approximate placement of the body."

"Quite so, my dear fellow. And look here—do you see these marks? These are certainly curious."

I looked to where Holmes was pointing, and I must admit that I did not really see anything but more grass.

"Look closely, Watson, and you will see where the ground has been disturbed in certain sections, almost as though divots have been repaired."

"Oh, yes!" I started, "I do see that now. I wonder what could have caused that?"

I had no doubt that Holmes had heard my question, but as was typical of him in such situations, he ignored it completely and continued to move about the rest of the right side of the lawn.

After he stood up and brushed himself off, he took one last look up at the balcony above and said, "That would certainly be a nasty fall, eh, Watson?"

Clearly his question had been a rhetorical one, as he immediately turned on his heels and marched up the front staircase to the front door, key in hand. The front door was situated under a small dome, and this only added to my sense of the house being somewhat gothic. The large double-door itself had a massive door-knocker in the center of it and was made of darkly stained oak. Holmes quickly opened the door and we were then inside the home of the late Professor Norton.

As exceptional as the exterior of the home had been, the interior was even more so. The floors were made of dark rosewood, which seemed to form patterns throughout the floor. In one section of the foyer, two book-matched pieces joined together to create the outline of a face. I was unsure where we would begin our investigation of the interior of the home, but I suspected that we would first make our way to the balcony that we had been viewing from the outside. Of course, I soon found that I was incorrect in my assumptions.

"No, Watson," said Holmes, apparently reading my mind, "I think it would be best that we begin our search in the place that would be most dear to an academic in his own home—the study."

I followed Holmes around the house until we located the study, a room that had tall, built-in bookcases on each wall that were filled with more books than I believe most library collections hold. However, unlike the many books that one typically finds in a manor, which are little more than decorative pieces to show off to one's guests, these books all showed signs of wear and usage, with the spines displaying the cracks and creases that come with repeated handling and reading.

"Have a look around, Watson, and I will take a look through the desk over there to see if there is anything of significance stored inside."

"Are there any specific items that I should be searching for, Holmes?"

Holmes shrugged his shoulders, "Who can say, Watson? After all, we have only just begun, have we not?"

It was certainly a study in silence during the hours that we spent in that room, as the ticking of the grandfather clock was the only sound to be heard other than my footsteps and Holmes's shuffling of papers. Now and then, I took different books off of the shelves and glanced at their contents. At one point, I had quite a surprise when I took down a rather large, leather-bound book from the shelf and found it to be a copy of the original King James Bible from sixteen hundred and eleven. Even with its rarity and import, the book was well worn; evidencing again that the professor was more interested in the Word than in simply keeping his book in pristine condition. Not wanting to damage the tome myself though, I soon replaced it and continued my search of the bookshelves.

At one corner of the room, I found a section where the professor had stored all of his personal and published writings, including a book whose title did not seem familiar from our earlier research. I took the book down from the shelf and found that it was certainly not a volume that had been produced for the masses. Other than the title and author's name on the leather-bound spine, there were no exterior markings. When I opened the book, I found that it was actually entirely handwritten, and the title *To Dream the Last Sunset* was written in an ornate script above an inscription to a woman named Sarah.

"Take a look at this Holmes," I said.

Holmes did not respond directly, as his attention was focused on a few sheaves of rather vintage paper and what looked to be a letter of some sort. He had a peculiar look on his face, and I wondered if he had found something of importance. He did not say so, but instead just folded the papers and put them inside his jacket pocket.

"Interesting, Watson," said Holmes. "Interesting indeed. My contact at the library mentioned nothing of the professor having written a novel. Be a good fellow and leave it on the desk there. Now we must move on, as the constable will most likely be returning with the remainder of the household within the next hour or so. That should give us just enough time to conduct our search of the professor's chambers."

Compared to the subtle extravagance of his study, the professor's bedroom was quite simple in its décor, there being little more than a bed, a table, an armoire, a dresser, and a mirror. Being situated in the front of the home, the bedroom windows offered a grand view of the front lawn. Holmes went right over to the balcony doors and began to examine them closely. He soon seemed content with his findings, and he abruptly threw the doors open and stepped out onto the balcony. The unbridled wind then poured into the room, and the mix of warm and cool added a freshness to the room that was certainly needed, as the house had become quite stuffy as the day had progressed.

I remained where I was and simply watched as Holmes stood in the middle of the balcony and looked over every visible section of it, including the short, decorative railing that barely came up to his knees. A few minutes passed, and he turned to look at the face and roof of the house. After nodding to himself a few times, he requested that I step outside and take a look myself.

"Do you notice anything of interest, Watson?" Holmes asked cryptically.

Try as I might, I did not see anything that would be of any importance to us in the course of our investigation.

"No, other than that this house is a truly remarkable example of expert craftsmanship."

Holmes chuckled, "It is certainly that. But I would call your attention to the areas on the walls there."

I directed my attention to the areas indicated, but I saw little more than minor imperfections in the stone.

"No matter, Watson. I am still not sure myself whether the pieces I have gathered fit together in some way or if they will ultimately form a tangible whole at all. On the face of it though, I would say it is a rather foul and nasty business."

I was about to respond when he stopped me and said, "But look there. It appears that we have company."

I first heard and then saw the familiar sight of Constable Taylor and his horses as they made their way up the driveway through the trees.

"Come, Watson. Let us go and greet the members of the house."

The reactions of the staff members to the situation and to the presence of Mr. Sherlock Holmes could not have been more different. Mr. James Peters, who we understood to be the groundskeeper, was a man of about thirty-five years of age, with a well-trimmed beard, slicked back hair, and a rather brash and arrogant air about him. He was dressed in clothes befitting his occupation, but he seemed to me to carry himself in such a way as to suggest that he was, in all actuality, simply a royal turned hobbyist. Standing next to him in complete contrast was a rather scraggly fellow who was well beyond the years of middle age. He had greasy black hair that was wildly unkempt and which covered the dark black of his eyes. He did not appear to be particularly interested in anything other than getting his cigar lit, but it was clear that he was watching everything that was happening with extreme interest. He was identified as Mr. Theodore Colby, and his role was to tend to the general structural upkeep of the residence, the workers' cottages in the backyard, and the various sheds.

Standing next to Constable Taylor was a woman whom I estimated was just reaching middle age. It was clear that she was inarguably, despite her age and obvious state of mourning and despair, even more beautiful than the woman from the train platform. In fact, so similar were their features, it could be said that the woman standing before me was simply a more matured version of the woman that I had seen earlier. There were some noticeable differences though. While the eyes of the woman from the train platform had been brown and vibrant with excitement, this woman's eyes were an olive green and betrayed an intense sadness. Additionally, even in her hour of grief, she moved with a sense of grace that our society was beginning to see less and less in our supposedly more modern and distinguished age. Not wanting to trouble her too much at that time, we avoided addressing her directly and learned that she was Ms. Roberts, the housekeeper and cook for Professor Norton.

Helping to console and support Ms. Roberts was a man who would best be described as the most prototypical butler one has ever seen. The elderly man stood tall and at attention, indicating that he may have had some level of military background, and his face remained stoic as the harrowed countenance of Ms. Roberts leaked tears onto the shoulder of his crisp black suit. However, an imperceptible tremble in his hand seemed to indicate that he held some amount of underlying sorrow over the loss of his employer. He was named as Mr. Stephen Bradshaw.

Having cast his all-knowing gaze over this diverse group in just a few seconds' time, Holmes finally spoke up.

"Please allow me to convey my deepest sympathies for the loss of Professor Norton. I regret that I must trouble you at this most difficult time."

"Obliged, sir," remarked Mr. Bradshaw.

"Th-thank you, Mr. Holmes," mustered Ms. Roberts. "It is certainly..."

"So what are you here for anyway, Mr. Holmes?" interjected Mr. Colby, sarcastically extending my friend's name.

Before Holmes could respond, Mr. Peters jumped in with a sense of calm and reason that I had not expected from him.

"I would ask that you please pardon my friend Colby here, Mr. Holmes. We have all been quite shaken by this unexpected turn of events. Professor Norton was a good man, he really was. I extend an offer of any assistance that I can provide you in your time here, sir."

Colby almost growled, his dark eyes disappearing behind another unruly wall of hair, and his mouth opened as if to speak again.

"Mr. Holmes, if it is all right with you, I think that it would be best if Colby and I took a walk so that he can calm himself down. He worked for the professor almost as long as Bradshaw here and actually built a lot of this place. We will be in our cottages whenever you should need to speak to us."

"Certainly, Mr. Peters. I think that course of action would be entirely appropriate at this particular moment. Expect my knock in about an hour's time."

With that, Peters led Colby by the arm around the left side of the house, the latter nearly tumbling into a rosebush as he tried to free himself from his friend's grip, and they were then gone from our sight.

"Mr. Bradshaw," Holmes began, "I should like to speak with you and Ms. Roberts in a few moments. Would you be so good as to take the lady inside so that she can have some time to collect herself?"

The butler nodded his head silently, and Holmes and I watched as Bradshaw slowly led the tragic figure of Ms. Roberts up the staircase and into the house.

"What would you like me to do, Mr. Holmes?" asked Constable Taylor.

"I imagine that our interviews here will take us into the early part of the evening. I suggest that you go home and join your wife for dinner. I am sure that she would be pleased."

"As you say, Mr. Holmes," the Constable agreed. "I will return at about eight o'clock this evening."

We said our goodbyes to the constable, and his carriage began to move down the driveway.

"Oh, I almost forgot," he yelled back to us as the carriage ground to a halt. "Professor Norton's wife arrived earlier today and has taken up a room at the inn. I assumed that you would want to speak with the others without having to deal with a grieving widow. She was none too pleased, if I may say so, but it seemed the right course. Although, Ms. Roberts herself is certainly torn up right good."

"His –" I began.

Holmes cast me a glance that indicated that this turn of events was not at all a surprise to him and thanked the constable for the information before waving him on his way. Once the constable was out of earshot, Holmes walked over to the rosebush that had almost claimed Mr. Colby and then turned to me and shook his head.

"Watson, you disappoint me. That the professor was married is certainly something that was quite apparent from the data laid before you."

"I guess I will just have to take your word for it, Holmes."

"Surely you noticed that in his earlier writings, the professor wrote about numerous different types of women, most probably women that he had loved or had wished for. But then in the few original works after that, he began writing solely about the same woman over and over. It seemed as though the professor had at last found his desired lady. That would also explain the decline in his output, would it not?"

"I had not thought of it like that, Holmes, but it certainly seems like a plausible enough explanation."

"Watson, I must say," said Holmes, chuckling, "you are always so willing to accept my explanations. I firmly believe that everything that I have just said is correct, so far as it goes, but I have also verified it in my investigation here today."

"So, in other words, you found something indicating that Norton was married?"

"More than that, my dear fellow, but we do not have the time to get into all of that now. I would call your attention to the portrait that is hanging over the fireplace in the sitting room. I happened to see it as we walked by that room earlier."

I did not have time to respond, as he had once again turned away and had made his way hurriedly up the staircase to seek out two people who he hoped would help to shed some light on the darkness of this mystery.

$$\mathit{el}$$

"You say that Professor Norton had been gone for just about two months, Mr. Bradshaw?" Holmes asked the butler as we sat in the sitting room.

Upon our entering the room a few minutes prior, I could not help but notice that above the fireplace hung a framed oil painting of the middle-aged professor and his considerably younger wife, who I was inwardly shocked to learn was the young woman who had so captured my attention earlier in the day.

"I would call your attention to the portrait that is hanging in the sitting room."

"Yes, Mr. Holmes," Bradshaw said. "Two months. He had seemed a bit unwell and had planned a holiday for himself on the Continent. He did not really elaborate on his travel plans, and it was not my place to ask him his destination."

"And when did Professor Norton return from his holiday, Mr. Bradshaw? Had he been back long?"

"That is the part of it that is quite unbelievable, sir. He had just returned home that rainy afternoon. We had received word from him earlier that morning that he would be home by evening time and that we were to return here at dinnertime."

"Return here, Mr. Bradshaw? Do you mean to say that all of you, including yourself, Ms. Roberts, Mr. Peters, and Mr. Colby, did not remain here in the two months that the professor was away?"

"No, sir. None of us did. While the professor was gracious enough to allow us all to live on his property and certainly trusted us all, he did not seem to like the idea of his home and grounds being open in his absence. Thus, when his bags were loaded, I locked the door securely, and it was not opened again until the professor himself turned the key that afternoon. We all stayed at the local inn."

"Interesting, Bradshaw," Holmes said mysteriously. "Very interesting."

Holmes paused for a moment and then asked what I considered to be a rather blunt question.

"Shocking to see that sight in the front lawn, was it not, Bradshaw?"

"One never quite gets used to seeing death, Mr. Holmes, though I had seen much of it in my time in the army. I was awakened by the loud cry from Mr. Peters and rushed to my window to see the horror outside. It was everything that I could do to get upstairs to Ms. Roberts in time and prevent her from making her way to the balcony herself."

The butler appeared lost in his memories for a few moments and then regained his composure.

"Pardon my manners, sirs. I have quite forgotten to ask you if you would care for any refreshments."

"Nothing for me, Bradshaw, but thank you just the same."

"Thank you, Bradshaw. I am quite well at the moment, but Holmes and I may be in need of something later."

"Certainly, sir."

"Upon your return here, did you find anything to be out of order in any way?"

"Not at all, sir. The house looked just as I left it, save for a few cobwebs that I quickly dispatched."

"How did you find it, working for the professor?"

"Easiest job I ever had, if I am being honest, sir, especially in these last few years since…well…it is not really my place to say."

Holmes nodded his head, "Admirable, Bradshaw. Your loyalty shows through for sure. But you may relax yourself, as I am already aware that the professor and his wife had been separated for some time. I will not pursue that line of questioning out of respect for you."

"Very good, sir. To return to your question, I was a bit lost after the passing of my wife and was simply looking to find employment that would allow me to be productive and yet have time to enjoy these last years of my life. This job afforded me that opportunity."

"And what of the professor himself, how would you rate him as an employer?"

"Professor Norton was a true gentleman, sir, a true gentleman. You will not find many men smarter or nicer than he. We were none of us ever treated rudely or like we were just servants. He treated us as friends of his, and as long as we did what was asked of us, we were given extended periods where we could do as we wished."

"Have you ever seen these documents before?" Holmes asked, removing the sheaves of paper from his jacket pocket.

Bradshaw flipped through the pages, but he did not display any indication of recognition on his face.

"Can't says that I have, sir. Seems just a bunch of gibberish to me, with the random letters and numbers and all, but the professor was a brilliant man, so it must mean something."

"Quite so. Tell me, what did a typical day in the life of the professor look like?"

Bradshaw smiled a bit and said, "Not exactly what you would expect from a retired man, I would wager, Mr. Holmes. He was very conscious of his time, and he did not like to waste even a second of it. He would awaken every day at about six o'clock in the morning, get dressed, converse with Ms. Roberts as they had breakfast, and then retire to his study and bedroom for much of the day, only leaving for meals and things like that. It is a funny thing, but because he was so efficient in everything he did, we all joked that it seemed as though he knew how many steps it would take him to get from one end of the house to the other."

"Holmes can certainly relate to that last bit," I said, realizing I had unnecessarily interrupted the butler's train of thought.

Holmes glanced in my direction with a look that indicated that he was unhappy that I had stopped the butler's recollection.

"Of course, Dr. Watson," Bradshaw replied politely. "Where was I? Oh, yes. Most days, I would bring lunch to him and Ms. Roberts as they sat together on the balcony, with her reading him the newspaper or passages from one of his many books. You have seen the library I am sure."

"We have indeed—a truly remarkable collection. Now, it seems as though Ms. Roberts was close to the professor, Mr. Bradshaw. I must admit that I gathered as much from her appearance earlier."

"You would be correct in saying so, sir."

"Is there anything else of interest that you can tell us about the professor before we speak with Ms. Roberts?"

"I do not mean to repeat myself, sir, but as I said, he was a true gentleman—always polite, always caring how we were all doing."

Then, the butler paused and closed his one eye as if a thought had just occurred to him.

"Now that you mention it though, and I would not think this has any relation to your presence here, but there was one startling habit that the professor had."

"Pray, tell us about it, Mr. Bradshaw."

"Well, I guess it would be incorrect to say habit, really. At times throughout the night, the professor would walk throughout the house as if he were caught in some sort of trance. I remember the first time that it happened, and I must say that it was a bit unsettling, what with the emptiness of his gaze and all that."

"Ah, I would say that it sounds as though he suffered from somnambulism, eh, Holmes?" I asked.

"Your diagnosis appears to be appropriate, Watson. Tell me, Mr. Bradshaw, what would these episodes of somnambulating look like?"

"Mostly just walks to the kitchen to get a drink of water or something like that. I do recall Mrs. Norton saying that every night in which they slept here in this home; he would rise from his bed, open the door of the balcony, and march up to the edge and just stand there as if he were taking in the night air."

"Have you experienced many such cases in your practice, Watson?"

"Yes, Holmes, on many occasions," I said confidently. "Though it appears quite bizarre to an onlooker, it is actually quite common really. I remember one startling case from when I was in Afghanistan. Every night, without fail, a member of our regiment would stir and walk around the camp at exactly three o'clock. The first time that it happened, we thought that an enemy solider had snuck into the camp."

Clearly my story had helped to lighten the butler's mood as he, and even Holmes, shared a laugh with me as I recounted the short tale.

"You have been incredibly helpful, Mr. Bradshaw," said Holmes, standing up from his chair. "I thank you greatly for your time and would ask that you please fetch Ms. Roberts for us."

"I am happy to be of service, Mr. Holmes," said Bradshaw. "I shall return with the lady momentarily."

"Bradshaw seems to be a good fellow, wouldn't you say Holmes?" I remarked after the butler had departed from the room.

"Indeed, and his testimony was certainly intriguing, was it not?" said Holmes.

"Did it help you at all, Holmes?" I asked.

"It would seem as though the pieces are slowly starting to fit into place," was his only reply.

⸮ʔ

The composure and demeanor of the woman who greeted us in the sitting room was far different than it had been when we had first witnessed her descending from the constable's carriage. The inherent anguish remained, but it appeared that she had made a conscious decision to hold her emotions in check so that she could speak with us as soon as possible so that we may take possession of any important information that her testimony might hold. As she sat down in her chair next to the fireplace, she smiled and what an attractive smile it was.

"I am so grateful to you, Mr. Holmes," she began, "and to you as well, Dr. Watson. Even now, it gladdens me to know that you would take the time from your own busy schedules to take an interest in determining what happened to Roddy….I mean Professor Norton."

"I have said it before, but it bears repeating that you have my deepest sympathies for your loss, Ms. Roberts," said Holmes in that calming and reassuring way that he always had with women.

"I cannot imagine what you must be feeling at this moment, Ms. Roberts. But please know that we are here for you," I added.

"Thank you both again," she said, her hand wiping at a tear that had begun to form at the corner of her eye.

"If you are up to the task, I would very much like to hear about your view of the professor and the goings-on of his household."

"Of course, Mr. Holmes. I will answer all questions as best as I am able."

"Very well. How long have you been employed here at the professor's estate, Ms. Roberts?"

"It would have been six years this August. I came on shortly after Rod... pardon me, Professor Norton...and his wife, Cassandra, got married. He thought that it would be good for his wife to have assistance around the house."

"Were there other staff in the professor's employ when you were hired on here?"

"Why, yes—Teddy Colby had remained on after helping construct this house, and he served to manage all of the upkeep. Stephen Bradshaw had served Professor Norton at the university and had continued his employ after the professor's retirement. Jim Peters was also here, and I was astonished at how he had built up the grounds, especially the roses—Cassandra always loved those."

I could not help but note the subtle scorn that was attached to each mention of Mrs. Norton's name. Thus far, we had learned very little about the widow, and I hoped that Ms. Roberts might educate us as our conversation progressed.

"Since you have mentioned her twice, I see fit to just ask you this now, Ms. Roberts. What was the state of affairs between the professor and his wife?"

Ms. Roberts shifted in her seat and appeared to make up her mind that if she were going to tell her story, it would be the whole story.

"They were happy in the beginning, of that there is no doubt. But such things that are impermanent ultimately pass away in time. I have come to learn that lesson."

"There seemed to be a considerable age difference between the two of them, though that is not necessarily out of the ordinary in the case of marriages in the higher-classes."

"About a quarter of a century, give or take. I only wish that his eyes had started to fail him before he ever laid them on her."

Ms. Roberts paused, collecting herself, the expression on her face one of the realization that she had fallen prey to her emotions once again. To her credit, she quickly regained herself.

"I apologize, Mr. Holmes. You must understand that this is an incredibly trying time for me. I truly adored Cassandra once, and it was with great pity that I found out what she was and began to despise her for it."

"Ms. Roberts, your apology is readily accepted but entirely unnecessary. Let me ask you a few more direct questions. Then, perhaps it would be best for you to tell your story in your own way."

"What is it that would you like to know, Mr. Holmes?"

"How long ago did the professor's sight begin to falter?"

"At least three years, but it was only within the last two years that the decline became much more pronounced—at first, it was not that bad, but after a time, it became difficult for him to read the smaller text of some of his books and for him to write as much as he once had."

"Was his trip to the Continent in any way related to the state of his health, Ms. Roberts?"

She nodded her head and said, "It was his sole purpose in going, Mr. Holmes. He had heard of some doctors who may be able to help him in some way and felt that it was worth the try if it could help restore his vision. And, if not, so be it."

"If his eyesight was as you say, Ms. Roberts, I find it interesting that he would choose to venture abroad without a companion at his side."

My friend had said those words as a statement, not a question, and the insinuation was clear. However, I noted that his eyes gazed somewhat sorrowfully upon Ms. Roberts as he watched her. Ms. Roberts stared at my friend and nodded to him as if they had reached an understanding with one another.

"I could not let him go alone, but the rest of the household was completely unaware of my accompanying him, you see. Roddy was not in as bad a way as all that, at least not then anyway, but there was no doubt of what was to come for him. To think that a man filled with such light would be faced with the inevitability of such darkness."

Before I could comment, Holmes pressed on, "Had you known the professor to walk in his sleep?"

"Roddy was always doing that," she said. "He believed it to be an inherited condition," she said.

"What of the last two years?"

"It would not happen as much, no," she said. "It seemed as though his condition really only worsened in times of great stress."

"Such as might be brought on by a letter from an estranged wife requesting an increase in payments?"

"I can see that you know a great deal more than I suspected, Mr. Holmes. I will tell you all that I know."

"Pray tell us what you can in your own way, Ms. Roberts. You will find that Watson and I are very good listeners."

"It is like this, Mr. Holmes. As I said, Roddy and Cassandra had been happy for a short while after their marriage, and they would travel and enjoy each other's company. But then, the cracks in the foundation started to show, and Cassandra became unruly and bitter. It was obvious that she remained here only to be able to afford her extravagant tastes. Eventually, they reached a compromise and agreed that they should take some time apart, and she went to live with her family in London. Her departure made a marked change in Roddy, and he was once again the man that I had met when I had first arrived here, so lively and enthusiastic. After a time, he and I became very close with one another, and I found myself rather taken with him. We would sit and have breakfast together, and over the last year, I would read to him out on the balcony. He always said that he liked the way my voice sounded when reading in the breeze. Anyway, every few months, he would receive letters from Cassandra requesting more and more money, as she felt that it was necessary for her to be able to keep up appearances. When we returned a few days ago, there was another letter waiting in the post."

"There you may be able to clear something up for me, Ms. Roberts. It was my understanding that you and the other members of the staff had taken residence at the inn in the professor's absence. Obviously, that is not entirely correct, being that you were with him on his travels. When did you return?"

"I arrived about one week ago. I had told the others that I was going to stay with some relatives in Sussex. After we returned to England, I came back here and took a room at the inn like the others and awaited Roddy's coming. He wanted it that way, as he felt that it would embarrass me otherwise. But I didn't care, as I was sure that the others suspected something. We were to have been married after the divorce was finalized, so what did it matter?"

"How did you find the house upon your return, Ms. Roberts?"

"The same as it always was, Mr. Holmes. There did not seem to be anything amiss. After all, no one had set foot inside since we left for our trip."

"Were you aware of the professor working on any original works in the past year, Ms. Roberts?" Holmes asked, shifting the conversation.

"No, Mr. Holmes," she said regretfully. "Unfortunately, he said that his creativity had faded with his eyesight."

"Have you any opinions on the other members of the house? Obviously Bradshaw seems to be quite the loyal friend, but what of Colby and Peters?"

"In my time here, I have done my best to keep my distance from them really. The way that Peters carries himself reminds me a lot of Cassandra, and I always found Colby to come across as devious if I am being truthful."

Holmes stood up, looking at the painting over the fireplace, and then turned back toward Ms. Roberts.

"One more question, Ms. Roberts. How would you have felt if Professor Norton had decided to try to rekindle the romance of his marriage with Mrs. Norton over these last two years?"

Ms. Roberts too stood up and walked over to stand next to Holmes, her hand falling onto the mantle.

"I had thought about that many times, Mr. Holmes, knowing that one day Cassandra could show up here and want to start anew. And one night, as I lie awake looking at the moonlight, I had my answer. I would have been truly happy for him."

"Watson, if you would be so good as to take the lady for a walk in the evening air. I have a few matters to attend to."

"Surely, Holmes," I agreed readily.

"And before you go, Watson, I would ask you this. What would you estimate the professor's height to be? I figured it at about three inches past six feet."

"That is about right I would say, Holmes," I concurred.

With that answer given, I did as Holmes requested, and with the lady on my arm, we exited the house and made our way down the staircase, soon feeling the crunch of the earth beneath our feet as we walked silently in the fading daylight.

ﻋﻠﻰ

We were not gone longer than an hour, and when we returned, we found Holmes pacing about the house and muttering to himself. Constable Taylor, who had passed us on our walk, sat with Mr. Bradshaw and did not seem to have any idea what was going on. Up and down the stairs Holmes would go, never quite going to the same place twice. I tried to keep pace with him, but as was usually the case in the middle of an experiment, he was full of such enthusiasm that he would not stop until he had reached whatever conclusion it was that he was seeking. Thus, it was not until a few moments later that he finally sat down at the desk in the professor's study and smacked his hand down in the middle of it.

"If I am correct, this is rather ingenious, Watson!" said Holmes excitedly.

"Very clever, indeed."

"What do you mean, Holmes?" I asked with some confusion.

"Tell me, Watson. How do you think the professor came to fall to his death?"

"Based on what we know, I would wager that he had an unfortunate accident in the middle of one of his somnambulatory episodes."

"Bravo, Watson!" he exclaimed. "I am glad to see that your deductive faculties continue to improve."

"I have absolutely no idea what you are talking about, Holmes," I said.

"Well, that is no matter. All will soon be made clear. Follow me."

I followed Holmes as we marched to the balcony from which the professor had fallen, and I stood outside next to the railing while Holmes took up a position next to the right side of the professor's bed.

"Now watch carefully, Watson. If the professor has calculated this accurately, it should be just twelve steps until I am standing with my leg against that railing there. Count aloud if you would, there's a good fellow."

Holmes began walking slowly toward me in a gait that was not his own. After I had reached the count of ten, Holmes stopped and turned to me with a grin.

"Here is the solution to it all, Watson."

I watched as his left foot came down on the floor of the balcony, marking his eleventh step. It was then that I realized that he could go no farther, and I watched in horror as his right leg began to rise up and make contact with the railing itself. I soon found that my worry was unnecessary, as Holmes had already regained his footing.

"With the time you have had to reflect on the matter, Watson," said Holmes, "what do you make of the marks on the wall? I would suggest that you continue pondering the matter."

I did not get to respond, as he had already begun walking back in the direction of the professor's study. Once again, I followed after him, and upon reaching the study, I sat down in a chair across the desk from my friend.

"This tale nears its end, and I could not be happier for that fact, my dear fellow," he said, lighting his pipe.

"I really wish that you would enlighten me, Holmes, as I clearly have not reached the same conclusions that you have."

"That is true, but then, I have come into possession of some more evidence while you were enjoying your nice country stroll with Ms. Roberts."

"Now, Holmes," I said, getting upset, "you were the one who sent me

"If I am correct, this is rather ingenious, Watson!"

with her in the first place."

"Settle down, Watson," he said, chuckling. "I did not mean anything untoward. I simply meant to say that I utilized that time to converse with Peters and Colby and then to that elderly gentleman we met earlier today."

"You mean the man who enjoys his walking? Whatever could he have had to say that would shed any light on this situation?"

"Only that he had heard the sounds of sawing and hammering in this general area over the course of the last two months."

"And what would that indicate, Holmes? I am sure that sort of thing goes on a lot this time of year."

"You can certainly be obtuse at times, Watson," said Holmes. "But as I stated, all will be clear to you soon enough."

In the next few minutes, he recounted the testimony of Peters and Colby, and it seemed to be rather in line with the information that we had already gathered from the other members of the household. When he was done speaking, he extinguished his pipe and rose from his seat.

"Come, let us see if my little gambit will pay off."

We soon reached the bottom of the stairs and were greeted by Constable Taylor and Mr. Bradshaw.

"We thank you again for your hospitality, Mr. Bradshaw. I would ask that you give Ms. Roberts our best."

"You are leaving, sir?" asked the butler, a hint of surprise showing in his voice.

"We are retiring to the inn, Bradshaw," said Holmes matter-of-factly. "There is little more to be done here tonight. Should anyone need our assistance, they can find us there."

"Very good, sir," said the butler.

The constable did not look to be shocked by this turn of events, and he led the way to his carriage without a word. Holmes remained silent as we rode down the driveway, and after about fifteen minutes, he rapped on the door, and the carriage came to a swift halt.

"I think that this is far enough, constable," said Holmes.

"What are we doing, Holmes?" I asked.

"Do you think that you have the energy for some nocturnal surveillance?" he asked in reply.

"This heat has been rather tiring, but I believe that I can manage just fine," I said.

"Good, now let us just join the constable."

Taylor, having hid the horses and carriage in the trees out of sight, seemed lively, no doubt filled with anticipation as to what lay before us. It was clear to me that Holmes had filled in the constable with at least the basic framework of his plans, but since I was not as lucky, I spoke up and asked about our destination.

"Why, back to the professor's estate, of course," said Holmes as though the answer were as clear as day. "We must ensure that we are in position before our final guest arrives. Be sure to have your revolver ready just in case for when we take them into custody, Watson. I surely hope that we will not need it though."

That was all that he would say, and I considered myself fortunate that he had even said that much. Ominous storm clouds had begun to roll in just after sunset, and what I estimated to be the eleven o'clock hour was a time marked by complete and utter darkness. Not one bit of moonlight was able to break through the cloud cover, and I struggled to keep up with Holmes and the constable as we trudged through the grove. Eventually, I could see some light escaping from the windows of the house, but even those were starting to be doused at this late hour. We kept to the trees and made a circuitous route to the rear of the property, directly behind the cottages that Peters and Colby called home. I could see light emanating from one of the cottages, and the windows were visibly raised, as the curtains fluttered outward with the gusts that had picked up over the last few hours.

All three of us knelt behind a hedge, and from our vantage point, we could see a shadowy silhouette pass back and forth rapidly. I could not tell exactly who it was, but I was sure that the man was nervous. Suddenly, a shadowy figure moved across the lawn, barely visible in the blackness. There was a slight tap at the door, and I heard the voice of Peters whisper sharply in the night as we watched both shadows converse in the glow of the light.

"What kept you so long?"

"I was delayed by that detective, Sherlock Holmes. The constable had informed me earlier in the day that Holmes meant to speak to me this evening, and I waited and waited until eventually a message was delivered to the clerk indicating that he did not wish to speak with me until morning after all."

"A lucky turn I think, Cassandra. I sense that he suspects something."

"Why should he? You said it would be impossible for anyone to determine what we have done."

"You're right, of course, but I have heard stories about him, and I do not want to leave anything to chance. We need to get this right."

"And then it is all ours, darling."

There was silence for a time, and the shadows rocked and swayed in the light. But then something happened that none of us, including Holmes, expected. We saw another shadow move from the darkened cottage and then throw open the door of Peters' abode with a loud crash.

"I thought I saw you scurrying about out there, little lady," said the voice of Colby with the slur of inebriation. "Think you are just going to hang it all on me and take all of it for yourselves, do you?"

I heard Holmes exhale a quick breath and mutter something to himself in apparent frustration for not having foreseen this outcome.

"Quick, Watson, you're with me. Constable, you go around the front. We must do our best to prevent any more blood from being spilled."

I held my revolver at the ready as Holmes and I crouched and made our way from the hedge to the window. I tried to get a good vantage point through the window so that I could fire if necessary, but it was already too late. Before Mrs. Norton or Peters could say a word, the thunder of the oncoming storm roared and Colby fired two deafening shots from the pistol he was holding. Turning at the sound of the constable's footsteps behind him, Colby aimed to fire again but was dropped by two bullets expertly placed by Constable Taylor.

"Are you all right, Constable?" Holmes yelled through the wind as we rushed inside the cottage.

"The heart is certainly pumping a bit, but I'm none the worse for wear, Mr. Holmes."

"Watson, check on Mrs. Norton. I will see to Peters."

Even in the dim light, I could see that the eyes of Mrs. Norton were staring vacantly at the ceiling, a single bullet hole in her chest still oozing blood.

"My God. She's dead, Holmes," I said.

"I feared as much," said Holmes with a shake of his head. "Peters is as well."

The rain had begun to fall outside, and after a few moments, we heard the sound of rushing footsteps across the lawn. Mr. Bradshaw had come to see what had happened, and upon seeing the bodies on the floor, his countenance was a somber one indeed.

"Bradshaw," Holmes said after a moment, "we shall require your assistance I think."

The butler swallowed hard and said, "Whatever you need, Mr. Holmes."

"Very good, Bradshaw. Then go back into the house and take Ms. Roberts to the sitting room. No doubt she has heard the gunshots and is aware that something is out of place. She need not see any of this. Please inform her that we will be inside within the hour, and I will explain everything."

Bradshaw retreated to the house, and Holmes again shook his head in annoyance as he contemplated the scene before him.

"This was certainly not an eventuality for which I had planned, Watson," he said. "A pity that I had not the foresight to prevent this."

After one last look around the room, Holmes turned to the constable, who seemed to be awaiting orders, and advised him that we would need to load the bodies into the carriage for transport to the coroner. The constable disappeared into the night to retrieve his conveyance, and I sat down at the table across from Holmes to await the constable's return.

"This certainly was a foul and nasty business, Holmes. You were right about that."

Holmes steepled his fingers before him and said, "Death always is, Watson."

We were all gathered around the fireplace, and Holmes was sitting much as he had been when we were in the cottage. Ms. Roberts had taken the news of what had happened as well as could be expected, but she could not stop tears from escaping at the mention of Cassandra's name being among the list of the deceased.

"The poor girl," she said, wiping her eyes. "I do not know what happened to her."

"Mr. Holmes," said Constable Taylor, "I was hoping that you would be able to explain precisely what has happened here."

"Of course, constable. I absolutely intend to do just that. I would first ask the lady if she wishes to be present for my presentation."

"There is no question of that, Mr. Holmes. Please proceed with your narrative."

"I thought as much, Ms. Roberts. As Watson can tell you, I was intrigued by the newspaper article describing Professor Norton's death, as brief and lacking as the reporting was. After careful consideration, I decided that even though it were certainly possible that a man could accidentally fall to his own death from his bedroom window, it was more likely that another party acting in a heinous manner would be necessary to bring about that result. At that time, I was unable to formulate any particular theories, as the evidence was scant. So I took it upon myself to try to gather whatever knowledge I could from the surrounding area in London. A review of Professor Norton's writings was essential in establishing the man's intelligence and frame of mind, and the fact that his once-prolific career had been reduced to a slow trickle was something for which I would have to find a satisfactory answer at some point in time. That he was also a hopeless romantic was an important point. Upon reviewing the coroner's report that had been obtained by Inspector Lestrade of Scotland Yard, I was sure that my discounting of death by misadventure was justified, as the professor showed no sign of having braced himself during the fall. The interesting thing to note is that I myself started to call into question that same evidence when I later learned that the professor suffered from bouts of somnambulation. Our personal examination of the professor's corpse offered little more explanation for his tragic end, but a white marking on the leg of his pajamas became of interest to me, especially when paired with the contusion present on his shin. Therefore, I was left with the notion that there had to be some sort of force involved in the fall. Though, as Watson can attest, there was no sign of the professor having been struck."

Holmes paused for a moment to drink a swig of brandy, and to say that the room was silent would be an understatement. It really seemed as though even the raging storm outside had quieted to allow Holmes the adequate atmosphere to conduct his grand performance. With a sound of his thirst having been quenched, he continued on with his explanation.

"A search of the professor's study offered interesting clues as well, though their importance was not abundantly clear at the time of their discovery. Surely the scathing letter from Mrs. Norton demanding more funds and refusing the professor's request for a divorce was quite telling of an underlying conflict between the two feuding spouses, but that, in and of itself, was not conclusive of anything else. Additionally, the significance of the cryptic lists of letters and corresponding numbers that I found did not immediately present itself either—at least, not until I interviewed Mr. Bradshaw and Ms. Roberts. Due to his declining visual faculties, Professor Norton had begun to chart the exact number of steps that he would need to take to successfully navigate from one point to another in the house. In some miraculous working of the human mind, the professor somehow recalled these calculations in his somnambulations, and this is why he could safely come to a complete stop at the very edge of his balcony when having an episode in the middle of the night. I satisfactorily demonstrated for myself that each of his calculations was accurate."

"But Holmes, the professor's calculation from his bed to the balcony was wrong, was it not?" I asked. "You showed me yourself that it was not twelve but eleven steps from his bed to the railing."

"Watson, clearly you have formed the wrong conclusion from the facts. If I had to wager, I would say that you believe that someone had climbed a ladder and pushed the professor to his demise."

I felt the shade of embarrassment cross my face and said, "You are correct, Holmes. That is what I thought."

"Certainly a plausible theory, my dear fellow, but not the correct one. No, the professor's foes were far too cunning for that. As they are all dead and cannot fully explain their actions, some of what I am about to say might be considered conjecture, but I would argue that it is supported by the totality of the facts and can be further supported by additional discovery. I submit that Mrs. Norton, fearing the loss of her stake in the professor's substantial fortune, made her way to town unbeknownst to anyone and quickly seduced young Peters whom she knew had always been mesmerized by her seductive figure. That they had met recently is confirmed by the presence of roses that he had clipped and given to her in one of their liaisons. The roses that I saw on her person at the train station were definitely a match for those growing in the bushes near the house."

"Ah, so that is why you inspected the rosebush, Holmes," I said.

"Just so, Watson. Between the two of them, they concocted a scheme to rid themselves of the professor, leaving the door open for Mrs. Norton to claim her fortune and soon after marry Peters. That is, at least, how Peters viewed the transaction, though I suspect that Mrs. Norton had little intention of continuing her relationship with Peters once her plot had come to fruition. How she intended to deal with that is something that we shall never know for certain. As for the means by which they would dispatch with the professor, that is something that would take a little more thought. However, I would not doubt that the final idea came from Mrs. Norton, as she would have the most intimate knowledge of her husband, and that would be crucial in the end. Soon after it was decided that they would devise a way to have Professor Norton fall to his death as though it were an accident, it did not take much effort to convince Colby to join in their plot, as he would have been more than happy to have his share of the fortune. The fact that Professor Norton was going on an extended holiday even afforded them ample opportunity to put their plan into action. Colby, who we were told had built most of the house, had already crafted the balconies once, so it was little effort for him to do so again. Peters and

Colby, needing supplies, stole wood and paint from Dr. Burnside's barn, and then Colby proceeded to build an exact replica of the professor's balcony. Well, to say it was *exact* would be incorrect, as it was actually a tad shorter in length. Ultimately, they assumed that no one would examine it close enough to notice that fact. Colby certainly did do fine work, as he was even able to mix the paint in such a way that it appeared just as aged as the other balconies. Their work did not go unnoticed, however, as a passerby heard much commotion around the professor's estate when he walked by on those days when it was not raining. I found marks dug into the ground underneath the balcony, and when I connected those marks to the scratches in the stone above, it was clear that a ladder had been used for some purpose. This evening, I located it, along with one other, in one of the sheds at the rear of the property."

"Amazing, Mr. Holmes," added Constable Taylor. "I do not know how you have accomplished this!"

"It is simple, constable. I merely observed and then formulated proper deductions from those observations."

"Incredible," the constable said.

"In case there are any further questions as to what occurred, I will provide a brief closing summary. Professor Norton returned from his holiday, and the only issue with the balcony was that the paint had not fully dried. However, with the professor struggling to see, this was not something that he would have noticed. On that fateful night, he had reviewed the most recent letter from his wife and had become overstressed. That he deeply loved Ms. Roberts is without question, and he wanted her to be able to marry him. But Mrs. Norton would not have that. So it goes that he arose from his bed and began his final somnambulatory stroll to the balcony. He must have been walking rather fast, and on his last step, he struck his shin against the railing and tumbled to his death. Of course, being virtually asleep and unaware of what was occurring, he did not try to break his fall. The only thing left to say is that Colby, thinking Mrs. Norton and Peters intended to deprive him of his share of the fortune, and possibly pin the entire scheme on him, took the unfortunate actions he did this evening and completed the tragedy."

Holmes removed another document from his pocket and handed it to Ms. Roberts. She opened it and stared at Holmes with a look of astonishment.

"But Mr. Holmes, this cannot be right," she said through gentle sobs.

"You will find that it is all in order," he said. "I suggest that you hold a meeting with the professor's solicitor when you feel up to it. With the death of Mrs. Norton, you will find it considerably easier to claim what is yours."

"I thank you, Mr. Holmes, but this does not comfort me in the least. There is nothing in this house that could not be replaced, except for Roddy."

"Perhaps not, Sarah, but I would pay particular interest to the book that is sitting on the professor's desk upstairs. I think that if you will ever find any comfort, it will be from the words contained in there."

With that remark, Holmes rose to his feet and flicked his hand towards me.

"Well, our work is done here," he said, walking towards the door. "No, no, constable. We appreciate it just the same, but I think Watson and I could do with a walk. We will see if we can catch a train back to London."

"Very well, Mr. Holmes. I cannot thank you enough for your assistance. It has been an invaluable lesson to me. I shall not forget what I have learned here."

"See that you don't, constable," said Holmes gravely. "Come, Watson."

As we walked down the driveway and reached the main road, Holmes turned around and regarded the path behind us. He took a moment to light his pipe and looked up into the darkness of the night sky.

"It is peaceful, the darkness, is it not, Watson? With the help of Ms. Roberts, I am sure that even Professor Norton came to think so. And after all, to be unable to see the blackness of men's hearts would be quite peaceful indeed."

THE END

THE PRINTED PAGE IN THE DIGITAL AGE

Several years ago, I spent my breaks and lunches at work reading newspaper articles from all over the world from the 1800s and early 1900s on a website called newspaperabstracts.com. In an age in which many people are not even reading contemporary newspapers, one might wonder why I would have had any interest in newspaper accounts from over a century ago. The only answer that I can provide is that many people have told me that I have an old soul. I have made this remark before, and every time someone makes that comment to me, I laugh because I wholeheartedly agree with that assessment. One thing I noticed about the articles from back then is that the reporting was far more direct and blunt than the articles written today. In some ways, that writing style inadvertently brought a humorous tone to even the most serious of articles, and my colleagues and I shared many laughs over countless strange tales from Luzerne County, Pennsylvania and Lackawanna County, Pennsylvania. Now, I do not want readers to get the impression that we were insensitive to the situations that those people faced; that was not the funny part. What made us laugh was the way in which the reporters presented the stories. Additionally, the fact that there was really no immediate means of determining what happened next added a level of intrigue to the stories. There were bizarre tales of crimes, people randomly getting struck by lightning, children fighting an angry deer in the woods, people being thrown hundreds of yards by tornados, and the list goes on.

Fast forwarding to October 2020, I had just submitted my second Sherlock Holmes story, "The Adventure of the Necrotic Needle", to Mr. Fortier, and I began to delve into the stories of Solar Pons, a consulting detective modeled after Sherlock Holmes; Pons's adventures take place in the 1920s-1930s and are chronicled by Dr. Lyndon Parker, a doctor turned biographer modeled after Dr. Watson. I would suggest that any fan of Sherlock Holmes immediately try to locate the Solar Pons stories. I personally find them to be just as enjoyable as the original Sherlock Holmes adventures.

As a result of all of this, my mind was filled with mysteries, and in the weeks that followed, I started to think about circumstances that might present an interesting challenge for the Great Detective in future stories of my own. My first two stories were somewhat fast-paced, and I wanted to try my hand at writing a more traditional Holmes tale, one that was more of a slow burn and included many clues along the way. It was not long after I had come up with a plot after waking up and trying to fall back to sleep one night (a story that will be entitled, "The Adventure of the Headless Pedestrian") that I was reminded of the website that I had visited all those years ago.

Revisiting the newspaper abstracts was a lot of fun, and I read countless interesting articles covering the happenings of my hometown and the surrounding area. I soon began to take note of numerous articles that stood out to me as being rather curious, horrific, mysterious, and baffling. One such article was from August 24, 1884 and was simply one line long, and it described a professor who had fallen to his death one night after walking out of his bedroom window. There was nothing more—no mention of a coroner's report, police investigation, suicide note, etc. The facts were simply that the professor had accidentally fallen to his death in a rather unfortunate manner.

Almost immediately, my mind began to craft the framework for a Holmes adventure that centered on a murder plot that results in a professor falling to his death in a way that appears to be the result of nothing more than an accident. Being a huge fan of "The Final Problem" and the many Holmes pastiches that include Professor Moriarty, the irony of creating a Holmes story that includes a professor plummeting to his death was not lost on me. Thus, I could not help but make a reference to that in this story. Also, to give the reader a sense of the genesis of the story, I thought that it would be fun for Holmes to learn of the main plot point from simply reading his newspaper and then have him work the scenario out in his mind, much as I did in crafting the story. I hope my readers will enjoy the story, and I hope that I have succeeded in my attempt to create a classic-style Holmes mystery. I can't wait to write the next one. As always, I am grateful to Mr. Fortier and Airship 27 Productions for continuing to allow me the opportunity to write stories for them.

JONATHAN CASEY—is an Early Intervention Service Coordinator from Pennsylvania who majored in the field of Criminology at Wilkes University. His first published story, "The Adventure of the Irregular Heartbeat", appeared in Volume 15 of *Sherlock Holmes: Consulting Detective*. His second published story, "The Adventure of the Necrotic Needle", appeared in Volume 17 of *Sherlock Holmes: Consulting Detective*. He enjoys playing guitar and spending time with his parents and his three West Highland White Terriers. He is still searching for The Woman. He does not use social media much these days but can be reached at Taylor67914@yahoo.com if anyone has questions or feedback.

Sherlock Holmes

in

A Quest for Guinevere

by
I.A. Watson

Of no more subtle master under heaven
Than is the maiden passion for a maid,
Not only to keep down the base in man,
But teach high thought, and amiable words
And courtliness, and the desire of fame,
And love of truth, and all that makes a man.

"Guinevere", *Idylls of the King*, Alfred Lord Tennyson

"I took one look at the murder and I sent for you," Inspector Lestrade told Holmes as we marched over Hampstead Heath towards the scene of the crime. The Scotland Yard man did not sound happy about sending for an outside consultant to help him with his case, but there was a resigned certainty in his voice that he would likely have to send for Holmes sooner or later, so he might as well avoid the lecture of allowing the evidence to be disturbed.

The Heath was still quiet, since it was not yet nine in the morning. A quartet of uniformed constables diverted the strollers and dog-walkers away from an area near the Highgate Ponds, that chain of waterways that drain through the Stock Pond, the Kenwood Ladies Pond, the Bird Sanctuary Pond, the Model Boating Pond, Highgate Men's Boating Pond, and the Number One Pond.

The main attention was on the path that ran beside the eastern waterways, where Lestrade and his fellows were clustered around a man being fished by boathooks out of the Model Boating Pond.

"Be careful with that corpse!" Lestrade demanded of the labourers who waded across the slippery shallow pool to haul the dead man from the water.

I did not need Holmes to warn me of cause of death. A long throwing-spear still protruded out of the corpse's back.

Lestrade guided Holmes and I and beckoned us past the police perimeter, towards the cadaver. "Sorry to drag you up here on Whit Sunday,"[1] he

---

1   Whit Sunday is the Christian feast of Pentecost, occurring on the seventh Sunday after Easter. Since Easter is a 'moveable feast' determined by lunar cycle, so is Whit Sunday. The day after Whit Sunday, Whit Monday, was until 1971 a British Bank Holiday on which shops and offices did not open. Many benevolent employers in the Victorian age also allowed a paid holiday on Whit Tuesday.

apologised, but not too hard since he was also having to work the holiday. "Come and see what you make of this fellow, Holmes, Watson! I've seem plenty of murders, but this is the first time with a lance-gay."

Holmes backed everyone away from the wet corpse. "The similarities are marked," he told Lestrade and I, "but this is not the traditional medieval weapon, the iron-tipped throwing lance. You will notice the unusual wood of the haft, the breadth of the blade and the different polishing processes. I'll venture that this weapon is manufactured from the dogwood *Curtisia dentate*, better known in English as the Cape Lancewood or Assegai Tree."

"Assegai as in the Zulu weapon?" I asked. "This is an African assegai?"

"And a rather fine one, Watson."

"So we might look for a murderer who has been to South Africa, a soldier or traveller," Lestrade suggested.

Holmes raised a warning finger to restrain the inspector's premature conclusions. By now the constables had hauled the corpse from the Model Boating Pond and laid it on the path. Two of the uniformed officers were wading further out to retrieve some large object that was mostly submerged a little way off.

The dead man had been a young, athletic sort. He was dressed in exercise fig, khaki shorts, a white singlet with a red horizontal band, and soft running shoes. His calves were wrapped puttee-style in linen bandages. He wore leather fingerless gloves. There was no sign of any hat.

Holmes fell upon the body with a thirst for evidence. He offered a kind of muttered commentary, either for my information or to prevent me from interrupting his thoughts as he moved over the cadaver. "Well off, military background, rides and hunts, right-handed, extremely fit... unfamiliar laundry mark on the shorts—not from London or the Home Counties, then... vest too large... empty tobacco pouch, unfilled for several weeks, carried by habit but was no longer smoking... red London clay on his soles, doused in the Pond, picked up with shards of path gravel, walked afoot at some time on the Heath, probably near Boadicea's Mound..."

Lestrade's officers finished their Pond retrieval, hauling out a wet high-wheeled velocipede, the kind that is now going somewhat out of fashion in favour of the chain-driven gear trains, pneumatic tires, and matched wheels of modern bicycles. This machine was of the sort the wags now call a "penny farthing", with one huge forewheel and a small stabilising rear wheel, and it was somewhat crusted with the slime one finds at the bottom of public ponds in summer.

"Ah!" Holmes cried, and rushed over to it. "It lay over there, yes? That matches the marks on the gravel by the path. You see, by the park benches? Our deceased was riding this cycle when he was assailed. For the bike to end up in the position it did, and the deceased to have tumbled into the Pond to drift, he must have been moving at around fifteen miles per hour."

"Holmes!" I objected, "That's as fast as a horse canters!"

"And requires expert balance and skill on a contraption such as that one," Holmes allowed. "Moreover…" He backtracked from the pool's edge and carefully sifted over the ground to the public path. Some traces of disturbed gravel and churned-up turf evidently satisfied him. "Moreover, Watson, the assegai that impaled the victim was hurled with sufficient accuracy and force to pierce him as he moved at that speed. From the entry wound it must have been thrown from directly behind him as he came onto this straight stretch of path. The range must have been…"

Again Holmes drifted off, vocally and actually, pacing backwards towards a stand of trees opposite the Bird Sanctuary Pond.

"Well," Lestrade huffed to me, "I hope I don't have to start combing through London for a Zulu."

"I trust not," I replied. "One Isandlwana was enough."[2]

"Here!" Holmes called to us. "But tread carefully. There are many useful signs on this ground."

He had found a patch of concealed land, an ideal natural hide for a man with a spear to lie in wait. The grass was trodden down, suggesting that the assailant had remained in place for some time before acting.

"Our murderer was six feet tall or close to it," Holmes suggested. "He wore old military boots with steel caps and frayed laces. They were perhaps hauled out of disuse for the vigil."

"And easily disposed of afterwards without their absence being noted," I suggested.

"Here's a scrap of fishing thread," Holmes pointed out. "And an indentation in the grass where some small canvas bag was laid. I'll warrant the murderer concealed his assegai as a fishing pole in an angler's bag."

Lestrade looked from the discovered ambush point to the road where the cyclist must have passed. "You're telling me that this fellow hid here, with his African spear, and nobody saw him until he somehow tossed his assegai, what, fifty feet, and hit a fellow moving at speeds as if he were on horseback?"

"We must follow the evidence, Inspector," Holmes chided. "We are seeking a killer who is expert with the weapon he used."

---

2   The Anglo-Zulu War of 1879 began with the Zulu victory at Isandlwana and ended with British triumph at the Battle of Rourke's Drift, ending Zulu dominance of South Africa and establishing British control of the area.

We trudged back to the body, which had now been detached from the spear and was being lifted onto a stretcher for the coroner's attention.

"Here are the marks where the cyclist faltered in his course. He had been hit by the spear and veered towards the water," Holmes read from the ground. "He hit the lip of the pool and flipped over it, coming off his machine, which bounced that way. The momentum of his crash floated his corpse in the other direction."

"But who is he?" Lestrade wanted to know.

"You must send to the police-houses of London," Holmes advised him. "This was a well-to-do young gentleman of station, taking a constitutional ride around a public park. He is likely to be missed when he does not return for breakfast. Enquiries will be made, and sooner or later someone will appeal to the constabulary."

"You cannot tell me his name and address now?" Lestrade twitted my friend.

"Only that he started his journey somewhere in Golder's Hill, that he borrowed his shirt from a friend, that he injured his left elbow last year in some sporting accident, that he used to smoke Virginian tobacco until a few weeks since, that he may also have been on a diet, that he fell off his machine earlier in his circuit of the park when he was assailed by a small fierce dog, and that he may have been in love. But all of that is self-evident. Do tell me when you know who he is, Lestrade. Good day."

Holmes likes to make an entrance, but he also loves an exit.

We did not have to wait long for a development. A little after noon, our landlady[3] Mrs Hudson sent up a card from a Mr Simon Presterwick of Golder's Hill, with a request from the gentleman to see if we were at home. Holmes bade that he be directed to our chambers.

The fellow turned out to be a healthy-looking youngster of similar age to the deceased, with cropped brown hair and a heavy jaw. He wore London day-dress and carried a stout walking cane with a carved bulldog handle. "Thank you for seeing me," he told Holmes as we made introductions. "The policeman told me that I should direct my enquiries to you, since you are an enquiry agent."

3   Watson is presumably simplifying his narrative here since at the likely time of this story he was not resident at Baker Street, having moved to a small Kensington medical practice with his first wife (at least according to the chronology presented by W.S. Baring Gould in his biography *Sherlock Holmes*).

"A consulting detective," Holmes corrected him. "I help out when other resource fails."

"I was hoping I might engage you on the matter of the death of my friend Mr Corcoran. I am… unsure of the protocol."

"Mr Corcoran was the man hauled out of the Model Boating Pond this morning," I surmised.

"The same. It was… more than a shock. Max and I have been friends since we were at school together."

"You must begin with the basics," Holmes told our new client. He sat Presterwick down in the battered old chair where we usually place our visitors—opposite Holmes and with me to the side where I can make notes and keep an eye on things—and quickly prised the core information out of him.

Presterwick and Corcoran were old comrades, survivors of preparatory school and classmates at Eton. They both had family connections in Shropshire and were part of the County Hunt there. Mr Presterwick had hopes of becoming affianced to Mr Corcoran's cousin Guinevere Lessup, who was apparently "the divinest creature who ever graced God's Earth."

Maxwell Corcoran customarily guested at Simon Presterwick's town house at Golder's Hill when business affairs required his presence in the capital. Such had been the case last Friday. Corcoran had stayed over for the weekend, and it was from Presterwick's domicile that the murdered man had set out that morning.

"I feel so terrible about it," our client told us, staring at his open hands as if they were covered in blood. "You see, Mr Holmes, Dr Watson, Max rode out today on my bicycle, along my training route, instead of me. He was doing me a favour. And he died for it."

"You will need to explain that more closely," Holmes told Presterwick.

The young man took a breath. "We are Olympians," he explained. "You know of the Shropshire Olympics? The Wenlock Olympic Games were founded in 1850 by Dr William Penny Brookes, 'to provide access to sport and the arts to people of every grade'. They are held mostly biannually, hosted by different towns in the county, with all kinds of events. They are patterned in spirit on the classical games of Greece, under the same aegis of sportsmanship and fellowship as then.[4] Max and I, we have both com-

---

4   This is all true. The Much Wenlock Games preceded the International Olympiad by half a century and set the pattern for it. Baron Coubertin, honoured as the founder of the modern Olympic Games, corresponded frequently with Dr Penny Brooks and visited him in 1890 to observe events especially put on for him. For Brooks's obituary, Coubertin wrote, "If the Olympic Games that Modern Greece has not yet been able to revive still survives today, it is due not to a Greek but to Dr William Penny Brookes." More is said of Brooks and Coubertin in the accompanying afterword.

peted twice. This was to be our third time."

"You were in training for a sports match," I realised. "The diet, the giving up of smoking..."

"We intended to enter three events each," Presterwick explained. "I am put down for the Gimcrack Race. Max was to do the Pole Leaping. We both signed for the Cycling and the Tilting."

I requested explanations and discovered more of the events of the Wenlock Games. Pole Leaping was a kind of vaulting using a long stick to aid one's parabola. Cycling was, of course, performed on those sit-up-and-beg high-wheeled bicycles rather than the new 'safety bikes'. Tilting was the old medieval knightly training exercise where a man a-gallop on horseback must place a lance through a hanging quoit and hook the hoop loose.

Most eccentric, but deucedly practical, was the Gimcrack Race where the rider must lace on his boots, rush to his horse, mount, ride, jump, dismount, drink a brandy, smoke a cigar, then repeat the process at set intervals. I must say from my military experience that this is the most practical sport ever invented for simulating an officer's day in the field.

"These games start on Whit Tuesday, the day after tomorrow," Presterwick reported. "People from all over England, from across Britain, and even from overseas will attend to compete and observe. There are small prizes, of course, but the prestige of winning is the thing."

Holmes drew the enthusiast back to his point. "You mentioned that Mr Corcoran took your place on your cycle training exercise today."

"That's right! Poor Max! You see, I do that route every morning. I time myself. But on several occasions I have thought that there might be someone watching me, spying upon me."

"As sometimes racing rivals sneak a look at the form of an opponent's horse?" I suggested.

"Yes, exactly. So I decided to find who it was and to... to confront them."

Remarkably, the Much Wenlock Olympian Games are still being held today, although the scheduled 2020 Games were cancelled due to Covid-19 restrictions.

Much of the information on the Much Wenlock Olympian Games used in this story came from two sources, the webpages of the Much Wenlock Olympian Society at http://www.wenlock-olympian-society.org.uk/ and a comprehensive article by Rob Gandy in *Fortean Times* #343 (August 2016, pg 46-50). Those wishing to delve further may wish to refer to *The Story of Wenlock Olympian Society and William Penny Brooks (Inspiration for the International Olympic Games)*, (2016, ISBN 97181861472205) or *Born Out of Wenlock: William Penny Brookes and the British Origins of the Modern Olympics* (Catherine Beale, 2011, ISBN 9781859839676).

I.A. Watson apologises to Much Wenlock Games historians for the minor fudges with dates of events and of procedures that were required to tell a Sherlock Holmes detective story against actual historical events. Let's blame Watsonian misdirection, shall we?

"Hampstead Heath is a public place," Holmes pointed out. "What had you hoped to do?"

"Well, to find out if it was who I thought it was, for one. And perhaps to have words with the fellow."

Presterwick's reddened countenance suggested that he might have expected more than a chat with the spy, but I said nothing.

Holmes summarised. "You asked Corcoran to take your circuit, dressed in your singlet, so that your unknown observer might assume he was you. It was your intention to also be on the Heath, to discover the man you thought might be watching you."

"That's right. I never expected that he might be there to kill me—to kill Max!"

"You saw him?" I asked.

"Not today. I expected him to be laid out on Boadicea's Mound, that old tumulus that overlooks the paths of South Meadow and Parliament Hill. I fancied I'd seen the reflection off field-glasses used by someone lying in the long cover there. When I got to the spot today, it was deserted."

"Could you see Corcoran?" Holmes enquired.

"Quite well for most of the route. There is a thicket of trees that screens the Ponds from the wind, and he was vanished behind them when… when something happened."

"You said you suspected who was watching you," I mentioned. "And that that fellow might be your friend's killer."

"Yes." Presterwick's face darkened again. "Miles Druden-Smythe. And he was not seeking to kill Maxwell. He thought he was murdering me!"

Holmes nodded, but not in acknowledgement of the young man's accusation. "You gave this name to Inspector Lestrade?"

"Of course I did. It must have been Druden-Smythe. He was my rival in every way, and the one who benefits the most from my death."

Again that required clarification. Holmes sought it.

"I mentioned Miss Lessup?" Presterwick reminded us. "Guinevere! Well, a paragon like that, beautiful, gifted, perfect in every way, and with a fortune as well… you would expect she would attract ruthless chancers, cads of low character and less morals. Druden-Smythe is one of them!"

"You said he was your rival," I acknowledged.

"He is my *bête-noir*!" Presterwick insisted. "He is the foulest blot on my life, and Gwen's, and… and now he has murdered Maxwell!"

Holmes extracted from Presterwick that Captain Miles Druden-Smythe was a serving officer with the L_____s, who were presently in barracks at Aldershot, and who was therefore at liberty in London and beyond to pursue his suit for the dazzling Miss Lessup.

"You named this officer to Lestrade," I noted. "There has been no arrest?" It seemed unlikely that the Scotland Yard detective would have forwarded the case to Sherlock Holmes had the guilt of Druden-Smythe been obvious or provable.

"The fellow is slippery," Presterwick growled. "But the three events in which he intends to compete at the Olympian are the Gimcrack Race, Tilting at the Ring… and the Zulu Contest, which is the hurling of assegais at a target sixty feet distant!"

"You told this to Lestrade," I surmised.

"Yes. But Druden-Smythe has managed to find three brother-officers who'll swear he was with them this morning up 'till seven a.m., playing cards—and there is no way for him to have got to Hampstead Heath in time to have killed Max."

"That does seem like an unshakable alibi."

"Not if you knew Druden-Smythe and his oily army pals. It wouldn't be the first time they'd borne false witness to protect each other, such as when one of them had been with a girl and the others swore to her father that he was in barracks all the time. I've heard the cad boast of it."

"Alibis can be verified or broken," Holmes observed. "But there is another reason for your enmity with this fellow."

Presterwick's mouth tightened and his scowl deepened. "Druden-Smythe and I… there is a wager."

"What kind of wager?" I wondered.

"An agreement. Miss Lessup has several admirers; she is a most admirable young lady. I daresay that I am foremost in her affections, but nevertheless there are others who aspire to her hand. Eventually, all four of us concluded that our suits would not prosper whiles the others continued their pursuit, and we resolved upon a way to determine which one of us should continue our courtship and which should remove themselves from the field."

"By gambling?" I rumbled.

"By a contest of skills. What fairer way to win the fair Guinevere, like the knightly romances of old? The four of us pacted that we would each compete in three events in the forthcoming Games. Whichever of us won the most medals, the others would step aside for him with Guinevere. In case of a tie we would settle the matter by tent-pegging."

Tent-pegging is an old cavalry game, where a rider with lance must charge past, flipping tent-pegs from the ground. It is a useful if showy military trick for a cavalry raid on an enemy camp, but it can go terribly wrong if the lance-tip buries into the earth and the rider is somersaulted from his seat.

"You gambled Miss Lessup," I accused, disapprovingly.

"We decided on a way to determine which of us would abandon our suit," the would-be swain answered. From his demeanour I recognised that I was not the first to indicate an objection. "Guinevere knows all about it, and does not object. She believes it to be romantic."

"You assert that your rival Druden-Smythe, uncertain of prevailing in this wager, set about to remove you in a more direct fashion," Holmes surmised.

"I am certain of it. I simply don't know how he managed it, yet. You are the consulting detective; I hope that you can accomplish that."

"What of the other two fellows?" I suggested. "You mentioned that there were four of you engaged in this dubious enterprise."

"If you are so disapproving then you need not concern yourself with it," Presterwick answered me hotly. "It was for Mr Holmes's opinion that I came here."

"Dr Watson is my dear and trusted colleague," Holmes warned our visitor. "You must accept both of us or neither for this case."

The Romeo subsided and answered my enquiry. "The others are Charlie Wheaton and Bill Cordwainer.[5] I doubt either of them would do such a thing. Charlie is ex-army, pensioned out after taking a shot in the shoulder in Burma.[6] He can still ride and jump, but he can't even throw a cricket ball. And Bill... well, Bill does not have the gumption to use violence. He is a pacifist."

Holmes questioned Presterwick further, until we were clear what each of Miss Lessup's four admirers intended to perform to win the prize:

Mr Simon Presterwick—Gimcrack Race, Tilting, Cycling
Captain Miles Druden-Smythe—Gimcrack Race, Tilting, Zulu Contest
Mr Charles Wheaton—Gimcrack Race, Tilting, Horseback Wrestling
Mr William H. Cordwainer—Pole Leaping, Throwing Cricket Ball, Cycling

To which we added:

---

5   Pronounced 'CORD-un-na'.

6   The Third Anglo-Burmese War officially ran from the 7th-29th November 1885 and ended with the British annexation of Burma and the folding of the nation into the administration of British-ruled India, but armed resistance continued until 1887, especially in the semi-independent tribal areas of the Kachin Hills and Chin Hills.

"You assert that your rival set about to remove you in a more direct fashion."

Mr Maxwell Corcoran (dec.d)—Tilting, Cycling, Pole Leaping

Holmes finished his enquiries by taking details of the principals in the case, including those of the much-quested-after Miss Guinevere Lessup. "Most everybody will be heading to Much Wenlock today or tomorrow, though," Presterwick cautioned us. "I shall be travelling up there myself this evening, to comfort poor Gwen."

"It may well be that Watson and I shall meet you there," Holmes told the young athlete. "We may also wish to attend these remarkable Games."

ه‌‌‌‌ل‌‌‌‌

Lestrade laid two more assegais down on his desk beside the one that had killed Corcoran. "We found them in Druden-Smythe's locker in his billet at Aldershot. They are identical to the murder weapon."

Holmes took his magnifying glass to the three war-spears, offering us a lecture as he checked them in fine detail. "The Assegai tree is considered very useful in its native habitat of Southern Africa. Untouched, it is a flowering evergreen that grows up to fifteen yards tall, with smooth bark and an unbuttressed bole. The flowers are cream-coloured, the berries white, sometimes tinged with pink. The Xhosa, Nguni, and Zulu coppice the plant, attaining straight long shoots than can be harvested for shafts like these. Spear-making is considered quite an art, and such a weapon is a native warrior's prized possession."

I noticed the Scotland Yard common room begin to empty. There had been some interest amongst the Detective Branch when Holmes had first arrived to see Lestrade—it was only days since my friend had secured the arrest of the terrible murderer Burt Stevens[7] by cunning observation of the blood-spatter on a cuckoo clock—but as he continued his monologue on botany and ethnology I could see the officers finding reasons to depart. Doubtless this was Holmes's intent.

Holmes turned the assegais over, examined them again, then moved on to the tips. "Such weapons are used for hunting and in war, for long-ranged attacks. Shaka of the Zulu additionally equipped his armies with shorter, two-foot staves of a similar nature, which came to be called *iklwa*, allegedly from the sound it made being pulled from a wound. These assegais are of

---

7   Watson also references this case in "The Adventure of the Norwood Builder" in *The Return of Sherlock Holmes* (1903). From this and other internal evidence, including the dates of meetings of the Shropshire Olympics, we may conclude that Holmes's present investigation took place from Sunday, May 29th—Tuesday May 31st 1887.

sufficient vintage to have been retrieved during the Zulu War, although the iron tips have since been replaced with practical Sheffield steel. Many such items were carried home by British soldiers as souvenirs of their adventures."

"That's what Captain Druden-Smythe's bunkmates had to say about them," Lestrade reported. "He had three assegais that he regularly practiced with at Aldershot, but one was missing when we looked."

"And these three match perfectly," I observed, looking to Holmes to check that I was right.

"It is likely that Corcoran died by Druden-Smythe's missing weapon. What does the Captain have to say on the matter, I wonder?"

"Well that's the thing, Mr Holmes. We can't find him. He has five days' leave from yesterday to attend those Games in Shropshire. Between the time I sent constables round to check his whereabouts this morning and the time I got there to question him myself—which would be around one p.m.—he left the camp and disappeared."

"Suspicious," I judged, "but legal, I suppose. Did you search his quarters?"

"Yes. Not much to find there except for a lot of unpaid tailors' bills and spirits vendors' dockets, a deck of illustrated 'French' playing cards, and whatever clothes he hadn't bothered to pack when he left."

"Did you confiscate his boots?" Holmes demanded. "Or at least measure them for size?"

"I didn't see any boots. He's presumably wearing them."

Holmes snorted. "I should have gone there myself, except I thought I might get a visit from Presterwick. I should have asked Watson to go."

"We are not incapable at Scotland Yard," Inspector Lestrade bristled.

"Will a search be made for Druden-Smythe?" I ventured, to divert the awkward confrontation that loomed between the Law and Holmes.

"We'll see. I suppose if he hasn't turned up by day-after-tomorrow he might surface at those events he's supposed to be in. We can take him there if needs be. But remember that he has three friends vouching for his whereabouts this morning."

"You must question them closely," Holmes advised. "Get each of them to describe the card game they played; who won each hand, what bets were laid, what the topics of conversation were. I'll warrant that they won't have fixed their stories in that much detail and a close questioning will rattle them."

I agreed. "This isn't some paternity suit, it's murder. That will shake the truth out of them, if anything does."

"Trust me to get confessions if confessions are due," Lestrade boasted.

"Only if they are due, if you please," Holmes told him dryly.

I looked at the three identical war-spears. "If the assegai that killed Maxwell Corcoran belonged to Druden-Smythe, he has much explaining to do as to how anybody else could have taken it."

"We will be certain to ask him about that, Dr Watson," Lestrade answered acidly. "When we finally find him."

ﷺ

Before sunset, Holmes and I walked Hampstead Heath again. Not, Holmes instructed me, because there were likely any traces left of the murder or the murderer, but rather to get a sense of the layout that might have been relevant to the crime. I was glad to see my friend in good spirits and tramping about in search of evidence. He had recently begun an unhealthy habit of dosing himself with a solution of cocaine, of which I disapproved, and from which only intellectual stimulation distracted him.

The Heath is a big place, nine hundred and seventy acres of grass and ancient parkland on one of the highest hills overlooking London. The sunset view of our capital city is unprecedented, reminding one just how attractive the spires and monuments of the largest metropolis in the world can seem from a distance. I have seen many other cities in the course of a long career, and to me none of them can match smoky old London Town.

The eastern perimeter of the Heath is denoted by a series of interlinked bodies of water, originally London's drinking reservoirs drawn from the River Fleet. It was into one of these pools that our murdered cyclist had crashed. From the western path beside the Ponds, the tall swell of Parliament Hill rises 322-feet high; the Palace of Westminster can be seen from there, six and a half miles away. Livestock is reared on the slopes for Smithfield Meat Market.

Technically, Parliament Hill was still in private hands at the time of Holmes's investigation, but already a campaign was underway to purchase it for the public (at the sum of £300,000!) to add to the common land of the Heath that was acquired by the Metropolitan Board of Health in 1875. The general public made little distinction regarding ownership of the site. So far as North Londoners are concerned, it was theirs by ancient right, a public park for their sport and recreation.[8]

Holmes and I hiked up the slope beside the Bronze Age burial mound,

---

8   Parliament Hill was purchased and reincorporated into Hampstead Heath in 1888, the year after Holmes and Watson tackled the case described herein. The site is now managed for the public by the City of London Corporation, municipal governing body of the City of London.

where someone had allegedly spied upon Simon Presterwick's training.

"If I wanted to set watch on someone going along those paths, this is the place I'd pick," I admitted.

"One would be pointing field-glasses downwards, north and east," Holmes observed. "But at this time of year, less than a month from the longest day, I cannot see how the lenses might have caught the sun and flashed, unless the observer was careless in lifting or setting down his instrument."

"Perhaps he was. Too many unfortunate military field scouts have been betrayed by their own inattention."

"Perhaps. Or it may have been intended as some form of intimidation, to let Presterwick know that he was under observation, to unnerve him for his training."

"Well, it's certainly easy to fall off those cycles."[9]

We dropped back down the bank towards the scene of the murder. The police were gone and all sign of the incident was now cleared away.

"Those high-wheelers don't have brakes like the new bikes," I mentioned. "The only way to slow down is to back-pedal. And the only way to get on and off is to stabilise the cycle against a tree or wall. Once seated, the rider's feet are a good twenty-four or thirty inches above the ground."

Holmes agreed. "Even if Corcoran had seen his assailant lurking over there in the foliage he would have been unable to do much about it. Stopping in time would be impossible. Turning away from the track onto the rough ground would have spilled him off, leaving him helpless."

"The murderer would only have seen his back, though, and that white singlet with the red stripe on to suggest it was Presterwick."

"Until the deed was done. And by then Corcoran's momentum had taken him and his vehicle into the Toy Boating Pool."

"An hour later and there would have been two score of children and their nannies here to witness it."

Holmes viewed the likely scene from where the killer had hidden. "It is entirely possible that our murderer never even realised that he had the wrong subject—if indeed he did. He may have made his getaway without any idea that he had failed in his objective."

"That must have come as quite a shock for Druden-Smythe later in the day, when police turned up to question him for the murder of Max Corcoran. Or if not Druden-Smythe, then whoever threw that assegai."

---

9   For example, the first winner of the Shropshire Olympian Three-Mile Cycle Race, Thomas Sabin of Coventry, is reported as "coming off, then remounting, cycling like fury, and still taking first place." Cyclists crashing into each other were also a common occurrence.

Holmes traced the distance to where the cyclist would have entered the pond. "You noted these divots in the ground this morning, Watson? They have been somewhat trampled now, but the grass is still a little disturbed. You apprehend their meaning?"

I looked at the displaced soil. "It looks as if they have been stabbed with a dibber or some other garden implement. Or... with an assegai? The killer *practiced* before doing the deed!"

"I am sure of it. There are fourteen such gouges. The smaller holes where wooden pegs were put out as range markers are no longer visible, but I was able to examine them this morning."

"This was carefully planned," I concluded.

"This was planned," Holmes amplified, "but not long in advance. As we have seen, the turf marks have scarcely survived one day of public access over this place. Had the practice been yesterday then all traces would have vanished under the shoes of little children running with their yachts, and of their younger siblings' perambulators. I venture we might allow our murderer to be too cautious to make more than one on-site foray to try his aim. So the whole exercise was likely conceived and executed very recently."

"What changed about Presterwick's chances with Miss Lessup that spurred someone to do away with him?"

Holmes stuffed his hands into the pockets of his longcoat and took a last look around. Finding nothing new to aid his detection, he gestured that we might return to town. "Will you be available to visit Shropshire tomorrow, Watson?"

"To see the Games? I should be delighted, Holmes."

"Then let us make our plans."

ڡڡ

On the 7.10 from Euston to Shrewsbury the following morning, Holmes briefed me on the results of his enquiries overnight.

"There is still no word of Captain Druden-Smythe," he began. "The fellow left Aldershot Barracks yesterday a little after noon, with a single grip but *without* his spears. His comrades-in-arms believe that he has another set in storage at Much Wenlock, along with his riding gear. He took a cab into London, discharged it at Trafalgar Square, and effectively disappeared. No other cabbie has responded to enquiries about transporting him after that time."

"He may be hiding from the police."

"It's possible. He did borrow five pounds and a clean shirt and collar from one of his brother-officers before he vanished, although that is evidently not unusual."

"There is always one of that type in barracks."

"My initial financial enquiries about Druden-Smythe are not encouraging. The fellow was a gambler, so his accounts were variously flush or empty at different times. He has a string of creditors chasing him. He was probably struggling to pay his regimental dues."

"He needed that heiress."

"Quite probably. The fellow's military record is undistinguished, but he did spend some time in South Africa just after the Zulu War. That is where he acquired his souvenirs and apparently developed an aptitude for them."

"If he has gone to ground, he may be hard to find."

"I have directed Lestrade's search to a number of establishments in Highgate, houses of ill-repute that are popular with military gentlemen. There may be employees there who know Druden-Smythe and his habits."

Holmes waved that aside and moved on. "Simon Presterwick is the younger son of a major Shropshire landowner. He has a private income from inheritance which he has supplemented with some shrewd property deals. His credit is good. At school he was an undistinguished academic but a keen sportsman, excelling in rugby, cricket, and riding. He has been known to the Corcorans and the Lessups for many years.

"Charles 'Charlie' Wheaton was a Captain in the 5th _____, serving in Burma until an injury caused his retirement around fifteen months since. He came to Shropshire and took on a horse farm, and has had some small success racing his stock. According to a thoroughbred breeder of my acquaintance, he is considered a hard bargainer, a good friend, and a dangerous adversary. 'No nonsense' was the term he used for Wheaton.

"William 'Bill' Cordwainer is a vicar's son, and indeed studied for the clergy at Cambridge for two years before deciding it was not his calling. He has a reasonable income from his mother's side of the family that allows him to pursue his interests without needing a profession. He is radical in his politics, liberal in his religion, and a dedicated and campaigning pacifist.

"And finally," Holmes told me, "there is the late Mr Maxwell Corcoran. He was the only son of Miss Guinevere Lessup's aunt. When he was not thrashing about on penny-farthings or tilting at the quoit he made his living as a surveyor. It was to present a recommendation to a client regarding land purchase in Shrewsbury that he came to London last Friday. He was also an avid member of the County Horse and Hound and one of the minor sponsors of the Shropshire Games. There is little more I can discern without more data."

"You have assembled quite a picture before ever arriving at Much Wenlock," I congratulated Holmes. "Have your researches suggested any further clue as to which of them may have been the murderer?"

"It may have been none of them," my friend cautioned. "Druden-Smythe has friends who may have offered him an alibi, who were with him in Africa. Was he the only one of them who mastered the assegai? Were the men who compacted in a modern quest for Guinevere the only competitors who might resort to a spear in the back to settle some problem? Also, the motive imputed by Presterwick for why someone might wish to murder him may be entirely wrong; Miss Lessup may play no part in the matter." He folded his hands together and rested his head back. "It is futile to theorise without good information, Watson. Let us merely enjoy the journey."

The Shrewsbury express drew in at 11.09am. From there we took a carriage across to Much Wenlock as the fastest way to travel to the home of the Shropshire Olympiad. There was a message waiting *post-restante* for Holmes at the local Post Office.

DRUDEN-SMYTHE TAKEN IN HIGHGATE HELD FOR QUESTIONING + STOP + CLAIMS SURPRISE OVER MISSING ASSEGAI + STOP + INTERVIEWING FELLOW OFFICERS SEPARATELY + STOP + HE DID IT DIDN'T HE? +STOP+ LESTRADE

"It's quite simple," Dr William Penny Brooks told Holmes and I as we discovered him supervising the layout of pavilions and viewing stands at the Linden Fields outside Much Wenlock, across from its ancient priory. "A healthy body means a healthy life. Physical exercise is good for children and adults alike—not just the regimented drills they do in school, but all-round physical education. It should be part of every curriculum, to encourage grown-ups to keep fit too. That's why we hold the Shropshire Olympiad."[10]

---

10   In addition to being founder of the Shropshire Olympian Games, the estimable Dr William Penny Brooks (1809-1895) was a local magistrate, Commissioner of Roads, Manager of the Much Wenlock National School, and played a significant role in providing the town with a gas supply, covered sewers, a railway line, an herbarium of rare and exotic plants outside the new railway station, and a museum of geology and archaeology in the rooms of the Agricultural Reading Society at the Corn Exchange. In addition, he was a lifelong campaigner for sports and health, lobbying at a national level for athletic curricula and public access to opportunities for self-improvement.

I was quite impressed with his vision and organisation. The field was bustling with activity in preparation for the start of the Games the next day, with dozens of people working to lay out the area in advance of the thousands who would come to spectate. "This is all bigger than I expected," I confessed.

"It has found a place," the country doctor assured me. "We started out quite small, you know, with just nine events, reviving the manly sports of past England. Then we added more military exercises, such as the Balaclava Melee and the Victoria Cross Race.[11] Gradually we have worked towards a more Olympian feel, such as adding the pentathlon or hurdle race, throwing a 32-pound stone, jumping for height and length, and climbing a 55-foot rope. Now we have become quite popular."

"Popular indeed," I recognised. "I see you have non-sporting activities in your tents too."

"Oh, as the original Olympics were cultural and artistic events as well as athletic, so we try to offer something for everyone. We have prizes for arithmetic, best poem and ode, essay writing, English history, scripture history, handwriting, solo singing and glee choirs, spelling... A brass band contest, of course. For the women there are a shirt-making competition, stocking-knitting contest, sewing contest—you would be amazed how fiercely contested they are! One year we even had a women's foot race for the over-thirties, with a grand prize of a pound of tea![12] That was a great success, but we deemed it a little dangerous for some of the more elderly contestants."

I had read the leaflet about the Olympian and knew that other events included drill displays, egg-and-spoon race, 50-yards hop, three-legged race, tug-of-war, jingling,[13] blindfolded wheelbarrow race, donkey race, pig

---

11   The Balaclava Melee was a mounted free-for-all in which contestants sought to use sticks to knock the plumes off their opponents' helmets. The Victoria Cross Race featured riders chasing across a field to retrieve full-sized straw dummies, representing wounded men, and delivering them safe to base.

12   The 'Old Women's Race For a Pound of Tea' was held in 1856, the only time that women competed in the physical Games during Dr Bookes's lifetime. The contestants were reported to have "acquitted themselves remarkably well, considering the disadvantage under which they laboured in not being provided with the 'bloomer costume' attire in which they would have run capitally." 45-year-old Mary Speake and 38-year-old Anne Meredith took first and second prizes.

An Australian Olympiad inspired by the Much Wenlock Games has recently revived this event.

13   Jingling was a kind of blind-man's-bluff wherein blindfolded children pursued a man wearing a suit covered in bells.

race,[14] climbing a greasy pole, prison base,[15] and putting a quarry stone.[16]

"Your Games have attracted a good deal of attention," I observed.

"Internationally," Penny Brooks assured us. "We try to support similar endeavours elsewhere. The Wenlock Olympian Committee sent £10 to Athens in '59 to support their Olympian Games, to cover the Wenlock Prize for their Long Race. And at the Queen's Jubilee, King George of Greece very kindly provided us with an inscribed silver cup."

I was fascinated by the bonhomie and teamwork being shown by the volunteers who were preparing the site. Holmes was less interested in the sporting and cultural programme, but watched the activities with his usual keen eye.

"You are aware of the competition regarding Miss Guinevere Lessup?" he asked the Games organiser.

"It has been much discussed," Dr Brooks replied. "I cannot say I approve of it, but nor can the Committee object to a purely private arrangement."

"The men involved have all competed before?"

"All except Mr Wheaton. He was only pensioned from military service last year. Mr Presterwick and Captain Druder-Smythe both won medals at the '86 event, for the Tilting and the Spear-Throwing respectively. They are both favourites to do well this year too."

"And Maxwell Corcoran?"

"That poor young man! Such a shock. He was runner-up after Presterwick at catching the quoit, and took the honours for Pole-Leaping. He was hotly tipped to take the Pole-Leaping medal again this time."

Unfortunately, Dr Penny Brookes did not have intimate acquaintance of the young men and could not apprise us of the history of their pursuit of Miss Lessup. He was able to tell us something of her family background and situation. "The Lessups are an old Shropshire name. Her late father was one of the sponsors of our first Games; he was a notable philanthropist. Most of the family's money is in land and rents. The majority passed to Miss

---

14   The Pig Race was more properly a Pig Hunt. According to the *Shrewsbury Chronicle,* 10th September 1858, pg 5, "The pig started in the middle of the field and led its pursuers over hedge and ditch right into town where it took ground in the cellars of Mr Blakeway's house and where it was captured by a man named William Hill." The winner got to keep the pig.

15   This mediaeval game was serial tag between two teams, with the objective of catching an opposition player before he could reach home base. It was so popular in the 14th century that King Edward III had to ban it from being played in the grounds of the Palace of Westminster because of its noise distracting government ministers from their work; the statute still remains in force.

16   This event was aimed at quarrymen, who were required to pitch a 56lb stone with each hand in turn; the longest distance won.

"Gradually we have worked towards a more Olympian feel…"

Lessup's elder brother, but old Mr Lessup left her and her younger brother incomes of around sixteen hundred a year, plus a lump sum of some eighteen thousand as dowry when Miss Lessup marries."

I whistled softly. That was a significant inheritance. Holmes and I had encountered several nefarious plots for lesser sums than that.

"What are the terms of the bequest?" Holmes wondered. "Is there some clause requiring approval of a marriage?" But our host did not know.

Penny Brookes directed us to the First Aid tent, where Miss Lessup herself was assisting with the unpacking of supplies for the nurses who would be on duty tomorrow. She was indeed an attractive young woman, golden-haired and pink-cheeked, looking as if she had just walked out of some Renaissance portrait of her Arthurian namesake. Her black mourning garb and veil did nothing to diminish her beauty.

She recognised Holmes's name; evidently Mr Presterwick had mentioned him when he had called upon her this morning. "You are the clever gentlemen who are investigating Max's death."

I offered our condolences and she agreed to help us with our questions.

"We have been apprised of the unusual agreement regarding the outcome of the forthcoming Games," Holmes mentioned.

Miss Lessup flushed prettily and looked down. "That was none of my doing. When I heard of it, my first instinct was outrage. But... there is something flattering to it, I suppose, and I have promised nothing. What my suitors choose to do, foolish or otherwise, is not my business."

"Your guardian does not object?"

"That would be my elder brother. He is presently in Ottawa on business, so cannot comment. My younger brother Talbot regards it as a great joke. Max..." She hesitated.

"Your cousin," I prompted.

"Yes... poor Max! Max said it was in poor taste, and they might as well have diced for me. He had some sharp words for Simon about it, but in the end he was reconciled."

"Corcoran favoured his friend's suit?" I wondered.

"Max introduced us, back in their school-days together. Max used to come to our house between terms, and sometimes he brought his chum along. But I cannot say whether Max favoured Simon's courtship of me; he never said." She dabbed an eye with her black-rimmed handkerchief. "And now he never shall!"

Holmes wanted to know about her other suitors, and she spoke about each of them. "Miles—that is Captain Druden-Smythe—is very much a soldier. He is plain in speech and bold in deeds. I met him here at these very Games last year, when I awarded the Nike medal to him after he took the Zulu Contest prize. He boldly proclaimed that he had rather have a kiss. I have known Bill since Max met him at a previous Games. Charlie rides with the County Hunt, as do Max, Simon and I."

Miss Lessup hesitated as she remembered that Maxwell Corcoran would follow the hounds no more, then struggled on. "Charlie was intro-duced to me at a Hunt Ball. He was also a soldier, though now discharged due to a war injury."

Holmes satisfied his curiosity regarding the lady's dowry. Miss Lessup's older brother must approve the match to release the funds, but she did not expect him to withhold permission for any gentleman upon whom she finally fixed her attentions. Her siblings could not profit in any way from the resources held in trust for her, and if she died those assets would be distributed to charity.

She had last seen "Darling Max" on Thursday, before he had departed for London. She had seen Druden-Smythe on Friday, near the refreshment tent that had just been raised for the Games. Wheaton had called to make his respects at her home the next day. Presterwick had come to see her this morning. She had not seen Cordwainer since Wednesday, at practice on the dressage square.

Holmes finished his interview with some more routine questions, then asked if any of Miss Lessup's suitors might be found in Linden Field today. The young woman directed us to the Tilting Yard, where many compet-itors would be practicing. Tilting was considered the main event at the Much Wenlock Games.

"I wonder if I should enter?" I speculated to Holmes. "I daresay I don't have the experience of these cavalry chappies and huntsmen, but I know my way around a good military horse."

"I am sure you would do your regiment justice, Watson, but we might do better judging the form of our suspects. A man who is proficient in the lance might also be an adept spear-thrower, whether he has taken the Zulu Prize before or not."

I dragged myself away from the tantalising sports contests and followed Holmes in search of his suspects.

ﻌﻠﻌ

Holmes interviewing Charles Wheaton at the paddock:

"You were aware of Mr Presterwick's pursuit of Miss Lessup?"

"Indeed. She is a popular young lady. I had hopes myself."

"You do not now?"

"So soon after the death of her beloved cousin? The time is not right."

"Are you familiar with other of Miss Lessup's suitors?"

"You mean Cordwainer and Druden-Smythe? One's a gossiping milksop and the other is a scoundrel. Neither are worthy of her."

"When you say scoundrel..." I intervened.

"One hears things in barracks. I may be pensioned out of service but I still have friends in the regiments. Druden-Smythe is not popular. He is suspected of cheating at cards. He is a known womaniser. I believe he chases Miss Lessup for her fortune, to cover his significant debts."

"And Mr Cordwainer?" Holmes enquired.

"Can't keep his mouth closed. Can't shut the man up at all. And he's a coward. Look at his choices of events—nothing where he faces another man."

"Where were you when Maxwell Corcoran took a Zulu spear in the back?"

"Training. Every minute of every day, training. Yesterday morning I was running a ten-mile chase from Edgebolton to Wrockwardine, here in the county of Shropshire, two hundred miles away in London. You can ask my batman."

"Your war injury does not interfere with your exercise?" I enquired, interested as a professional and as a veteran who was similarly pensioned out.

"I took a single bullet from a sniper as we were clearing some rebel-supporting village in the Katchin Hills, which damaged some of the muscles and nerves in my right shoulder. It restricts certain forms of overarm movement but doesn't interfere with me running or riding. But in the hospital I caught a fever which led to a prolonged period of sickness and delirium. I'd been marked for discharge and sent home before I even realised what was happening to me. I am now fully recovered, except for a little twinge now and again. I prefer not to make a fuss about it."

"You cannot hurl an assegai," I understood.

"Why would I want to? Heathen weapon, ridiculous contest."

Holmes pressed on. "Other than rivalry over Miss Lessup, do you know of any reason why anyone might wish to harm Simon Presterwick—or Max Corcoran?"

"Presterwick's a damned oik, lacking the manners and breeding of his class, but if we shot all such men we'd lose half the blue blood of England, wouldn't we? I know of nothing against Corcoran. Didn't know him well, but seemed a decent enough type. I was sorry to hear of his death, and not only because it put a stop to my hopes regarding his cousin."

"The wager is now off?" I supposed.

"It was a d___d stupid bet in the first place. Blame late night drinking at the Hunt Rally. Now, if you have finished your interrogation, I need to get back to my regime. I may no longer be playing for a chance at Miss Lessup's hand, but that doesn't mean I don't want to grind Presterwick, Cordwainer, and Druden-Smythe into the dirt!"

۩

Holmes interviewing William Cordwainer in the tea pavilion:

"Can you account for your whereabouts yesterday morning, Mr Cordwainer?"

"Yesterday? I spent the better part of it changing trains to get up here in time for the events tomorrow. If you pressed me for a timetable then I'd say I left London about 11 o'clock. Before that time? When poor Max was murdered? I left my town lodgings about 9 a.m. and picked up some supplies before heading out to Much Wenlock. Before that? Late breakfast, old boy. Have to keep my strength up for the competition, you know. Faint heart never won fair lady."

"Never," I agreed, from an experience of women on three separate continents. "How proficient are you at tossing an assegai?"

"The Zulu Contest? Not my thing, old chap. I am a pacifist by doctrine. I believe that we should have evolved beyond savagery and the use of force by now. I will not take up arms for any reason, even for a sporting match."

"You have never held arms?"

"Not since I came to my convictions, nearly two years ago now."

"You have tossed an assegai before that," Holmes suggested.

"Before I was enlightened, yes. Not since."

"Describe, if you please, the circumstances of your coming to know Miss Lessup and the origin of the rivalry between her admirers."

"Oh, that's a proper tangle," Cordwainer confided in us, speaking rapidly and eagerly. "I suppose Maxwell was the common denominator between all of us, before Guinev... Miss Lessup. Max and Simon were school pals. He met Charlie Wheaton through the Hunt, and he introduced her to his cousin there. I believe he'd encountered Captain Druden-Smythe playing cards in a London club, and made him known to the rest of us, including his cousin. I became friends with Max through our participation in the last two Olympiads; we had a friendly rivalry, and he invited me to his home several times, which is where I met Guinev... Miss Lessup."

"There was a wager," I prompted him.

"Oh, yes. That. Barbaric, isn't it, that four men should make such a pact in the nineteenth century? We were all in our cups, of course, when we spoke our oaths. It wasn't like me at all."

"Who suggested the contest?" Holmes wanted to know.

"I'm not actually sure," Cordwainer frowned. "It just came up as we were asserting our affections for Gu... Miss Lessup."

Holmes was adept at reading men, and he had certainly caught the reservation in his interviewee every time he spoke of Corcoran's cousin. "Your affections for Miss Lessup have changed? Cooled?"

"No. No, why would they?"

"You blink and look away when you speak of her. You have been accustomed to using her Christian name and now amend it to a more formal title once more. Your body language changes as you discuss her, your spine stiffening and your fingers becoming more rigid. Moreover..."

"All right! All right! I confess that I am... *less* keen on winning the lady than I have previously been. She is... not entirely what I hope for in a wife."

"You will need to explain that," I told him.

"Best not. Enough harm has been done already."

I remembered that Wheaton had called Cordwainer a gossip. "What have you heard or said that might cause harm?"

Cordwainer shook his head, but Holmes is persistent. "A man has died, Cordwainer. I intend to discover the reason for it and the man responsible. If you are the person of conscience that you claim to be, a despiser of violence, then you will assist me in my discovery."

"In confidence, then," the pacifist demanded. "You see... I have good reason to believe that Miss Lessup's... her purity may have been compromised. I would not wish a wife whose purity had been... compromised."

"On what do you base this assertion?"

"I was told it, by the man who had compromised her. He boasted of it to me, to prove his triumph over her virtue and the futility of my further pursuit. 'You're too late, old fellow. I've been there first.' And other vile things."

"Who was this Lothario, and why did you believe him?" I asked.

"I have said enough. I will not further soil Guin... Miss Lessup's reputation by naming her seducer."

"And to whom did you impart this information before?" Holmes asked coldly.

Cordwainer blanched. "You have to understand. I was upset. Very upset. I blurted the truth out without thinking. Sometimes I do that, speaking before I take consideration of…"

"To whom did you speak of it?"

"Well… when I heard of it, earlier this week… there is a drinks tent here, of course, a sort of makeshift bar, open for those of us who came early to practice, and I had been at it rather hard. I was somewhat in my cups when I encountered Captain Druden-Smythe and… mentioned what I had learned."

Was that another black mark against the "bounder" officer, by way of a possible motive? "You believed Simon Presterwick to have made Miss Lessup his mistress? And you told Druden-Smythe about it?"

"I did not say Presterwick," Cordwainer insisted. "To you, I mean."

"But you did to him," Holmes followed the gossip's convoluted statement to its logical conclusion. "When was this?"

"Last weekend. During the prizegiving for the children's three-legged race."

"And what was Druden-Smythe's reaction."

"He called me a fool and told me to shut up. Then he walked away."

My estimation of the officer notched up a fraction.

Holmes asked whom else Cordwainer might have spoken to about this matter. "I spoke about it to Miss Lessup's brother, Talbot, but he laughed in my face. I thought of telling Max, but I did not see him between last week-end and the time of his demise. I… I shall not discuss this further!"

Then Cordwainer was called away to take his turn at the vaulting pole, leaving us with more complications but few answers.

♪

Holmes interviewing Presterwick again, as he arrived at the stables:

"I am not employing you to grub about in my affairs, Holmes. But since you ask, yes, I told some lies to that prig Cordwainer. Haven't you heard that all's fair in love and war? I knew that any rumour about Guinevere's unchasitity would send Cordwainer scurrying to clutch his Bible and put him out of the running. There is, of course, no truth to any story of her infidelity. She is quite perfect."

"And yet you blackened her name," I accused.

"I made a few hints to a prissy eccentric. The rest of the imputation was his. What does that say about his own supposed purity of mind and body, eh? Nor did I send him running off to get drunk on half a pint of shandy ale and blab his secrets to his rival in love."

"You knew about him speaking with Druden-Smythe?"

"Of course. The fellow thundered round to confront me about it. He was halfway to challenging me to a duel before I laughed him out of it and told him it was all nonsense."

"You did not mention this in your previous account."

"Well, by then I was feeling rather sheepish about the fib I'd told. It was unworthy of me and of Gwen. I could hardly repeat it to you as a particular reason why Druden-Smythe might want to see me dead. Poor Max! I told you I felt responsible. Now you know the full reason why."

⁂

Captain Miles Druden-Smythe had not arrived at Linden Field to practice for the coming contests like his rivals. A telegram from Lestrade explained the reason.

"The Inspector has arrested him," Holmes revealed to me.

He handed over the latest wire that had been sent from the Post Office. Lestrade had simply written "DRUDEN-SMYTHE ALIBI BROKEN + STOP + ARRESTED THIS MORNING BAILED THIS AFTERNOON + STOP + WHAT NOW? + STOP + LESTRADE

"Bailed?" I asked. "Why would Druden-Smythe be released from custody with a murder charge against him?"

"The judge must have felt that Lestrade's case was very weak; which indeed it is. There is no evidence to place Druden-Smythe at the scene of the crime. A competent defence barrister would eviscerate any prosecution."

"But if Druden-Smythe's alibi was false, something offered by his cronies to protect him as they have before, then surely that makes him the foremost suspect? He was the prize-winning spear-thrower. He had just been told of Presterwick's supposed corruption of Miss Lessup, and he had every reason to believe that the man in Presterwick's cycling singlet on Presterwick's bicycle was actually is bitter enemy."

"Indeed," Holmes agreed. "And yet there are aspects of this case that are yet to be uncovered."

He returned the runner-boy with a brief reply to Lestrade. + WHO PAID BAIL? + STOP + HOLMES

That accomplished, he turned suddenly and stalked away. "Come Watson! Our enquiries proceed!"

We spent the rest of the day watching more preparations being made for the grand opening, while the preliminary trials and eliminations took place across the field. There were many schoolchildren present, evidently being brought from across the county for the educational experience, and Miss Lessup awarded a prize to the writer of the best essay.[17]

That evening Holmes and I were put up at the Lessup estate, technically the property of Miss Guinevere's overseas brother but presently the home of the two younger Lessup siblings.

"You will not be competing in the Games tomorrow?" I asked Mr Talbot Lessup over the dinner table.

"Catch me breaking my neck on one of those bicycles!" Miss Lessup's brother replied. He drew another snort of brandy; it was not his first.

"Talbot is not of an athletic mind," our hostess warned us.

"I don't mind watching other men make fools of themselves falling off horses or dropping heaving-stones on their feet," Talbot assured us. "I have little desire to try it for myself."

"You are an artist," Holmes observed of him. "You prefer watercolour to oils. Some of your work adorns the walls of this house."

"How did…?" Talbot inspected his fingernails and cuffs, his top pocket, and then the placement of framed pictures around the dining room. "And you are the detective that Simon Presterwick has engaged to solve the murder of our cousin," he replied. "Any luck yet?"

"A number of distinctive features in events and evidence suggest a solution," Holmes assured him. "However, I prefer not to vocalise my theories before I can adduce proof."

"Mr Holmes is evidently quite the sleuth-hound," Miss Lessup instructed her brother. "Simon asked around about him before engaging his services. He recently proved that a lady in the Scottish Borderlands was not killed by a lighting strike as everyone believed but was in fact done away with by

---

17   Writing contests are still held at the Much Wenlock Games today; see http://www.wenlock-olympian-society.org.uk/creative/

"And yet there are aspects of this case that are yet to be uncovered."

murder,[18] and he was involved in the capture of a notorious fellow named Stevens who had evidently killed several people most gruesomely. He is known as the detective's detective, to whom other refer when their cases grow too difficult."

"Holmes has some extraordinary capacities," I agreed, but seeing my friend was uncomfortable with the direction of conversation I asked Talbot, "Have you entered your artwork into the Games' arts competition, then?"

The young man shook his head. "I do not believe that art should be competitive. That is not what it's for. Besides, the Games Committee has a taste for landscapes with horses, or sentimental portraits of innocent-faced urchins, or still-life fruitbowls."[19] He snorted. "They prefer their models to be clad."

"And Talbot prefers his models otherwise," Miss Lessup twitted her sibling.

Talbot refused to rise to the bait. "The human form is the best way to convey mood and theme. The unclad human body, transgressive as it can be in our modern age, requiring some historic motif to legitimise it for prurient viewers, is the ideal way to deliver the message of the artwork."

"And in this way he convinces young ladies to remove their garments for him."

Talbot lifted his drink and saluted her. "My sister is ever convinced that I am a wastrel and a roué. Her suitors come and disapprove of me, tell her that when they are wed they will help her to take her disreputable brother 'in hand'. I assure you that they will not."

"You do not have a high opinion of Miss Lessup's admirers?" I sensed.

"Let's say that I'm glad that Presterwick excused himself from dinner here tonight, but not as glad as I am that Cordwainer, Druden-Smythe, and Wheaton were never invited."

"Talbot!" Miss Lessup chided her brother.

"Simon Presterwick was to be present with us?" Holmes verified.

"He chose a last-minute practice," Miss Lessup answered. "Simon is a more frequent visitor than the others, since he has known us since we were

18   This may be a reference to "the Death of Mrs Stewart, of Lauder" that Watson mentions in "The Adventure of the Empty House" (1903, collected in *The Return of Sherlock Holmes*). Curiously, the historic Tollbooth in Lauder, Berwickshire, is recorded as being hit on 18th July 1793 when a "ball of fire struck the steeple above the Tollbooth, [that] did considerable damage".

19   Actually, the art competitions had been discontinued by this time since the Games were aimed at amateurs and many of the art entries had been from professional painters.

all children. For that reason, though, he is wont to cancel his engagements at table as casually as a family member."

"He thinks himself already half-wed to Gwen," Talbot objected. "He commands the servants as if he was part of the household. I know they have remarked it. But he is at least able to hold good conversation at dinner. All Druden-Smythe will talk about is sports, and Wheaton about military campaigns. I don't care how many days it took them to trudge through the swamps of such-a-place, or of their problems with lice and dysentery. Not through the soup course."

"And Mr Cordwainer?" I enquired, fascinated by Talbot's excoriation of the suitors.

"Bible passages and pacifist tracts and the most narrow-minded liberalism one could possibly contradict oneself with. He certainly disapproves of my art. I should show him the 'Guinevere and Lancelot' painting I did with Gwen posing as her namesake. He'd probably die of apoplexy, choking on his own sermon."

Miss Lessup blushed charmingly. "It is a watercolour-and-chalk of the queen receiving the knight into her boudoir," she explained to us. "Guinevere is clad in but her golden hair as she reaches to her lover, who has broken the bars at her window to come to her. It is quite tasteful, but I confess that we do not display it on the walls."[20]

I remembered Cordwainer's puritan response to Presterwick's imputations about Miss Lessup and had to agree that he might not have approved of her modelling.

I was surprised when Holmes took an interest. "Who posed for Lancelot?"

Miss Lessup's mischievous mouth-quirk vanished abruptly. Her eyes

---

20   Sir Thomas Malory's *Le Morte D'Arthur* Book XIX covers the story of Sir Meliagrant's kidnap of Queen Guinevere, and of Sir Lancelot's one-man rescue of her. The night after her rescue, while Guinevere sleeps in the bedroom where she had been formerly imprisoned, with several wounded Knights of the Round Table slumbering in an outer chamber, Lancelot climbs the walls of the tower and tears away the window-bars to lie with her for the first time (Chapter VI). His bloodied hands leave marks on her bedclothes which lead to charges of her infidelity with the injured knights beyond her door. Lancelot defends her honour in a duel since those charges are untrue; her actual infidelity goes undiscovered.

Malory's version of this story is drawn from several earlier sources, starting with the early 12th-century Latin *Life of Gildas* by Caradoc of Llancarfan, then as the central plot in Chrétien de Troyes' *Lancelot, the Knight of the Cart*. Many other variants of Meliagrant's name appear in all of the versions. Lancelot coming to Guinevere in her prison tower was a popular theme for medieval and Renaissance art and images of their liaison were in vogue right to the end of the Victorian era; see Wilhelm List's erotically-charged picture at https://en.wikipedia.org/wiki/File:Ritter-und-Dame_(Sir_Lancelot_und_Guinevere)_Wilhelm_List_52x35cm.png watered with tears. "It was Maxwell, of course. Who else could it be?"

We completed our repast in careful and respectful silence.

❧

The Olympian Games began with a grand procession. A huge brass band led the parade through the town, with bearers carrying flags and banners, followed by a march of children drilled in lockstep, and then a show of carts from local tradesmen. There was a much larger crowd than I had expected; several thousand strong, cheering and waving streamers.

Holmes and I had a good view of the march-past, perched at a window-sill of the Corn Exchange, though we had to jostle for elbow-room with other guests of the Committee and sponsors who had met the costs of the celebration.

After the drilling boys and girls came the civic dignitaries, not only from the town but from across the county and beyond. Several wore sashes depicting the colours of foreign nations they represented; observers were sent from other parts of the world which were interested in the Olympian ideal and might wish to encourage similar events in their own countries. There was even talk of reviving an international competition in Athens.

Then came the contestants, some riding, many afoot, a few even balancing precariously on those dangerous two-wheeled high cycles. These sportsmen received huge approval from the gathered audience, who cheered and huzzahed as they swaggered past. I recognised Presterwick atop a splendid bay, and some way apart from him was Cordwainer. They paid no attention to each other.

Many of the men were common labourers. Several of the events were especially aimed at the lower classes and were evidently highly contested by their participants. Other groups wore matching uniforms, the drill teams and gymnastics troupes who would compete in units; a few demonstrated their athletic skills by cartwheeling and hand-walking, playing to the crowd.

There were other players and judges yet to march past us, but Holmes touched my shoulder and led me away from our vantage spot. "There are fifty-one contestants entered for the various riding events," he told me, "and fifty-one men on horseback down there in column."

"You mean that Captain Druden-Smythe is amongst them?"

"He received his parole on bail. He is at liberty to come here and take part in the Games."

"You want to find him, interview him."

"Indeed I do. He is the bewhiskered fellow on the rangy bay at the furthermost side of the troop."

"How…?"

"His military bearing, the habit of leaning loose in the saddle adopted by all soldiers who have campaigned in the more hot and humid parts of Africa, the cavalry strapping on his mount, and the way he keeps stealing vicious glances at Simon Presterwick in front of him," Holmes mentioned casually. "We shall move to the assembly field and catch him while the speeches are being made."

"Should we not try to find Inspector Lestrade?" The Scotland Yard man had arrived in Much Wenlock that morning to attempt his own enquiries.

"Lestrade may amuse himself. He has already had his interview with the notorious Captain. Let us see how we fare."

We skirted the route of the procession, dodging through the waiting spectators to find vantage at Linden Field, where the parade would terminate with the singing of Olympic hymns and the Games would be declared open. The assembly square was adjacent to the racetrack and athletics area where the main events would be held. A line of tents we had seen erected and furnished yesterday were already populated with the volunteers, staff, and vendors who would operate them.

It took ten minutes for the procession to catch up with us. The band assumed position to one side as marshals directed the various members of the column to their assigned places. Dr Brooke led the important guests onto a raised platform where they could see and be seen.

Holmes neatly intercepted Captain Druden-Smythe as he entered the field. "A word, if you please," he asked the soldier.

"Who the devil are you?" Druden-Smythe demanded of him. "Can't you see I'm busy?"

"I see that you are a worried man. You have come here under a shadow, and you fear that the Committee might hear of it and decide you are unfit to compete. You have slept poorly and you are wearing yesterday's borrowed shirt and collar. I am Sherlock Holmes, engaged to make enquiries into the death of Maxwell Corcoran. It would be best if you found the time to talk with me."

The angry rider realised that he was trapped. "After the opening, then," he conceded. "At the further corner of the refreshment tent. But I want to hear this ceremony." Evidently the Games mattered quite a lot to him.

Holmes and I retreated to the rendezvous location and listened to the guest speaker's opening speech. He alluded to the classical origins of the Olympic tradition, but reminded his audience that it was British endeavour that built a wholesome society for the future. Another very important person rose to offer a prayer. The band played the national anthem, with choral accompaniment. A third distinguished guest declared the Olympiad open.

Druden-Smythe passed his horse off to a stable-hand and attended his promised meeting with us. "I suppose you want to ask more pointless questions about my whereabouts yesterday."

"Your alibi is broken," I warned the champion assegai-thrower. "Your card-playing comrades could not remember the hands they played whilst they were supposed to be warranting that you were not murdering Max Corcoran."

Druden-Smythe snorted in frustration. "I suppose you have come to arrest me again. Anything to keep me from my victory!"

Holmes regarded the competitor with close attention. "You had best answer my enquiries with exactitude. Your freedom and your life may depend upon it."

"What's the point? The evidence is damning. False—but damning."

"You claim innocence still?" I challenged Druden-Smythe.

"I *am* innocent. Of that. I'll admit that it was I who kept watch on Presterwick as he cycled his circuit. He in turn had taken the trouble to time my ride as he prepared for the Gimcrack Race."

"You were only gaining intelligence on a sporting rival, is that it?"

"What's sauce for the goose is sauce for the gander. If Presterwick was to seek advantage like that, why not me? The wager is substantial enough. Oh, I don't mean the initiative to court Gwen. There's also a matter of a hundred guineas between us. For that I intend to go all out for victory. The filly Miss Lessup is a nice little bonus prize."

"There is a financial stake as well as a romantic one," Holmes understood. "This in no way clears you from the suspicious circumstances of Corcoran's demise."

"I wasn't in that grove, dash it!" Druden-Smythe protested. "I told that policeman and I'm telling you. I saw the cyclist—I thought it was Presterwick at first—and I watched him as I had three other days, timing his progress until he went behind the trees by the Ponds. I was puzzled on Sunday when he didn't come out the other side of the treeline."

"You went to check?"

"No. I had to pick a different line of sight at Whitsun. Some wretched dog ran wild, even knocking Corcoran off his bike. It was prancing all over Parliament Hill, its owner chasing after. I had to shift position downslope, which meant I couldn't even see what I could usually spy from my customary hide. When I lost view of that the cyclist and couldn't spot him again I headed off back to barracks. I have my own training regime, you know."

"You said that you thought it was Presterwick 'at first'," I prompted.

"That last day? Yes, until I saw his technique. Presterwick is a very good bike rider, d__n his eyes. Corcoran can cycle too, but not so well as that. His time was slower. I imagine the dratted dog didn't help."

"It was your assegai that killed him," Holmes reminded Druden-Smythe.

"The devil you say it was! I can't see how it's possible. I have six lance-gays from Africa, three here in my lodgings, three at barracks for practice there. The three with me are all present. I don't see how anyone could break into Aldershot Garrison and steal one of the others. But they must have. There's no other answer."

"Except that you used one yourself," I suggested.

"Really? Why would I use my own easily-traceable weapon to kill a fellow I had no quarrel with? Even if I had thought the cyclist to be Presterwick, why go after him in such a ridiculous manner? If I want a man dead I'll call him out in a duel, law be d_____d, and I'll finish him too!"

Holmes inclined his head slightly in acknowledgement of the point. "You had reason to believe from Mr Cordwainer that Mr Presterwick had been improper with Miss Lessup."

Druden-Smythe snorted. "Temperancer prudes shouldn't down strong brews when they're shocked and heartsick! Yes, I heard Cordwainer's bleating accusation. And I admit, I jollied him along a little by pretending outrage, just to see how worked up I could get the little worm—which was quite a lot as it turned out. Great fun! But really, I expect that Presterwick was doing the same to our little pacifist as I was, seeing if he could get him to put up a fight after all. Scaring a rival off with some crude boasts and a bit of bluff."

"You did not believe the accusations?" I queried. "It did not spur you to plot a bizarre revenge upon Miss Lessup's traducer?"

The soldier snorted. "You've seen Guinevere Lessup? *I'd* traduce her if I got the chance, and I expect Presterwick has had a go as well. For looks like that, and a fortune to boot, who cares is she's a little soiled? A girl with a bit of experience can be a jolly thing, what? I doubt she dallied with Simon Presterwick, because she's got taste, but if she did then it just means there's hope for me to make a pass."

I did not like hearing a young lady discussed in those terms and told Druden-Smythe as much. He sneered at me and turned to go, but then returned to add, "Look, I've had my legal fellow onto this arrest charge. He pointed out to the Beak[21] that there's not a scrap of evidence places me at the scene of the crime. Someone might well have stolen my assegai to incriminate me, either to get me out of the Games or away from the delicious Guinevere altogether by seeing me hang. But there's not enough proof to hang a dog, and that's why I'm here today as a free man—and I'm going to win my wagers too, just watch me!"

Having said his piece he cut us dead and returned to the festivities.

⚓

"Druden-Smythe, here?" Lestrade objected when we found the inspector wandering the showground. "The impudence of that man. Where is he? I need to interview him again."

I indicated that the officer was probably about to begin the Gimcrack Race, that endearingly authentic summary of a cavalry officer's field life. "I gather that he's favourite to win, ahead of Presterwick and Wheaton."

The Inspector's brows rose. "Really? Then why...?" He took a breath. "Holmes asked me to discover who had posted bail for Druden-Smythe, given that the man was ear-deep in debt and didn't have two crowns to rub together. Well, those same brother-officers who offered him a false alibi came forward with the money. But you'll never guess who gave *them* the hundred guineas on promise of anonymity!"

He looked at Holmes triumphantly, then was disappointed when Holmes told him. "It was Simon Presterwick."

Lestrade's jaw dropped. "How did...? How could you *possibly* know that? Why would Druden-Smythe's rival release him to beat him in the very contest they both strove at so hard?"

"After dinner last night, Miss Lessup's brother spoke of the unofficial betting odds for the events today. It offered some interesting data."

I tried to recall what Talbot had told us. "Druden-Smythe was tipped for the Gimcrack Race, not surprisingly given his cavalry experience. If he was not participating, then Wheaton was the next-favourite. Presterwick is the odds-on favourite for the Cycling. Cordwainer is expected to take the medal for Pole Jumping now that Corcoran is out of the running."

"What about the Zulu Contest?" Lestrade reasoned. "Surely

---

21   Slang for 'magistrate', the judge who heard Druden-Smythe's bail appeal.

Druden-Smythe would be champion there, his second win."

"Druden-Smythe is only ranked third in the Spear Throwing book this year," I reported. "And the Tilting is anybody's guess, though Presterwick has the odds by a narrow margin."

"Therein lies the interest," Holmes told Lestrade and I. "If Corcoran had not died, then the odds suggested that Presterwick would take the Cycling, Druden-Smythe the Gimcrack, and Wheaton the Horseback Wrestling. Corcoran himself would have been favourite for the Pole-Leaping, and any of these men except Cordwainer might have triumphed in the Tilting."

"Meaning all but Cordwainer would have one medal, and the result of their private contest for Miss Lessup would depend on the outcome of a deciding Tent-Pegging match."

"Indeed, Watson. But with Corcoran scratched from the card, Cordwainer became favourite for the Pole Leaping, and I believe took those laurels about a half-hour ago. Had Druden-Smythe been unable to compete because he was in police charge, the favourite for the Gimcrack would have been Wheaton."

"So then Wheaton would have two medals to his credit before the Tilting began. But if Presterwick arranged for Druden-Smythe to compete, and the Captain won as was expected, then all four of Miss Lessup's suitors might have one victory apiece."

Holmes nodded. "And if none of them triumphed in the highly-contested Tilting then their wager came down to Tent-Pegging between the four of them."

Talbot Lessup had not indicated what kind of odds we might expect at that endeavour. A contest of lance skill between professional military horsemen and experienced hunt riders would be hard to predict.

"So Presterwick was being clever when he paid for his enemy's release," Lestrade understood.

"He is an ingenious gentleman," Holmes observed.

A great cry rose from the crowd by the dressage paddock. Captain Druden-Smythe had won the Gimcrack Race.

There was not much to do while the day's contests continued. Holmes and I took a light lunch at the refreshment tent and chatted with Talbot Lessup as we consumed our cheese and pickle.

The main events so far had played out as the book-keepers had predicted,

"So Presterwick was being clever when he paid for his enemy's release."

except for one upset.

"Here's to Mr Sabin of Coventry!" Lessup toasted with his hip-flask, already cheerful despite the hour. "What a setback for the ambitions of Simon Presterwick!"

Just before the midday break in events the aforementioned cyclist from Coventry had defied the odds and pedalled to triumph in the Three-Mile Bicycle Race.[22] This must have seriously thwarted Holmes's client's results mathematics. Presterwick must now triumph in the Tilting to stay in the competition for the fair Guinevere Lessup. I confess that I was hoping he would not.

"You do not approve of an alliance between your sister and Mr Presterwick," Holmes noted to Talbot.

"He is a clinger-on," the artist answered, his opinions perhaps made freer by his flask. "Always has been, since he was a snotty schoolboy battening onto Simon for the holidays. Father working in India, you see, and nowhere else to go between terms, I suppose. But I could tolerate him, up to his recent slanders of Gwen."

"What he said to deter Mr Cordwainer's suit," I recognised. "Cordwainer also approached you."

"Ah, you've already heard about that. Yes, the prig Cordwainer came to see me, day before poor Simon died. Expected me to shoot Presterwick or something. I told him to go put his head in a bucket."

"You did not believe him."

"Of course not. But when that fellow gets a bee in his bonnet he just won't shut up about it. He'd already appealed to Druden-Smythe and Wheaton about it. Told him to call Presterwick to order and punch him on the snoot, but that's not Cordwainer's style. Violence, you see. Expect he wanted me to give Simon a serious ticking-off and cut off his access to my sister. Maybe shut her in a tower as if we were actually in Camelot. Said he would write to my brother in Canada about my lack of care for Gwen. I offered him a stamp. Oik."

"Did you hear from Druden-Smythe or Wheaton?" Holmes asked.

"No. Both probably have more common sense. Charlie Wheaton did visit Gwen unannounced about that time, so maybe he just asked her about it directly."

"How might your sister have reacted to hearing of the allegation?"

Talbot shrugged. "Well, Gwen can have a temper. She wouldn't faint, but she might throw things. At Simon, hopefully. But she hasn't, so maybe <u>Wheaton didn't</u> mention it after all. He wasn't with her for long."

22   Mr T. Sabin went on to win the contest in the 1878 Games also.

"What day was this?"

"Saturday last."

He finished his sandwich and rose to go. "Hope you can find who did for Max, Mr Holmes. He was a lovely man, a gentleman and a sportsman, and he didn't deserve a spear in the back."

∾ℓ∾

Charlie Wheaton was wrestling on horseback. The objective was to grapple an opponent from his seat. First man to touch the ground lost.

Miss Lessup was watching the contest, a semi-final, and Bill Cordwainer was in attendance to her. Evidently the scepticism of everyone to whom he had reported her supposed corruption had convinced him that he had been duped. Certainly the young lady herself looked like the very flower of innocence, though pale in her mourning weeds for her cousin.

"Congratulations on your triumph in the Pole Leaping, Mr Cordwainer," Holmes told Miss Lessup's companion, after we had lifted our hats to her.

"Thank you," he replied, then glanced at Miss Lessup and added, "Of course, it was a bittersweet victory given that poor Max would probably have taken the medal had he not... had he been..." His gallant attempt at tribute collapsed to incoherence. He was not a natural at courtship.

"I believe these would have been Max's Games," Miss Lessup told us sadly. "He had trained so hard, improved so much since last time."

"He was very talented," Cordwainer toadied.

"He *was*," the young lady agreed. She clapped as Wheaton dragged his opponent from his saddle and dropped him to the turf, winning his place in the final, but her mind was elsewhere. "Max disagreed with this contest you set up about me, Bill. He said it was unseemly."

Cordwainer flushed, unhappy at the criticism. "We never intended any discourtesy, Guinevere. It was a... a foolish thing agreed when we were not... not at our best. If it offends you then let all idea of it be put away forever."

"As I have said, it is not for me to determine which gentlemen come to pay me court. Despite my name I am not some medieval damsel who stands as prize for some tourney victor. If you or any of my callers elect to withdraw from association with me then that is your business between you. I have promised nothing on that matter. Nothing."

"Of course not. I never intended..."

Holmes interrupted the struggling swain. "You also contested in the bowling match, I believe," he mentioned to Cordwainer.

"I came fourth, alas."

"Might you have about your person a cricket ball? And may I borrow it?"

Cordwainer was caught out by the enquiry and request, but owned that he had such an item and loaned it to my friend. I knew better than to ask Holmes his purposes in front of others.

There was more movement in the yard. The crowds cheered as Wheaton and his last opponent took to the field and paraded round before engaging.

"I will be convening a small meeting shortly," Holmes told Miss Lessup and Cordwainer. "It concerns the death of Maxwell Corcoran and the circumstances behind it. Dr Brookes has been kind enough to lend Inspector Lestrade the administration booth for the occasion. There should be time for our conversation before the Tilting competition begins."

Miss Lessup looked uncomfortable. "Who shall be present?"

"The relevant participants in the contest," Holmes answered gnomically.

We paused to see Wheaton engage his adversary. Miss Lessup watched intently. Cordwainer watched her, unhappy at the attention with which she followed his rival.

After a hard and thrilling match, Charlie Wheaton managed to unseat the opposition. There was a resounding cheer and applause from the audience, though Miss Lessup's clap was polite rather than wholehearted. Wheaton raised his hands in acknowledgement of the accolades.

As the judge came out to formally announce the winner, Holmes called out to the victorious horseman, "Wheaton! Catch!"

He tossed the cricket ball high at Wheaton, and the mounted man stretched up by reflex and captured it in his right hand.

"Tell me, Watson," Holmes asked me in quiet tones. "Does that motion betray a man whose arm was permanently damaged by enemy fire?"

I had to own that it did not.

❧

"What is all this about?" Presterwick demanded as we all assembled in the privacy of the administration booth. "Some of us have to prepare for the final event, you know!"

"You engaged me to uncover certain truths," Holmes answered him. "Now some truths shall be revealed."

In addition to our irritated client, Inspector Lestrade had gathered Miss Lessup and her brother, Miles Druden-Smythe, Charlie Wheaton, and Bill

Cordwainer. Few of them were happy to be there.

"Mr Holmes has made some observations and wishes to impart his views," Lestrade explained to the others. "It is best in my experience to allow him to have his say."

"So long as it's quick," Druden-Smythe demanded, impatiently.

Holmes gathered the attention of the room and made his explanations. "Let us begin with the evidence; that is, the imprints on the ground at Hampstead Heath. There were fourteen divots where practice shots had turned up the turf. If the spear-thrower had had access to three assegais would there not have been a number of gouges divisible by three? Might we venture that the assailant had but a single spear to try out?"

Wheaton was unimpressed. "It might well be coincidence, miscounting, mere supposition."

"Next we come to how different participants came to knowledge of certain events. How did Druden-Smythe know to position himself to spy on Presterwick cycling on the Heath? Answer: he bribed Presterwick's domestic staff to watch their master's comings and goings—just as Presterwick had slipped cash to learn of Druden-Smythe's comings and goings. But it was former Captain Charlie Wheaton who had the access and familiarity with Aldershot barracks to easily pass through camp security to avail himself of Druden-Smythe's locker. He had stayed there before his pensioning out and his old batman knew the right sentries to bribe."

"That's an outrageous charge!" Wheaton thundered, rising to his feet.

"Sit down!" barked Holmes. "Next we come to who told what to whom. That begins with Presterwick's slur on Miss Lessup to Cordwainer, who in turn passed on the allegation to her other suitors and to her own brother. Of these, it was Wheaton who approached Miss Lessup directly to seek veracity, and it is from him that she learned of the challenge to her reputation."

"Ungentlemanly and unwarranted!" Wheaton persisted.

"Gwen, you have to believe that this was a joke—a lark!" Simon Presterwick assured the pale-faced young woman, but she turned away from him.

Cordwainer looked unhappy and guilty. He would not meet Miss Lessup's glare.

"Mr Cordwainer repeated what he had heard from Mr Presterwick," Holmes carried on inexorably, as he did when he was unravelling the facts. "He even went so far as to threaten a letter to Miss Lessup's older brother in Canada. He *did* pen a letter to Miss Lessup's cousin, the protective Maxwell Corcoran."

Guinevere Lessup looked up in surprise; this was news to her.

"The letter never reached him," Holmes revealed, "It went to his Shropshire address and he was already in London with Presterwick. But Presterwick certainly suspected that Cordwainer had penned such a missive."

"And I retrieved the post at Mr Holmes's advice this afternoon," Lestrade informed the room.

"Presterwick now had a serious problem," Holmes went on. "His passionate pursuit of Miss Lessup would certainly be harmed by her discovery of his deceit. Moreover, according to his servants, Mr Presterwick received a visit from Captain Druden-Smythe at his Golder's Hill home on Saturday. The two shared an angry exchange behind closed doors. From what the domestics could hear the two not only accused each other of mutual spying, but Druden-Smythe threatened Presterwick with a duel for his slandering of the lady. Far from being sanguine about Presterwick's imprecations, Druden-Smythe was furious."

"I was and am," the Captain maintained. "I didn't mention it to the Inspector because he didn't need any more reason to accuse me of murder."

"The objective of the argument was not to spur you to murder," Holmes told him. "It was to make it appear you were the murderer."

"Then who...?" I gasped.

"There was another, less noted unpleasant conversation before that," Holmes suggested. "Was there not, Miss Lessup?"

"I... I don't know what you mean," the young lady gasped.

"You heard of Presterwick's slander from Wheaton on Saturday night. Wheaton had already travelled to London and back earlier that day—the ticket office attendant at Shrewsbury knows him from his frequent journeys for his horse-trading business. I can trace his route to and from a meeting with Presterwick. Mr Wheaton, did you too confront Presterwick about his behaviour to Miss Lessup, before taking the matter to her?"

"I did," Wheaton confirmed. "The bounder tried to bluff it out and then to laugh it off. I told Gwen as much."

Presterwick flinched again. "Gwen..."

"That was when Miss Lessup decided to live up to her namesake," declared Holmes. "She gave Charlie Wheaton a quest. She sent him to kill Simon Presterwick."

"What?" Talbot Lessup asked, confused and surprised. "Why?"

Presterwick gave up any pretence. He threw his hands up. "Because it was true. Everything I said to Cordwainer—true!"

Miss Lessup buried her head into her hands and burst to tears.

She shrugged off her brother and made her confession. "It's true!" she agreed. "Not just about Simon and me… but that I sent Charlie to kill him. I promised Charlie my hand if he would avenge my honour. But he killed Max instead!"

Wheaton half-rose from his seat again, then slumped hopelessly.

"You faked a greater injury than you really took," I surmised of the discharged veteran, disgusted. "You got out of hard service in the army and came home without disgrace, a wounded hero rather than a fellow who had become shy of enemy fire. But you are more than able to hurl a spear. And you had experience of lance-work in the hills of Burma."

"Your manservant gave you a false alibi for Sunday morning," Holmes revealed. "You took the last train back to London on Saturday and took the overnight post train to Aldershot. Lestrade will be able to trace the banknote with which you purchased your tickets. You returned to London on the early milk train and hired a Hansom to Hampstead. My young Irregulars have located the cabbie who recognised your description, 'a sporting cove with a soldier's walk, perhaps heading out for some Whitsun river-fishing'. A short walk and you were all set for murder—the wrong murder."

"What point denying it now?" Wheaton agreed, staring disconcertedly at Miss Lessup. "It is all done. She gave me a task and I bungled it beyond redemption. There is nothing left for me now but the long drop."[23]

"*You* stole my assegai," Druden-Smythe accused the man. "You tried to have me swing for it!"

"There is some more," Holmes told us. "You see, Mr Presterwick likes plots. He had several problems and decided they could be made to form one solution."

"Holmes, that's enough from you," Presterwick interrupted curtly. "As your employer, I…"

"You will be silent!" Holmes thundered at the cad, and such was the expression on his countenance that Presterwick shied away and complied. "You determined to use your enemies against each other. Druden-Smythe looked to challenge you to a duel, else give you the drubbing of a lifetime. When your friend Corcoran received word from Cordwainer, you would be done in Shropshire. Your romancing of Miss Lessup had gone awry. So you provoked Wheaton to a murderous jealous rage, so that he determined you must die. But you also put into his head that he might set the blame on

---

23   That is, the gallows execution.

his other rival, the unworthy Druden-Smythe. Your watchers told you how he had acquired the assegai late on Saturday night, while its owner was in the stews of Highgate. So you told Simon Corcoran about the mysterious watcher on Parliament Hill and asked him to play decoy on Whitsuntide."

"Presterwick was never on Hampstead Heath that Sunday," I realised. "Had he been seeking his mysterious watcher he would have been at Boadicea's Mound, might have encountered that exuberant dog, would have seen Druden-Smythe flushed from his usual hide and been seen by him. Instead he wanted to be well clear. He set up all and simply kept away."

Miss Lessup looked up from her weeping with red, angry eyes. "You took my revenge and used it to murder Max!"

"I never even touched a spear," Presterwick assured her.

"You never needed to," Holmes replied. "You eliminated all your rivals with nothing but words."

"It still makes you an accessory to murder, Mr Presterwick," Inspector Lestrade assured the viper.

"There is a little more yet," Talbot Lessup added regretfully. "It might as well all come out. Max… he loved you, Gwen. He pitied you, yapped after by these curs, gambled between them like a bauble toy. Maxwell intended to enter the Games and beat them all. The Pole-Vaulting was his to take. The Tilting too. Maybe even a third, the Cricket Ball Toss or the Rope-Climbing. But he didn't intend to win them to win you. He intended to win them to *save* you from these unworthy matches." He drained the last of his flask. "That is what you have lost, Guinevere. I am sorry."

Lestrade was sorry too, but he had a duty to perform. "It so happens that I must place Mr Wheaton, Mr Presterwick, and Miss Lessup under arrest for murder or conspiracy, and let a court sort it out. There's evidence aplenty now, for which I thank Mr Presterwick for bringing Sherlock Holmes into the matter."

"Damn you!" Presterwick told the policeman. "And damn Holmes. Damn you all!"

Miss Lessup moved swiftly then. Holmes intercepted her before she sank the dagger she had previously concealed to use on Wheaton into Presterwick's heart, but he took the blade into his upper chest, which was bad and bloody enough.

I was able to stanch the wound in the nearby and excellent medical tent, despite my better judgement. Presterwick's pectoralis major muscle was badly sliced, so his sporting days were over, but he lived to get some exercise in a prison yard.

And thus another Guinevere's love life ended in tragedy and destruction, and nobody was happy.

Who then won the Nike medal and the laurel wreath for the Tilting contest, you wonder? In the absence of some of the favourite competitors, the prize went to Dr John H. Watson.

THE END

THE GAMES
ARE AFOOT

I.A. Watson reveals forgotten Olympian secrets

In 1850, according to Mr W.S. Baring-Gould in his seminal biography of Sherlock Holmes,[24] Siger Holmes was resident as Squire of Mycroft in the North Riding of Yorkshire, with his wife Violet and two young sons, Sherringford and Mycroft. They were four years off completing their family with a third son, whom they would give an ancient Anglo-Saxon name meaning "Fair one" or "Shining": Sherlock.

That same year, concerned to promote sport for public health and well-being, the Wenlock Agricultural Reading Society formed an 'Olympian Class' "for the promotion of the moral, physical and intellectual improvement of the inhabitants of the town and neighbourhood of Wenlock and especially of the working classes, by the encouragement of outdoor recreation, and by the award of prizes annually at public meetings for skill in athletic exercise and proficiency in intellectual and industrial attainments." The Reading Society's secretary and driving force was local benefactor Dr William Penny Brookes, who oversaw the first Games in October of that year. Events included cricket, football, athletics, and quoits.[25]

In 1870, the sixteen-year-old William Sherlock Scott Holmes was accompanying his parents on a second bohemian tour of Europe, having departed to St Malo, Brittany in September 1868 and reached the Basque Pyrenees town of Pau that October. To 'toughen' Holmes, his father was teaching

---

24   Now usually published as *Sherlock Holmes of Baker Street*, ISBN-10: 051703817X, ISBN-13: 978-0517038178

25   This antecedent of the modern Olympic Games was cited in the British Olympic Association's successful bid to host the 2012 Games, along with a much earlier "Cotswold Olimpick Games" held annually near Chipping Campden between 1612 and 1642. Much Wenlock's role in Olympic history was acknowledged at those 2012 Games by naming one of the Games' mascots Wenlock. The odd answer to the trivia question "What was the most-visited British tourist destination outside London in 2012?" is remarkably "The small Shropshire town of Much Wenlock".

Special mention for Olympic forebears should also go to Revolutionary France's L'Olympiade de la République festival held annually from 1796 to 1798, and Olympic games in Ramlösa and Stockholm, Sweden in 1843.

him boxing, and he had been entered into the exclusive fencing salon of Maître Alphonse Bencin. Meanwhile, thirteen-year-old John H Watson had been sent to boarding school at Wellington College, Hampshire, and was perhaps considering a career in medicine or the military.

Unfortunately, Baring-Gould neglected to reveal his documentary sources for those parts of Holmes's life that were not included in the Canon of accounts prepared by Dr Watson and literary agent Doyle, and so much of the information regarding Holmes and Watson's junior years remains unverified.[26]

What can be more certain is that on 16th July 1870 the French Parliament voted for war on Prussia. French forces were on German soil by 1st August. The German Army under Otto von Bismarck turned out to be significantly better trained, better led, better equipped with modern technology, and more numerous than the invaders. The conflict went badly for France, with battle losses at the Siege of Metz and at Sedan culminating in the capture of Emperor Napoleon III and then Paris itself. The clash tipped the balance of power in the Continent to Bismarck's favour. France was again the loser in the hardball politics of middle Europe.

That same year, Pierre de Frédy, fourth child of Baron Charles Louis de Frédy, Baron de Coubertin, and Marie–Marcelle Gigault de Crisenoy, turned seven. As an adult, inheriting as Baron Coubertin, he became an influential philosopher, writer, and French leader, who attributed France's grievous military losses against Germany to his nation's lack of physical fitness and to lack of the moral and mental disciplines that were engendered by sport and exercise. He corresponded with and visited Dr Arnold, the headmaster of Rugby School made famous in *Tom Brown's Schooldays*, to see how a regime of healthy activities bred boys who grew to build the still-expanding British Empire.[27]

And somewhere along the way, Coubertin received a letter from Dr William Penny Brookes. Brookes's Shropshire Olympian Games had already become a great success, replicated in several other countries across

---

26   In other words, *caveat lector*. I.A Watson follows many other modern Holmes writers in generally adhering to the Baring-Gould timeline, but shies away from verifying some of the biographer's less likely theories about Watson's Australian upbringing, Moriarty being Holmes's boyhood mathematics tutor, and Inspector Althelney Jones being Jack the Ripper.

27   Coubertin recorded his conclusions in his book *L'Education en Angleterre* (Paris, 1888), which praises the British system.

the world.[28] After long cordial correspondence, Penny Brookes[29] invited Baron Coubertin to view the 1890 Games. This was around the time that Holmes was addressing the cases of Morgan, the Poisoner, Merridew of Abominable Memory, and the disappearance of champion racehorse Silver Blaze.[30] Since Coubertin was unable to get away for the scheduled Shropshire event, Brooks kindly arranged another Games for the Baron to see later the same year.

Coubertin was impressed. He wrote, "The Wenlock people alone have preserved and followed the true Olympian traditions." He and Brooks discussed the possibility of setting up an international Olympic revival in Athens.

In 1894, Watson discovered that Baker Street was no longer unoccupied and that his great friend Holmes had not perished over the Reichenbach Falls.[31] He subsequently sold his Kensington medical practice and returned to share lodging with Holmes. The reunited duo uncovered the Repulsive Story of the Red Leech and the Terrible Death of Crosby the Banker, addressed the Addleton Tragedy and the Singular Contents of the Ancient British Barrow, tracked and arrested Huret, the Boulevard Assassin, and tackled The Famous Mortimer-Smith Succession Case, the Shocking Affair of the Dutch Streamer *Friesland*, and the Adventure of the Golden Pince-Nez.[32]

---

28   In lauding Brookes for his role in reviving the Olympic spirit, one must not overlook the importance of figures like Greek-Romanian philanthropist Evangelos Zappas, who funded a Greek and Ottoman Olympiad in 1859 and restored the ancient Panathenaic Stadium in Athens to host it.

29   Like Arthur Conan Doyle, William Penny Brookes was often referred to by his middle and last name together.

30   Holmes investigates the vanished racehorse in "Silver Blaze" (1892, collected in *The Memoirs of Sherlock Holmes*). Morgan and Merridew are mentioned in passing in "The Adventure of the Empty House". I.A Watson's retrieval of the affair of "The Abominable Merridew" appears in *Sherlock Holmes, Consulting Detective* volume 5 (2013) and *Sherlock Holmes Mysteries* volume 1 (2015).
I.A. Watson has further uncovered additional Holmes casework for 1890 in "Dead Man's Manuscript", "The Problem of the Western Mail", "The Last Deposit", "The Lucky Leprechaun", "The Woman Who Collected Queen Victoria", and "The Lady on the Ledge", in *Consulting Detective* volumes 1, 2, 2, 3, 13, and 15 respectively, collected in the *Sherlock Holmes Mysteries* compilations.

31   "The Adventure of the Empty House".

32   "The Adventure of the Golden Pince-Nez" (1904) was collected in *The Return of Sherlock Holmes*. All the other cases are mentioned in that story, save for Friesland, which

Meanwhile, Baron Coubertin assembled the first Olympic Congress to discuss the possibility of an international Olympiad. Dr Brooks was unable to attend due to ill-health and advanced age, being then 85 years old, but he was listed as an honorary member of the committee; he died in December the following year.

The first modern international Olympic Games took place in Athens in 1896. Holmesian scholars refer to this as "the lost year", for no Canon stories cover the period from November 1895 ("The Adventure of the Bruce Partington Plans" in *His Last Bow*) to October 1896 ("The Adventure of the Veiled Lodger" in *The Case-Book of Sherlock Holmes*), so there is no reason why Holmes and Watson may not have attended the event. If so, much of it might have been familiar to them; the International Olympic Committee borrowed many of the forms that Brooks had revived for his Much Wenlock Games—the opening pageant of flags and competitors, the Nike medallion showing Winged Victory, and the crown of olive leaves presented to the winner.

All of which is to memorialise the founding of Olympian Games in a spirit of cordial competition and a celebration of sport, arts, and crafts. There is no doubt that the world owes a debt to Dr Brooks. I hope that dropping a murder-mystery on an otherwise happy occasion does not offend or otherwise mar a sterling tradition.

IW
March 2021
Aiming for gold.

۔لی

I.A. WATSON is a veteran of the *Sherlock Holmes Consulting Detective* series, having previously provided stories for eighteen previous volumes, plus the novel *Holmes & Houdini*, the anthology *The Incunabulum of Sherlock Holmes*, and the forthcoming *The Paralipomena of Sherlock Holmes*. A full list of these and other Holmesian tales, plus a roster of his twenty additional novels and fifty-plus other anthology stories are available on his website at http://www.chillwater.org.uk/writing/iawatsonhome.htm

---

was referenced in "The Adventure of the Norwood Builder" (1903, also in *The Return of Sherlock Holmes*), and Huret, namedropped in "The Adventure of Wisteria Lodge" (1908, collected in His Last Bow). I.A. Watson uncovered more about the Boulevard Assassin in "The Adventure of the Anarchist's Apprentice" in *Sherlock Holmes Consulting Detective* volume 16 (2020).

Since he tries to make each of his "About the Author" pieces original despite how many he had had to generate, I.A. Watson takes this occasion to confess that he cannot type the word "Consulting" at speed without error, and indeed has set his computer to correct the mistake automatically. Let the Freudians make of this what they wish.

Sherlock Holmes

in

THE RHYMES OF DEATH

by
Ray Lovato

I sit here at my desk writing up our latest adventure that took place last May still in awe of Sherlock Holmes' brilliant unraveling of the rhyming clues and those cryptic verses that accompanied every murder as he strove to save lives in an obtuse game of death. Never has a case so frustrated and perplexed the great detective than that series of maddening clues pointing to a murder yet to be committed, but perhaps tied to the robbery of a book. Only going on snippets of poetry suggesting the identity of the next victim, but just vague enough to construct a puzzle that tested the very wit of Holmes. It was no mere child's game that was being played between the detective and the mysterious killer, but lives hung in the balance with each couplet, each verse. Poems that hinted at the method of death, frustrating him at every turn. Holmes had to figure out the rhymes of death before more people met the grim reaper.

It was a little after ten on a slightly chilly Monday morning when I dropped a small lump of coal onto the embers of the fire in the fireplace and then stirred the ashes with the poker. Holmes was firmly ensconced in his usual easy chair wearing his purple dressing gown and slippers and had just about finished with the Daily Mail, having read the Daily Chronicle which lay discarded on the floor before him. Before I could return to my seat there was a gentle knock on our door.

"Come in Mrs. Hudson," Holmes said, "and please show Inspector Lestrade in."

The door opened slowly and our landlady ushered in the Inspector, bowler in hand.

"How the deuce did you know that Lestrade was at the door?" I inquired.

"Quite simple, old man. I heard the familiar shuffle of his feet on the steps as he ascended the stairs. Then when he reached the landing outside our door, I recognized the muffled cadence of his 'thank you' to Mrs. Hudson. It's always the same."

"Inspector Lestrade, it's so very nice to see you," I said. "May I take your coat and hat?"

"Good morning Dr. Watson. Good morning Mr. Holmes," Lestrade said handing his coat to me.

"Good morning, Inspector," Holmes rejoined. "Please have a seat and warm yourself by the fire."

"Thank you," he replied, stepping over to the grate and bending forward to rub his hands together for several seconds. As he leaned forward, his watch fob slid out of his vest pocket and dangled on its chain.

"I see time is of the essence to you, Lestrade, as it is to me. So please, tell me what is the nature of your business and how may I be of service to Scotland Yard?"

He fumbled slightly catching the swinging watch and placed it securely in his pocket. He moved over to the settee and crossed his legs in a comfortable manner, being in the presence of two men he considered his partners in fighting crime. He straightened the crease in his trouser leg and took out his note pad from his suit pocket.

"It concerns a robbery with a few twists to this tale, gentlemen. It's probably best if I tell it in order to let it unfold in its natural way."

"Quite a good way to tell a story," Holmes said dropping the paper to the floor and crossing his legs, then slightly canting his head. "Please begin."

"Well, this takes place last Saturday evening, the fifteenth, at the New London Literary Depository where they keep all those old books of famous poetry."

"I'm familiar with the building," said I. "They have an exhibit space in the front of the hall for special works of poetry."

"That's right, Doctor. That's where the burglary took place."

"This had better be more than a common burglary, Lestrade, if you are to keep my interest," Holmes said matter of factly.

"Yes, it is. I assure you," he continued. "The best we can reconstruct the crime is that the thief hid in the janitor's closet just inside the exhibit hall for about four hours until the Depository had closed."

"Four hours," said I. "why wait so long?"

"He had to wait until the guard at the front desk went to fetch his lunch," the Inspector continued. "There are two guards on duty; one at the front desk and the other sitting in the back of the exhibit hall. When the first guard, an older gent called Winthrop," he glanced down at his note book, "left to go fetch his lunch, the thief must have left the closet and snuck into the hall. The object of his thievery was a small book of poems by Thomas Moore held in a small glass case in the center of the room."

"Thomas Moore, an Irish poet who fell into favor with British royalty," Holmes said as he uncrossed his legs and then crossed them to the opposite side as he shifted his weight in his chair. He brought his right hand up to his pointy chin and rested one finger along the side of his angular cheek bone. I wasn't sure if he was still interested in Lestrade's story or if boredom was setting in.

"When did you become interested in literature?" I inquired. "It isn't your usual forte."

"Why, Watson, you cut me to the quick. I brushed up on my literary knowledge last winter for that case you wrote up as the Spineless Poet."

"It was the case of the Spineless Book. And, yes, you were quite knowledgeable on your English poets and writers in that instance."

A slight smile crossed his lips.

Lestrade continued, "By a small book of poems I mean it is only ten inches by eight inches and about thirty pages long. Not a big deal if you ask me."

"Please go on," Holmes said with a wave of his hand.

"From the evidence, the thief used a glass cutter and cut a circle big enough for his hand and the book to fit through very quickly as Winthrop only stopped to talk to Tucker for a few minutes, he's the second guard sitting in the back of the hall where Winthrop had to go for his lunch. Here's where the tricky part comes in. The thief set up a candle with a long wick attached to a string of fireworks next to the base of the case and must have run back to the closet. There was no other way out besides a door opposite the second guard which was also locked."

"Fireworks and back to the closet? What was the purpose in all that?" I said.

"Obvious," Holmes said, "to create some type of diversion. He couldn't escape by the front doors as they were still locked also."

"Obvious," I repeated, embarrassed that I had missed the connection.

"The guard, Winthrop, must have just settled in back at the desk when the fireworks went off. Both guards ran to the center of the hall leaving the front desk unattended. The thief then ran from the closet and took the front door key from behind the desk and let himself out," Lestrade concluded.

"Well, that was very uninteresting, Inspector. The simple burglary is solved and unless you have any clues at the scene that you are trying to interpret as to the identity of the thief and that you wish me to examine I have very little interest in this simple heist." Holmes placed both his hands on the chair's arms as if ready to rise.

"But that's not the good part, Mr. Holmes. It's not only what was taken; it's what was left behind. The thief left some notes at the Depository."

The detective's hands immediately shifted to both of his knees and he leaned forward.

"First tell me more about these notes, Lestrade."

"Well, at the Depository, right there on the front desk, was several pieces of paper left behind by the thief. One of them was a poem what said, 'Jack be nimble, Jack be quick. Jack jump over the candle stick.'"

"Interesting," my companion observed, "probably referring to the candle used to light the fireworks."

The Inspector nodded, then continued, "A second one read:

My Days Among the Dead Are Passed
by Sir Walter Scott

My thoughts are with the dead, with them
I live in long past years,
Their virtues love, their faults condemn,
partake their hopes and fears,
And from their lessons seek and find
Instruction with a humble mind.

My hopes are with the dead, anon
my place with them will be,
And I with them shall travel on
through all futurity;
Yet leaving here a name, I trust
that will not perish in the dust. "

"Quite fascinating," Holmes said, "who is concentrating on the dead past and why do they want their name remembered. What lessons did they learn?"

"I couldn't make hide nor hair out of it myself," Lestrade admitted looking up from his notes. "But there is still more."

"Do continue," the detective leaned back and steepled his fingers in front of his chin, his piercing gaze fixed on the Inspector.

"Then there was a paper that said, 'This Is The First One ':

Where supped you yesterday
Dear son mine, noble and wise?
Oh I am dying. Oh him ise!
What supper did she give you
my gentle knight?

An eel that was roasted,
Mother, dear mother.
I am sick at heart,
How sick am I!
An eel that was roasted.
She began to shake,
She began to cry, Lawk a mercy on me,
This is none of I.

Little Bo Peep
She cried wag-tails, come and be killed
for you must be stuffed and my customers filled.
Dilly, dilly, dilly, dilly come to be killed
for you must be stuffed and my customers filled.

Holmes sprung from his chair so suddenly that it even set me aback. He began to pace back and forth before Lestrade and myself, one arm tucked behind his back and his other arm raised to his chin. "Someone who ate something bad. Is stuffed and sick. What does stuffed and sick have to do with our two guards? "

Lestrade flipped his small note pad quickly and looked up at Holmes, hoping to get a word in before the detective continued.

"Mr. Holmes, if it refers to the old guard Winthrop, then it might refer to his death."

"His death?" my friend exclaimed, not expecting that pronouncement any more than I had.

"Yes. When I went to his home Sunday afternoon to ask him some follow up questions, I couldn't find him. His door wasn't locked, so I let myself in. His shoes were beside the door and his jacket was hung up behind the door, so I expected to find him home. But I found his kitchen to be in disarray. A right awful struggle went on there. For a geezer in his sixties, he must have put up a fight; but there was plenty of blood about."

Holmes flung himself into his easy chair, sat with his profile toward Lestrade and rested his chin on his right hand. His eyes were frozen with that far away look of deep concentration that gripped him when his great mind began to take hold of a present conundrum.

The Inspector paused for a moment then continued. "I followed the bloody trail out to his yard in back and the stench was overpowering. The door to his privy was torn off and Winthrop's body was jammed down into the hole with all the shite. All that stuck up was the knees and feet of the man. If he was still alive when he was shoved down the hole it was one hell of a way to die."

"What a way, indeed," the detective said. "But I see no immediate connection between the cryptic poems and this Winthrop's death. And why would the thief go and kill the museum guard after his successful robbery. It makes no sense."

"Well, here's something else that makes no sense to me," Lestrade continued, "There was a note left on the table in the kitchen. Another poem."

"Another poem," said I. "What in blue blazes does this poesy have to do with this ghastly murder?"

"This one," the Inspector said, "says, 'This Is The Second One.'"

London Bridge is broken down.
London Bridge is broken down.
London Bridge is broken down.
My Fair Lady.

Set a man to watch all night.
Watch all night, watch all night.
Set a man to watch all night.
My Fair Lady.

Give him a pipe to smoke all night.
Smoke all night, smoke all night.
Give him a pipe to smoke all night
My Fair Lady."

"This is the second one. A watchman smoking his pipe," my companion said withdrawing his hand from his chin. "Who does that refer to? One of our two guards from the robbery Saturday night? What does this have to do with Winthrop's death? Was Winthrop a smoker? Lestrade, who else knew about the routine of the two guards?"

"The only other person would be the curator, a Mr. Perpence," Lestrade said. "And he has the only other key to the Depository. But he is beyond reproach. Why would he go through all that bother just to steal from the Literary Depository?"

"I would be satisfied if we could find out his movements on that night?" Holmes said. "But the question remains, why kill a guard who can't identify you or is not in any way a threat to you?"

Holmes spun about in his chair. "In the meanwhile, I would appreciate it if you could have copies made of these poems and sent here to Baker
Street. I will visit the Depository and Mr. Winthrop's domicile later to see
if there is anything to be learned there. And, Lestrade, thank you for bringing such an interesting case to me."

"Mr. Holmes, sometimes you've been quite helpful on some of my cases,
and I probably could use a little of your assistance on this one." He tipped
his hat and showed himself to the door.

"I'm always glad to be of service to Scotland Yard, Inspector," Holmes
said with a sly grin as Lestrade left.

"Well, Holmes, it looks like we've got a case of poetry, puzzles and a pur-
loined book," I said quite pleased with my alliteration.

"Not to mention a load of shite," he rejoined. "It looks like it's time to literally get into the mind of a literary thief."

It was around eleven o'clock when Holmes and I left for the Literary
Depository. There we found one Bobbie standing watch at the front desk
along with the usual Depository guard. The Yarder recognized Holmes and
me and ushered us into the exhibit hall. Holmes spent approximately half
an hour examining the broken case where the book of Thomas Moore's
poems had once stood. He spent another fifteen minutes looking over the
front desk and the small closet where the thief purportedly hid.

"Quite ingenious tying the fuse of the fireworks to the wick of the candle.
It gave the thief time to hide back into the closet, where I found signs that
the man indeed had hidden, and giving the guard time to return to the
desk," he said.

When Holmes was finished with the Depository, we took a hansom over
to the modest apartment of Winthrop. The kitchen was in a state of disarray with blood stains still marking the floor. My companion did a thorough
search of the entire house, looking for the smallest of clues that would tell
him anything about the elder guard. He was satisfied that Winthrop was
not a smoker; so the poem about the watchman smoking probably had
nothing to do with him. As far as I could tell, he found nothing else that
tied Winthrop to the crime.

It was out in back where the investigation took a decidedly unpleasant
turn. Next to the damaged privy was a pile of shite that had been removed
from the loo to recover the body of the guard. The stench was over-power-
ing. Any useful clues were totally obliterated by the digging, the pile of waste
and the trampled ground. I was glad that our visit to the scene was short.

After concluding that there was nothing else to be learned there, we returned to Baker Street. There was a package waiting there for us. It contained copies of the poems left at the scene of the crime by the thief. Also included was a note from Lestrade saying that the curator was at home all night doing research on the writings of John Keats. Holmes unwrapped the package and sat at his desk spending the early afternoon reviewing the poems from the scene of the crime.

After an hour he said, "It puzzles me. The seemingly unrelated threads of events and cryptic notes. And there is no apparent reason for the crime against Mr. Winthrop. All very curious."

"And all for a book of poems by Thomas Moore," said I. "If our perpetrator had robbed a jewelry store I could see some profit in his effort, but a book of poems. It's worth something only to an unscrupulous collector. What is the street value in that?" I took out my pipe and reached for the tobacco sitting on the small table next to my chair.

"It's that particular book of poetry that is stuck in the back of my mind, Watson. There is something familiar about it. Something from the far distant past."

"Maybe it's the thief's unusual fascination for the writings of Moore?" I answered. "Or maybe it's because he couldn't be bothered to steal a larger book of poems by Johne Dunne," I said in jest.

"Aha, I have it!" Holmes said clapping his hands together. "It was over a decade and more ago, when you and I first met. There was an attempted theft of that very same book from the Depository. But as I recall, it was foiled and the thief was apprehended."

"I barely remember that, Holmes, but if you say it happened, then it must have. I wonder if there is some connection between the two cases?"

"Perhaps. Or perhaps it is just a coincidence. But either way, we should not overlook the fact. We should get more information about this first attempt." He got up from his chair, crossed the room to his desk, and began to write two notes. When he was finished, he carefully folded them, reached into the pocket of his suit and retrieved two coins.

"I shall return shortly." With that he descended the stairs. I got up from the table and moved to the window where I observed him flag down one of his Irregulars and hand him the notes and the coins. He dispatched the lad and returned to our room.

I was again seated when he entered our parlor. He rubbed his hands together and stepped over to the fire to warm himself.

"There, one letter to Lestrade requesting the file on the case of the original attempt on the theft of the book. One can only hope that Scotland Yard's archives are complete from a decade and a half ago. That should give us the particulars of the attempted theft."

"And the other note?"

"The second note went to my brother, Mycroft. With his political sway, he can most certainly obtain the court transcripts of the case when it went to trial. There might be something useful in those records that could shed some light on this mystery. Until then I shall dedicate the rest of the day to contemplating the particulars of this current case."

ِِِِِِِِِِِِِِِِِِِِِِِ

It was early Tuesday morning, Mrs. Hudson had brought breakfast up to our quarters. Holmes had finished nibbling at his toast and eggs and biscuit and was reclining in his usual chair by the fireplace when I walked into the room. His clay pipe had just been recently lit and a plume of smoke rose from his lips as he bade me good morning.

"Good morning to you," I returned. "I trust you slept well?"

"Hardly a wink. I was preoccupied with our new case."

The next hour was spent in silence as the detective ruminated about the strange case that lay before him. Shortly before nine o'clock, Mrs. Hudson appeared at our door with a package from Scotland Yard. Inspector Lestrade had sent over the case file for the break in and theft of the Thomas Moore book and informed us that there were no further breaks in the case.

"Ah, I see that Scotland Yard is better at record keeping than they are at investigating," my friend said. "How very kind of Lestrade to furnish these old files so promptly." He spent the better part of the morning seated quietly in his chair combing through the file, absorbing every word scribbled down on every page and contemplating the Depository crime and the two strange poems left behind. He hardly noticed when Mrs. Hudson brought up our mid-day meal and placed it on the table. I thanked her with a smile and she left us to our solitary pursuits.

It was approximately one hour later that Holmes stood up and announced, "I've given this problem all the attention that it deserves for today, Watson. I must occupy my mind with another task to cleanse my palate."

"Speaking of your palate, why don't you come over here and try one these delightful sandwiches that Mrs. Hudson has prepared?"

"Oh, I've no time for that. I'll eat something later." I was saddened to hear that familiar refrain.

"Ah, I see that Scotland Yard is better at record keeping than at investigating,"

With that he moved over to his files in the corner of our room by the other window facing the street and pulled the chair out from the small desk. He opened up the first drawer of his card filing system which contained index cards on every crook, scoundrel and scalawag in London that was known to Sherlock Holmes in perfect alphabetical order. He reached over and secured a pencil from the desk and brought the point up to his tongue.

"Abbie Carl Abbott, what a blackard. Now we can discard him. Deceased," and he flipped the card over his shoulder and onto the floor. "Jake Alcott. Still in Black Gate, I believe." He set the card down on the desk and made a notation on it. And so the afternoon went as my companion steadily went through the file of London's underground to keep himself occupied. But I was sure that his mind was in two places, still contemplating the Depository crime while also sorting out his rogue's gallery.

It was around seven when he finished going through the card files. He sprung up, as fresh as a daisy from hours of tedious work and walked over to the table.

"Why is our supper cold?" he demanded.

"That's because it's been sitting here for over an hour," I responded. "Now come and sit down and I'll call Mrs. Hudson and have her warm up some of this delicious stew for you."

"How can I eat stew when I have such a perplexing case on my mind?"

"You'll eat it like any other person. With a spoon and with your napkin in your lap," I said and promptly took the pot down stairs for Mrs. Hudson to warm up for Holmes. I was going to make sure that he was going to eat something.

After eating a hearty bowl of stew, Holmes retired to his chair by the fireplace and was off into that state he gets into when he puts blinders on to the rest of the world and enters his own reality of deep concentration. I knew he would be occupied there the rest of the evening, possibly forsaking sleep itself.

We were both up at the crack of dawn on Wednesday morning. I was glad to see Holmes in his dressing gown, meaning that he had, indeed, gone to bed sometime during the night. After breakfast Holmes took up his seat in his usual chair with a telegram on the table next to him. He was thumbing through the morning paper skimming the articles for anything that might interest him, the case file scattered on the floor before him, his breakfast still untouched, when he looked up and said, "Ah, Inspector Lestrade is here to see us."

I thought that he was completely engrossed with the newspaper, but not even the slightest noise escaped his notice.

"You recognized him by his footsteps," said I.

Mrs. Hudson knocked gently at the door, opened it, and announced the Inspector.

"Thank you, Mrs. Hudson for stating the obvious," Holmes said with a wave of his hand.

She gave him her usual sour look in return and showed Lestrade in.

"Any further news for us today?" my friend said.

"Good morning Mr. Holmes. Dr. Watson. Yes," he replied. "Another murder and another poem."

"We are looking to be making progress on this case," Holmes said. "Thank you for sending over the case file on the original Depository attempted burglary from fifteen years ago. And I received a reply earlier today from my brother Mycroft and now you come in here and say you have another murder. Well, let's have it, man."

"Well, there was a fire about two this morning," the Inspector began taking a seat on the sofa, "on Blockard Lane by the St. Jermaine Episcopal Church. It was a shed out back of a row of apartments. When the fire boys had put the fire out, they found a body. That's why I got called out. When we canvassed the area, we discovered that Mr. Tucker, the guard from the Depository lived in the building. We couldn't account for his whereabouts, so I sent one of my boys into his apartment and he found it in shambles. Mr. Tucker didn't leave it peacefully."

Lestrade shifted his weight on the sofa and stroked his unshaven chin. "It so happens that one of the neighbor ladies that was kind of sweet on Tucker knew that he wore a St. Christopher medal around his neck and carried a small crucifix in his back pocket." Lestrade turned slightly to face me. "Well we got lucky and found the medal and small cross in the burnt flesh of the body. The size of the corpse and what features remained were enough to identify him as Tucker."

"And so," my companion said forcefully, causing the Inspector to turn quickly back to Holmes, "what else can you tell me about the body?"

"It was tied to a chair with ropes as far as we could tell, but the chair and ropes were burned in the fire and spread all over the ground."

"Just like any clues were," Holmes muttered. "What can you tell me about how the fire started?"

"There was a can of kerosene in the corner of the shed that still stood. The Fire Department did a good job of saving the shed. Put the fire out quickly, they did. But it was strange that I noticed that the entire floor of the shed was spread with tobacco."

"Tobacco?" said I.

"Yes, tobacco. Hands full of tobacco that you would stuff into your pipe."

"Is our Mr. Tucker a heavy smoker?" Holmes asked.

"Yes sir. I checked on that with his neighbors straight away. And we found several packets of cigarettes in his place."

"Quite observant, Lestrade. I can see why you're a Chief Inspector," Holmes said.

"What do you make of it?" I asked.

"It's a sign of some kind." my companion replied. "Didn't you say there was another poem involved, Lestrade?"

"Yes. Yes. Constable Hogan found it tacked to the table in Tucker's apartment." He pulled a folded piece of paper out of his suit pocket.

"If you'll be so kind, Watson?"

"Certainly, Holmes," I said taking the paper from Lestrade's out stretched hand.

"There was a man had three sons; Jeffrey, James and Jake.
The one was hanged, the other drowned,
The third was lost and never found.

Barefoot Boy by John Greenleaf Whittier

Blessings on thee, little man,
Barefoot boy with cheeks of tan.
Never on forbidden ground;
Happy if they not sink in
Quick and treacherous sands of sin.
Ah! That thou should know the joy,
Ere it passes, Barefoot Boy.

"Rather cryptic," said I. "Full of drowning and sinking in."

"Rather,' Holmes said. "I see a connection to Tucker's murder and the second clue of London Bridge. The watchman *Set a man to watch all night. Give him a pipe to smoke all night.*' But I still find no sense to the first clue and Winthrop's death in the feces."

"And now we have a third clue to another murder and no idea who the victim might be," I said. "We've run out of Depository guards on duty."

"That's what bothers me," Lestrade said sheepishly.

"Lestrade, if you would be so kind, could you allow Dr. Watson a few moments to make a copy of that latest poem for our file on this case. So I might study it."

"Of course," he replied.

I moved over to our desk in the corner of the room and began to transpose the poem.

Holmes sat there, absently tapping his forefinger to his pointed chin. "One clue could make sense, but what does the first one have to do with the other?"

Lestrade just sat there shaking his head.

"Well, we have a lot to do today, Inspector. I've got to go over the case file from the first attempt to steal the Thomas Moore book. Now, I want to drop into the Depository and reexamine the scene of the crime and speak to the curator, Mr. Perpence. Perhaps he can enlighten us as to who we might be overlooking as to anyone who might have any involvement in this crime besides our two guards. But first, my brother has made appointments for us at Oxford to speak to two prominent professors that he thinks might shed some light on our investigation. A professor of literature and an alienist. Though I can't see how anyone who has invested time in those two unscientific fields of study can be of any help."

"Holmes is doing it just to humor his brother," I said softly to Lestrade.

"Thank you for dropping by, Inspector," Holmes said standing up," I'm sure that you will keep us abreast of any further developments in the case as I will of you."

After Lestrade had left Holmes suggeested, "Why don't we go out for an early lunch and start over to Oxford. After all, we don't want to be late for the learned academicians."

As I grabbed my coat and hat, I knew that this was not going to be a very pleasant visit.

ﷺ

A student whose face we could barely see behind the large stack of books that he was carrying gave us directions to Professor August T. Scott's office. As we walked down the corridors, the musty smell of the halls of the learned institution brought back memories of my own collegiate days. I enjoyed my academic studies. The thrill of discovery. The conquest of the human body. Filling my head with hitherto unknown knowledge. Part of me envied these youths.

Shortly we were at the door of Professor Scott. We knocked and were bade entrance. There behind a very neatly organized desk sat a tall, dark haired gentleman in a tailored suit that showed off his obvious healthy physique. He rose smartly. "Mr. Holmes, Dr. Watson. Mycroft Holmes said you'd be stopping by this afternoon. Please have a seat." He gestured to the two Queen Ann chairs in front of his desk.

"I prefer to stand, if you don't mind," Holmes said.

"Thank you," I replied and took a seat opposite Scott. There was a silence that fell over the room; so I took it upon myself to begin the conversation.

"We are here to ask for your opinion about some poems that were discovered at the scene of a recent theft. Well, one poem was left before a first murder. Then a second poem was left before a second murder. Now we have a third poem and no idea how it might fit into the case or if it refers to a third victim."

"Interesting," Scott said sitting down behind his desk. "How can I be of service?"

"We were wondering what can you tell us about this man? The murderer." Holmes said abruptly.

"What do you mean, Mr. Holmes?"

"I man exactly what I asked. What type of man steals a book of poems and then murders two men who can't possibly identify him or harm him in any way? What type of man leaves nursery rhymes and Sir Walter Scott as clues to his next murder? Is there any logical connection between the poems?"

"I don't know. I haven't seen the poems. I don't know the circumstances of the crime," Scott offered.

"Dr. Watson, would you please be so kind as to fill in the Professor of the particulars of the crime and let him read the poems that you have copied down on your note book."

I began to relate the tale of the burglary, followed by the two murders and the poems connected to each one. Scott read the poems carefully, taking in each line. All the while, Holmes slowly circled the room taking in the copious bound volumes of literary masterpieces that lined the shelves that rose like the Hanging Gardens of Babylon around us. A credenza was lined with neatly placed trophies, awards and photos.

"From what Dr. Watson has told me about the men in this case, I can see no correlation between the poems and their style of death except for the obvious one of the tobacco. But why single out the smoking of that guard?"

"Precisely," I said.

"But the methodical, organized way that he carried out his heist was quite astounding. And to dare to leave clues, no matter how obtuse, almost to dare Scotland Yard to catch him is bold, indeed."

"I rather think it all quite vulgar," Holmes said, placing a plaque from the Royal Shakespeare Literary Society back on the credenza next to a rugby trophy.

"Quite the contrary, Mr. Holmes. From an academic viewpoint, his knowledge of old English nursery rhymes and classical Sir Walter Scott shows certain sophistication."

"There is nothing sophisticated about murder, Mr. Scott. But if you say there is no discernible connection between these rhymes, then we have taken up enough of your time. Come, Watson, we have another appointment to keep. Thank you, Professor Scott for your opinion on our case. It is much appreciated."

I stood and bid the Professor good day and followed Holmes out the door. Once out into the hallway, I had to quick step it to keep a pace with my companion.

"Slow down, Holmes. We have plenty of time to make our next appointment."

"It's not where I'm going, Watson, it's where I'm getting away from. That was a complete waste of my time. The comparative study of poetry. One might as well compare the length of pig's tails. If our visit with this alienist is as wasteful, I must surely thank Mycroft for this goose chase he has suggested."

We traveled down several long corridors and across the Quad to another ivy-covered building to arrive at the office of Professor Phineus Wilford Dardenbury, Dean of Mental Alienation. I found the study of the subconscious mind a fascinating topic. Since the turn of the century, the academicians have been theorizing that the mental aberrations and resulting insanity were caused by heredity, environmental or weak moral nature. And these conditions caused the person to become alienated from oneself. A mental alienation. It is, of course, the most inexact science. But nonetheless, we were about to step into the office of Oxford University's preeminent alienist.

"Good afternoon, gentlemen," Professor Dardenbury said pointing to the two chairs opposite his cluttered desk. The papers and books piled up on top of each other looked like they were about to topple over any second.

"Thank you," I said. "Professor Dardenbury, I'm Dr. Watson. This is Sherlock Holmes."

"Of course you are. I'm Phineus Dardenbury. Please be seated."

"I'd prefer to stand if you don't mind, Professor." Holmes said a matter of factly.

"Of course. Of course. What can I do for you gentlemen?"

"Well, we're here to seek your insight into the mental state of a man who can commit a simple burglary and then two gruesome murders and leave clues at the scene of the crimes pointing to his next victims."

"Very interesting," Dardenbury said.

I proceeded to tell him the entire story of the theft and the grisly murders and let him read the rhymes. When this was accomplished he sat back in his chair and stared at the ceiling for several minutes.

Holmes meanwhile had occupied himself by surveying the room just as he had in Professor Scott's office. Only here he found bookshelves jammed with books pushed sideways, and piled on top of one another on each shelve. There was a stack of framed diplomas and awards in a pile resting on top of one another on the credenza against the back wall. The pictures that hung on the wall behind Dardenbury's desk were all askew. Even I noticed this. How the man could function amidst such chaos was beyond me.

Finally the Professor fixed his eyes on me and began, "Your man is an egotist of the first order. He has a very elevated opinion of himself. He believes that the poems that he leaves for the police are a clever way of living on the edge by giving the police the false hope of capturing him with subtle clues to his next method of dealing death. But the clues are so purposely vague as to be useless because he doesn't want to be caught. The use of poems are a construct of his mind."

"Yet the second clue about smoking all night was a reference to how our Mr. Tucker was found murdered," Holmes called out.

"Yes, that is so. But the other poems are jumbled. He is showing signs of being removed from reality."

"Do go on, Professor," I implored him.

"His actions suggest to me that he is suffering from a severe case of obsessive compulsive disease."

"Obsessive compulsive disease? What might that be?"

"As simply as I can put it, it is the obsessive concern with one's own sins and the compulsive performance of religious devotion to right them. Things must be done in a certain order under pain of sin. There is a compulsion to complete them in a preordained order. First he must leave a poem. Then he must kill the person who the poem refers to. Then he leaves another poem and must kill the person that poem refers to. Then another in that strict sequence. No variation. He is compelled to do it in that order."

"So the poems are linked to the murders," Holmes said.

"Yes, I might amend my thinking to agree with that. But the rationale of the meaning of the poems seems to have no context to what you have given me of your case."

"Well, I might have more context later when I review a transcript on a similar case," my companion said. "Thank you, Professor Dardenbury for your time. We must be going. We'll show ourselves out."

With that, Holmes spun and made his way out of the room with me fast on his tail.

"That man could not reach four if he had two horses and two horses standing right in front of him," I said.

"I'm not so sure of that, Watson. Although his suppositions had no solid scientific basis or facts behind them, they were based on deductions reached at by careful reasoning and logical progression. Perhaps with scientific study and confirmation, the study of the criminal psyche might someday be a useful tool in criminal detection."

I wasn't sure if Holmes was making a jest or was serious about his last comment.

"Let's grab a cab and stop at the Depository and see the curator before we call it a day, shall we?"

After a slow ride through afternoon traffic, we arrived at the Book Depository. The Bobbie was still stationed at the front entrance along with the Depository guard as we went in and Holmes went down the hallway to the right directly to the curator's office. We met the curator in the doorway as he was exiting his office.

"Good afternoon, Mr. Holmes."

"Good afternoon, Mr. Perpence," Holmes tipped his hat. "Dr. Watson and I were wondering if you could spare us a few moments of your time and answer a few questions about the theft last week?"

"But of course. Please come in. Have a seat."

We followed him into his comfortable office and sat across from his desk. Holmes settled in quickly and crossed his legs. It was the first time that I had noticed how tall the curator was. He was almost as tall as Holmes with a sturdy physique.

"I see by the books on your shelf behind you that you are a connoisseur of Old English poetry and classical texts. Is that your specialty?" Holmes began.

"Yes, that was my specialty. The simplicity yet the force behind the words has always fascinated me."

"Mr. Perpence, Are there any other guards employed by you during the week?" my friend asked.

"Of course. On Thursday and Friday evening we rotate Harrington, Borring and Rachett on those two nights. It's hard to hold on to good part time help."

"So Winthrop and Tucker worked the rest of the week together?"

"Worked together. Why those two worked together for over seventeen years. But I could hardly say they worked. Winthrop was around fifty when he started. Tucker was only thirty. Laziest pair of wastrels I've ever seen."

"Why would you say that?" Holmes inquired.

"Winthrop was too old for the job now. And Tucker just sat on his duff and read the paper in the back and barely made his appointed rounds. I would have sacked the both of them if they weren't so well entrenched and liked by the board of directors. I've only been in this job for about five years and don't have enough clout to do them in."

Perpence stopped and sat back in his chair realizing that what he said might have sounded a little harsh under the circumstances.

"I mean, God rest their souls. But it didn't take me long to find good replacements."

"And there are only two sets of keys to the front door?" Holmes continued.

"Yes. One stays with me everywhere I go. The other used to hang behind the front desk. Now it stays on the person of the front desk guard as long as he's on duty."

Holmes uncrossed his legs, ready to end the conversation.

"Mr. Holmes, may I ask you have you made any headway on deciphering those rhyming clues that were left behind?"

"Not really. One seems to fit one of the murders. But the other two still hang uncertain."

"It's a wicked web we choose when we start to leave clues," Perpence said.

"Thank you, Mr. Perpence," Holmes said raising an eyebrow. "You've been quite generous with your time." As he got up, he paused and motioned to the back wall. "I see you've got a pair of old boxing gloves there on your

"Mr. Holmes, have you made any headway on those rhyming clues?"

table. Do you indulge?"

"Yes," he smiled, "once upon a time. Back at Durham University. I was quite a good heavy weight in my day. Do you box, Mr. Holmes?"

"Only when I have too," came his reply.

It was a while later when we were back at Baker Street and seated in our familiar chairs. Holmes had just finished starting a small fire and I had gathered the evening editions of the paper. Waiting for us was a packet from Mycroft with the transcript of the trial of the first robbery of the Thomas Moore book.

"After dinner I shall spend the rest of the evening reviewing the case file from Scotland Yard on the recent heist last Saturday and the transcript of the trial of the first successful heist supplied by my dear brother."

After a delicious meal, I settled down with the evening paper and Holmes filled his lap with the thick folder of the trial of a Mr. Philip Morton, unsuccessful burglar of the Thomas Moore tome some fifteen years ago. On the table next to him was the file from Lestrade containing the particulars of the last actions of Mr. Winthrop and Mr. Tucker. At ten I said good night to Holmes who didn't raise his head to acknowledge me. I knew he was lost in the minutia of court reports and would be for most of the night.

☙

It was half past ten on Thursday morning before I joined Holmes in our sitting room having rolled over and taken another forty winks upon waking early this morning. The breakfast prepared by Mrs. Hudson was still covered and warm waiting on the table; mine to be eaten, Holmes' apparently to be ignored. After wishing my friend a good morning and he reciprocating, I sat down and began to eat.

Holmes, sitting in his purple dressing gown surrounded by a flurry of papers scattered on the floor around him, looked up and said, "You know, Watson, this is the second time this week that the Pearson's Market has been held up and no arrest has been made. Scotland Yard should simply pick up Bartholomew Eldridge and Snuffy Caniffer and the entire affair would be solved in an hour."

"Quite so, Holmes. Why don't you inform Inspector Lestrade the next time you see him."

I reached over and poured myself a cup of coffee, still warm enough to send a wisp of steam into the air.

"It seems that you've been working all night on the two files before you.

Have you made any headway?"

"Yes, the trial of Mr. Philip Morton, the perpetrator of the heist of the Thomas Moore book some fifteen years ago was quite interesting. It seems that he was foiled by an unfortunate series of circumstances beyond his control that went counter to his careful planning."

"How so?" I asked.

"I shall endeavor to begin at the very beginning. As the testimony bears out at his trial, Philip Morton was a student of literature and poetry having obtained his degree at university who could only get a job teaching secondary school. He did, however, manage to publish three unsuccessful books of his own poetry which bankrupted him. Not only did it make his livelihood more difficult, it also cost him his marriage and his young son, they left him and moved out of the country to France. He had to take on odd jobs along with his teaching duties just to survive. His expenses continued to exceed his income and he turned to a crime to make ends meet."

Holmes spun in his chair to better face me and crossed his legs.

"Apparently, his first foray into crime was only partially successful. He snuck in at night and tried to steal the proceeds of an auction, only to be surprised half way through the attempt. He narrowly escaped with several rare books. Quite ironic, don't you say, Watson?"

"Very," I replied.

"He took the books to a pawn broker and received a small sum and considered that a sign that he should make that his course in thievery. He admitted to breaking into a hardware shop and pilfering a handful of tools and pawning them a week later, but didn't get the same amount as he did for the books. That's when he set his sights on the books in the Literary Depository. He admitted to scoping the Depository out for several weeks coming back at night to peer into the windows to learn the routine of the guards to concoct a fool proof plan. It was very good, too. But the night he put it into motion, unforeseen circumstances came into play."

"How so?" I inquired, taking the last bite of my biscuit and raising my coffee cup to my lips.

"As he tells it, he hid in the front closet, the same as our recent bandit did, and was going to wait until the guard, Winthrop, who was in his late forties at the time, left to get his lunch. Only Winthrop was going and coming back and forth at odd intervals all evening. As it turns out, he was suffering from a bad stomach and had a case of diarrhea. There was no way that he could be away from the front lavatory for any long period of time nor had any appetite for food. That caused Morton to have to estimate when

Winthrop would have gone to get his lunch and carefully crawl along the floor into the large hall to access the Moore book."

I reached across the table and grabbed the coffee pot and picked it up to pour myself another cup of coffee. I held it up in Holmes' direction offering him a cup. He waved his hand.

"If he guessed properly," I said, "then I assume he had the time right when the second guard had gone on his rounds and the coast was clear."

"There you would be wrong. The second guard, our friend Tucker, then a young man of thirty years of age, had abandoned both his post and his patrol duty to step out of the side door, the only other exit from the Depository, to take a smoke. That left poor Mr. Morton with no other exit from the building and stuck cowering in the shadows in the corner."

"But surely he could wait until Tucker was done with his cigarette and then steal the book and make his exit through the side door."

"Absolutely not. For just as Mr. Tucker was extinguishing his smoke, Inspector Bristol came upon him while making his evening rounds and they began a conversation which started with yet more cigarettes."

"Mr. Morton testified that he panicked and saw his window of opportunity closing, so he made the bold move to creep into the exhibit hall and took out his glass cutter and cut a hole in the protective glass encasement. He took the Moore book and wrapped it in cheese cloth and stuffed it into his coat and quickly retreated to his corner once again. From his vantage point he could observe Bristol and Tucker finally finishing their conversation. He said he now feared that Tucker would stroll back through the hall in a different pattern that would bring him right to where he was crouched. So, he decided to make a run for it."

"Good Lord, Holmes, the man is trapped like a rabbit in a bramble."

"Precisely. He made a dash for a window in the back of the hall, smashed it with his elbow, and climbed through it. The noise alerted Bristol who immediately gave chase. They ran two blocks south and turned into High Brook Park with Bristol closing the gap between them. It was then that the book slipped out from Morton's coat and slid to a halt on the grass."

"In the court record, Bristol said that he felt that the book was in a secure position and he was closing in on the suspect, so he continued with the pursuit. It was then that further misfortune struck Mr. Morton as he slipped along the bank of the large pond in the center of the park. He was immediately swallowed up by the thick mud along the shore. As he initially struggled, his shoes became stuck in the mire and were pulled off. The more he struggled, the deeper he was swallowed up in the mud. He was easily captured then. At the end of his trial he was sentenced to twenty years."

"Apparently he got swallowed up by the judicial system," said I. "Isn't twenty years a bit harsh for a robbery?"

"Apparently the Right Honorable Manfred Stanford Peckinbridge didn't think so. He referred to the Monuments and Royal Documents Act in the sentencing because the book was by Thomas Moore."

"I remember that judge, Holmes. A real stickler for heavy sentences in his day."

"Be it as it may, the prosecutor was a Richard Yardley, a familiar name around Old Bailey."

"I've heard of him too. A real hard-nosed barrister. Would go to any length to win his cases," I said over my cup. "There are some similarities between the first robbery and the second robbery, but being so far apart," I shook my head. "Is there any connection with any of the other names involved with the case?"

"None that I could find, Watson. No connection to any of the names involved in our present day case. We have just a string of murders and poems."

"That's a shame. But it was worth a try, Holmes."

"There is a new name that came up in the trial record. A Mr. Samuel Pellitree whose name was mentioned by Constable Bristol, a fence of stolen property specializing in books and documents down on the lower East End. But Bristol said Pellitree had no connection to the case. But, perhaps, he might be a name that we should pay a visit to in our present investigation."

"Sounds like a splendid idea, Holmes," said I, brushing a few crumbs from my moustache with my napkin. "Just let me finish here and we shall be off."

In two hours we were in a cab heading slowly towards the East End, the unsavory part of London, where we would find Mr. Pellitree after availing ourselves of the knowledge of Shinwell Johnson. It only took him less than an hour to learn the location of Pellitree. Mr. Johnson's ability to move freely within the circles of the London underground made him an invaluable asset to Sherlock Holmes. His knowledge and contacts again proved indispensible to Holmes. After serving two terms at Parkhurst, Shinwell decided that staying on the straight and narrow was a safer choice in life. When he met Holmes, this newly reformed criminal struck up a strong friendship with the detective that was mutually beneficial to both parties.

We pulled up to a nondescript small shop nestled between two brownstones. The sign in the window simply read, "Properties". I followed Holmes inside to a dark, dusty space with wall to wall shelves containing all sorts of odds and ends displayed for purchase. Behind a counter in the back of the store sat a wizened older man with more lines in his face than the morning newspaper. Next to him stood s rather tall, stocky fellow with a neck and face that resembled an ox. The phrase for where we presently stood that came to me was a den of thieves.

"Mr. Pellitree, I presume," Holmes said.

"And how would you know that?" came the gruff reply.

"Quite simple because of the monogram on the handkerchief tucked rather smartly in your tweed breast pocket."

Pellitree simply sniffed.

"I'm Sherlock Holmes and I've come to ask you a few questions. I'll get right down to the point. You're a business man. Your business is dealing in stolen property as you so slyly advertise on your storefront. What is your involvement with the stolen Thomas Moore book?"

The hefty thug balled up his fist and almost snorted at Holmes and me, obviously ready to defend the not so sterling reputation of his boss.

"I would think twice before you do something rash, my good fellow. I have three ways to stop you by breaking several small bones and two ways that lead to the fracturing of your skull. So, please give up any idea of an assault on us."

"O'Hare, it's alright," Pellitree said.

The brute stood there in silence. Then he slowly unclenched his fist.

"It's obvious you're not the police," Pellitree said. "The Moore book is worth a small fortune to certain collectors, especially with the notoriety its theft has gained. But, alas, I have not come into contact with it. If you do know who has it, please give them my name and express my interest in the book."

"Thank you for your candor, sir," my companion said. "I'll trouble you no more." And with that, we left.

"Do you believe him, Holmes?" I asked as we rode away in the hansom.

"Yes, I do. When we spoke, his eyes locked into mine. He never looked away. There was no change in the timbre of his voice. No pauses or skips He was telling the truth."

The rest of the ride was filled with small talk as the London traffic was interminably slow. It was past two when we arrived back at Baker Street. Holmes immediately set to reviewing the two files that lay spread out on the floor of our apartment.

"It all sounds so familiar, Watson. Like it's almost the same story. I can't help but think they are somehow related."

"Perhaps one is like a bad relative and won't go away?"

"Or, Watson, they aren't related, but rather one continuous story. We have the connecting thread of Winthrop and Tucker. Both guards were present at both robberies. It's as if the second robbery was a copy of the first one, but with a successful outcome. So why kill the two guards? The difference is that they foiled the first attempt. Is it to punish them for thwarting the first robbery?"

He bolted up from his chair as if he were shot out of a cannon.

"That's it, Watson! It's all about revenge for the first failed attempted robbery. We were looking at the wrong theft. I've been as blind as a mole. Someone is exacting revenge on the personages involved in the heist from fifteen years ago. First there was Winthrop. He was prevented from making his trip to get his lunch by his bad case of diarrhea. His death was arranged by drowning him in pile of his own shite as retribution, preceded by the poem about *'what supper did she give you. An eel that was roasted. Now I'm sick at heart.'*

"Tucker abandoned his rounds by stopping for an extended cigarette break causing Morton to alter his escape plan and go out the window, alerting the constable. Tucker's death was being burnt alive in flames stoked by tobacco. His poem was *'London Bridge. Set a man to watch all night, give him a pipe to smoke all night.'*

"Next was Constable Bristol, who chased down Morton into the muddy banks of the pond where he lost his shoes. Unless I miss the pattern of these murders, Bristol is the one who caught the *'Barefoot Boy with cheeks of tan, never on forbidden ground. Happy if they not sink in, quick and treacherous sands of sin.'*"

Holmes stopped his pacing and pointed his finger at me and said with great certainty, "And the murders happen every other night. Tonight is Thursday. The night the next murder would take place."

Holmes dropped to his knees and began rummaging through the papers strewn on the floor. He caused a blizzard of white sheets before he pulled two pieces out and bolted to his desk where he began frantically writing a series of names on a sheet of paper. When he had finished, he grabbed a few coins from his pocket and rushed down the stairs to the street. I watched from the window as he began waving wildly and one of his Irregulars came dashing to his side. After barking out directions, he deposited several coins in the boy's hand and watched him run off. Satisfied, he once again joined me in our room.

"The lad will get to Scotland Yard in record time, Watson. I'm sure of it. Now we must hurry. We possibly have a life to save. Please bring your pistol," he said as he walked over to the desk and took out his small revolver and checked that it was fully loaded.

"The game is afoot."

It was a short ride north of Baker Street to our destination. On the way there Holmes related our mission.

"The letter I sent to Scotland Yard was to Lestrade instructing him to get his boys to the homes of the persons listed on the paper. They are the names of the people involved in the trial of Philip Morton. Every one of them is in danger from Mr. Morton and his diabolical plan for revenge, if it indeed is Morton carrying out these murders. Morton was sentenced to fifteen years in Black Gate and his time still has three years left on it. So, someone must be carrying out these crimes on his behest. Tomorrow I will devote the day to figuring out just who that might be and why now. But tonight we are setting ourselves to protect retired Inspector Bristol."

"Why Bristol?" I asked.

"Because he was the first name alphabetically on the list of names that I found on the transcript involved with the court case. The names and addresses were listed in the appendix and I sent the others to Lestrade. His men should be rushing now to protect the other participants."

"I just hope that they all live at the same address as they did back then," said I.

"Let's hope so for their sakes, Watson."

The carriage pushed on through the London fog to the address we gave the driver and eventually pulled up to a modest but newer home; a two-story white brick house nestled between others just like it. I paid the driver as Holmes ran to the door and knocked vigorously. There was no answer.

"Perhaps he's already retired to bed," I offered.

"Nonsense. It's only half past seven. It has just turned dark."

"Then perhaps he isn't home."

Holmes reached down and tried the handle. The door slowly swung open.

"Very curious," my friend exclaimed as he stepped inside. He quickly entered with me following closely behind. The parlor light was dim. It was a new electric light. And a stand up lamp was still glowing with the soft luminescence of its flickering bulb in the back kitchen. It would appear that Bristol was home.

"Shhh, do you hear that Watson? The sound of splashing water in the lavatory."

I quickly looked around for the location of the indoor facility. The sound seemed to come from behind a door in the far corner of the house.

"Over there, Holmes," I pointed.

Neither of us was prepared for what we encountered next when we arrived at the loo. There stood a large hooded man in a loose fitting robe standing over Bristol, holding him under the water of his tub that was overflowing with dark, muddy water. Holmes rushed forward, only to receive a severe block to his chest by the big man's shoulder. That sent my companion tumbling back into me, knocking us both to the wet floor. Holmes tried to grab the man's foot, only to be greeted by a boot to his head. The intruder hopped over our fallen bodies and made a run for it out the front door. By the time that Holmes regained his senses, the thug was gone.

"Holmes, are you alright?"

"Yes, I think so." By then, Bristol was sitting up in the tub, spitting the brackish water out.

"What in God's name is going on? Who was that man? Who the hell are you? Untie my hands."

I obliged and while loosening his bonds I noticed that Bristol was fully dressed except for his socks and shoes. Bare Foot Boy, I mused.

After an introduction and wrapping him in his robe, we moved to the kitchen to sit at the table where we found a note folded in half. Holmes picked it up and immediately recognized the handwriting of the murderer. It was another poem.

The Beasts Confession by Jonathon Swift

While others of the learned robe
would break the patience of a Job;
No pleader at the bar could match
his diligence and quick dispatch;
Nor kept a cause, he well may boast,
above a term or two at most.

Pity Poor Barnett by Anonymous

Pity poor Barnett, no longer has his bark.

Doomed by his priest, to be hanged by his clerk.
I pray good sir, weigh right his case.
Hang clerk. Hang clerk. Hang in his place.

"Watson, would you copy this down before we give it to Lestrade."

What followed was an explanation of the circumstances as to how Bristol came to be in his present circumstance. We assured him that he would get protection from Scotland Yard here on out. He was flabbergasted and in disbelief but after fortifying him with several glasses of his own brandy we bade him good night.

We had flagged down a brougham and on our way home I said, "You were correct in your supposition that the next murder was going to be tied in to the chasing of Morton into the water and his losing his shoes. The muddy water was a nice touch."

"Yes, it fit the narrative that the murderer has established."

"And did you notice the size of that hooded scoundrel?"

"I did notice the size of his boot," Holmes replied gingerly touching the side of his head.

"We must get some ice on that as soon as possible," I said. "But his size and the loose fitting robe did little to hide a strong physique. Do you think it might be that O'Hare fellow or possibly Perpence, the curator, because of their size and both their interest in the book?"

"Either one is a likely candidate for the present murders, but do not fit in to my theory of it being tied into the original robbery. If the killer stays with his pattern, there will be no murder tomorrow night. The next one will happen Saturday. We got lucky by our guessing to take Bristol tonight. We can't guard everyone who was involved with the trial forever. There must be another pattern besides the every other night."

"And the poem?" I asked.

"That might make our task a little simpler. I deduce that it refers to a barrister. *'Others of the learned robe. No pleader at the bar. I pray good sir, weigh right his case. Hang clerk. Hang clerk. Hang clerk in his place.'* The prosecutor in Morton's case was Yardley. He must be the next target. And a noose probably awaits him. I'll ask Lestrade to keep watch on the others on the list while you and I take Yardley. And pray that I'm right."

"I deduce that it refers to a barrister. *'Others of the learned robe...'*"

Friday morning brought fresh sunshine into our parlor as I sat reading the Daily Telegraph while waiting for Mrs. Hudson to bring our breakfast up. It amused me on page five to see the police report of yet another burglary at Pearson's Market. Holmes had not yet had time to pass along his information to Lestrade. There was a knock at our door and I quickly jumped up to hold it open so that Mrs. Hudson could gain entry with the toast, jam, soft boiled eggs and applesauce. On her way out she met Holmes coming out of his bedroom.

"Mr. Holmes, you look positively dreadful today," she chirped.

"And you look positively underfoot. Good day, Mrs. Hudson."

She immediately left our presence in a huff.

"Holmes, how is your headache this morning?"

"Dreadful, Doctor. Simply dreadful," he moaned.

"How would you like some more laudanum to ease the pain?"

"Oh, no, Watson. After taking it last night, I had the most disturbing dream. I dreamed I was riding a chestnut stallion under water and there was a bull walrus there trying to play the violin. And he was just awful."

"It sounds like you're back to your own normal self," I said just taking the last drags on my morning cigarette.

He just turned and gave me a wry smile. I could see that even that caused him some measure of pain.

"Did you send the poem to Lestrade?" he asked.

"First thing this morning," I replied.

"Good. Good. I was thinking after I awoke from that ghastly nightmare that I have much more work to do on my theory. I have a pretty good supposition as to who is next but have no idea why. If I could just figure out who is behind these ghastly murders, we can put an end to this madness. If I continue to go by the trial transcript, I have a list of all the people who were involved in the actual trial.

"We start with the guards Winthrop and Tucker. Next there is Constable Bristol. I appears next could be barrister Yardley. But who comes after that? The court clerk? Morton's own defense attorney? The bailiff or the court reporter? Of course, there's the judge; but he's deceased. There were two witnesses who were called to testify that they saw Morton running from the scene. Do we go past the court and include the prison warden? Too many variables. What am I missing?

"Does the killer go back and try to murder Bristol, finish off the job, or does he move on?"

I took a long drag on my cigarette. "It surely is a cacophony of options.

There is no judge to yell order in the court."

"What did you just say, Watson?" Holmes asked excitedly.

"Order in the court," I said.

"Brilliant. That's the pattern," he said clapping his hands together, and then rubbing his head.

"The order in which the clues, the poems, are laid out. First the two Depository guards. Then the constable. Next the barrister. He must move on. He can't go back. It's what that Dardenbury fellow had hypothesized that the killer must do things in order. He can't deviate. He must follow the pattern that he has set for himself. The poems will point us to the next victim. Now we have to figure out who is perpetrating these crimes and why. And when this ache in my head has subsided a little I have many places I must visit today."

"How can I help, Holmes?"

"Watson, you can stop by Scotland Yard and bring Lestrade up to date and have him make sure that he has the updated addresses for all the people on the list I gave him plus the witnesses and the prison warden in case the killer escapes us Saturday night. We might as well be prepared for any eventuality. But I find that highly unlikely. Have him ready to send his men Saturday evening to watch over the same persons he did last night just for good measure. You and I will take Yardley with the Inspector as our back up."

"Are you sure you're well enough to go running around London today?"

"I'm not going to let a little headache stop me when we are so close to identifying our quarry. I feel that we are soon going to put a close to this affair."

I convinced Holmes that a little nourishment would help him recover from his headache and he happily obliged me. It was slightly past nine when he set out on his mission to his many places and I went to Scotland Yard to meet with Inspector Lestrade. It was a brisk May day but the sun was shining brightly. Perhaps Holmes was right; today was going to be the day that we unwrapped the riddle of the poems and the killer behind them.

Holmes didn't return until way after six that evening. Mrs. Hudson was kind enough to hold our dinner until she heard his footsteps on the stairs. The door burst open and he positively sashayed into the room reflecting his ebullient mood.

"Holmes, are you alright?"

"Watson, I'm better than alright. I've had the most productive afternoon than I've had in a long time. Birds are chirping. The sky is blue. Except for the fact that it is getting dark out now. And I should be positively exhausted from all the running around that I've done. But it was all worth it, my friend. All worth it. I have so many facts in my head that I barely contain them all. Let's have some supper while I digest what I've learned today and put the pieces of this puzzle together."

He threw his coat and top hat on the sofa.

"Oh, Mrs. Hudson," he yelled, "Where is our supper?"

After he finished the last spoonful of his custard pudding, he twirled out of his seat and threw himself into his chair next to the fireplace.

"Watson, would you mind starting a small fire while I weigh the evidence that I have collected today." He smiled and put his hand to his chin and closed his eyes. I knew he would be sitting there for hours like that mimicking Rodin's Thinker. I took up the evening paper and started at the front page and began to read every word to pass the time. About ten o'clock I was starting to doze off; so I got up and whispered good night to Holmes who was still deeply engaged. His train of thought must have hit a whistle stop at that moment as he looked up and replied with a "Good night, Watson." With that I was off to bed, leaving the detective to wander the great halls of his magnificent mind.

ﷺ

I didn't enter our sitting room until a little after eight on Saturday morning. I immediately made a fire. I was surprised to find Holmes' chair vacant as I assumed that he would have been up all night. But the door to his bedroom was closed. As was her way, Mrs. Hudson brought our breakfast up when she heard me stirring a floor above her.

I decided not to wait for Holmes and finished my meal and was reading the Daily Telegraph when Holmes made his appearance about half past eight. He still wore that pleased smile on his face.

"Good morning, Holmes," said I. "Is your head any better today?"

"Yes. I feel splendid. Thank you for asking. I slept like a baby. The head ache did start to come back late last night or was it early this morning. So I went to lie down. I slept soundly. Except for a nasty bruise on my sternum, I am as fit as a fiddle."

"That is good to hear. May I ask what good news you came upon yesterday that made you so happy when you returned from your travels?"

"Well, besides a tortuous ride to Black Gate that was made even longer when two carts collided and one horse came up lame and the unfortunate animal had to be put down there in the middle of the street, blocking traffic for a half an hour while they dragged the carcass of the dead beast away." Holmes paused to take a sip of his coffee.

"Yes, it sounds like a very hazardous journey," said I. "Your discoveries?"

"Ah, yes, Watson. My discoveries. I found out that Mr. Philip Morton is dead."

"Good Lord, Holmes, how does that help us?"

"It means, Watson, that he is not responsible for these crimes. At least not directly. He can hardly commit them from the grave. He must have a confederate working for him. A relative, a former cell mate, a lover, someone he perhaps paid with some hidden ill gotten gains that Scotland Yard had not known about?"

Holmes picked up his napkin and availed himself of a piece of toast and jam.

"He died by his own hand, Watson. Suicide after about thirteen years. Hung himself about four weeks ago. The warden said he was quite sick. Didn't have long to live. By the way, it is a new warden. The old one died several years ago, so we can fortunately scratch him off our revenge list."

I shook my head at my friends' choice of words.

"But he did leave something interesting behind. In his belongs there was a poem by Sir Walter Scott. Crumpled up by whoever the reader was."

"Another poem. This time by the original thief who attempted to steal the Moore book." I almost spit my coffee back into my cup.

"Yes. The warden was kind enough to give it to me as it was of no importance to him." Holmes went over to his desk, picked up a piece of paper, brought it back and handed it to me.

"If you'd be so kind."

I read:

My Days Among The Dead Are Passed by Sir Walter Scott

My hopes are with the dead, anon.
My place with them will be,
And I with them shall travel on
Through all futurity;
Yet leave here hope a name, I trust

That will not perish in the dust.

"Why that's the exact first poem that was left at the theft of the Thomas Moore book last Saturday," I exclaimed.

"Yes it is, Watson."

"Who was the note for?" I asked "Who read it and crumpled it up?"

"That I do not know yet. The warden has no knowledge of who claimed the body. I intend to find that out today. Then I spoke with every prison guard to see if they remembered who came to see him in prison lately and none could recall him having any visitors. I went to the Hall of Records and did research on every name on the court transcript list for any connection to Morton and there were none to be found. His wife and child left for France right after his conviction. Two of the witnesses have since died. But I have a trip to the morgue planned for today.

He took another bite of his toast and reached for his eggs.

"Holmes, how can you eat like that knowing you're headed for the morgue with the smell of cadavers awaiting you? It can make even the strongest man a little queasy."

"It's not the dead that bother me, Watson. It's their secrets."

I had neglected my rounds for about a week now; so I spent the rest of my day going about London stopping in to see my usual patients. It was a day spent pleasantly tending to the infirmed or the ones who imagined that they were sickly. I returned at approximately five to find Holmes lying on the sofa with his eyes closed. I didn't know whether to disturb him or let him rest peacefully. My quandary was solved immediately.

"Good evening, Doctor. How was your day?"

"Splendid, Holmes. And yours?"

"Quite illuminating. I began at the morgue where the most salient clue started me on a chase for the eventual answer to our puzzle. Then onto a learned institution, then to Scotland Yard to set up our plan tonight with Lestrade."

"What did you find out, Holmes?"

"I believe that I've solved it. I have found that our criminal is a very crafty mastermind indeed. It has been so well plotted that there really were no clues leading back to him or to be able to accuse him without concrete evidence. It would be a waste of time. Yesterday, I figured out the pattern to his crimes. Today I believe I have identified the criminal himself. He will strike tonight. His target will be the barrister, Yardley. "

"If you know who the murderer is, shouldn't we pick him up now?"

"No, as I said, we only have circumstantial evidence. We must catch him in the act to make it stick. Besides, he's not going anywhere tonight but into our trap."

"Well, who is he then" I asked.

"It's better if I do not say. I'd hate to spoil the surprise for you. It's like if you were to reveal the ending of one of your stories in the Strand magazine in the first chapter until waiting for the proper end where it belongs. But you and Lestrade will learn soon enough. Allow me to see that my theory bears out."

I knew it would be fruitless to press him any further on the matter; so I sat there and finished my breakfast contemplating tonight's events when we would catch our rhyming murderer.

At six o'clock sharp Lestrade pulled up to our house with a Bobbie in tow. We joined him in his brougham and settled in for the cross town ride to Yardley's house. On the way, Holmes laid out his plan for the evening. Lestrade informed him that Yardley reluctantly had agreed to it but not before exclaiming that he didn't care a deuce what Sherlock Holmes wanted. Lestrade said that he then threatened him with that Yardley could do this the way that Mr. Sherlock Holmes suggested or that he could do it Lestrade's way and he could assure the barrister that he wouldn't like his way.

I was quite pleased with Lestrade's forcefulness in the situation in the way that he handled the barrister.

"Well done, Inspector," Holmes said "So, we are all in agreement with the plan?"

Everyone nodded yes. It took approximately a half an hour to reach the home of Yardley. Inspector Lestrade had the key and let Holmes and me in, he and the policeman staying hidden outside. We moved to the large living room where a small fire greeted us. I stoked it and threw two more logs on. Looking around, I chose to take my place behind some heavy brown curtains off to the corner of the room. When I turned around, I had lost sight of Holmes, but I knew he was carrying out his part in the plan.

Within the hour there came a noise coming from the back of the house. Someone jimmying a window, trying to be as silent as he possibly could. The sound of the crackling fire almost disguised the sound if you weren't listening for it. But I was on the alert and picked up the sound immediately.

From my vantage point behind the curtain I saw the large form of the hooded man creeping up on the figure seated in the chair opposite of the fire. He held a noose in his hands. When he stood almost directly overhead of the seated figure I yelled out, "Holmes, behind you!"

The detective immediately sprang to his feet and put his hands up deflecting the attack of his assailant. The noose caught Holmes' left arm encircling his forearm. With that, my companion turned around facing his attacker. The hooded man let loose of the rope with his right hand, gripping it tightly with his left and swung a clumsy overhand right hook to Holmes' head. The blow momentarily stunned the detective. As the thug raised his arm to deliver another blow, Holmes lashed out with his right hand and caught the ruffian with a glancing shot to the side of his head. The villain staggered backwards, pulling Holmes into the chair. Then the detective hit the brute with a looping punch to the left side of his face. It caused the attacker to pause. Holmes regained his balance first, kneeling firmly in the chair, he unleashed a furious right cross to the rogues' nose, shattering it and sending a torrent of blood squirting over both combatants. Enraged, the thug hammered Holmes' shoulder with a heavy downward fist that slammed into the detective's shoulder like a trip hammer. Holmes now had both of his feet firmly planted on the carpet and delivered a devastating right jab to the jaw of his assailant sending them both tumbling to the floor with the chair in between them. His attacker was now unconscious. The fight was finished before I reached the combatants. Holmes was victorious.

"Bloody good show, Holmes."

"I couldn't have done it without your support, old man," he breathed heavily. "Call Lestrade."

"Of course," I replied and took my police whistle out of my coat pocket and summoned the Inspector who was in the house with the policeman in moments standing over the body.

"Of course you'll want to take the hood off of Mr. Scott," Holmes said.

Lestrade reached down and removed the black hood off the unconscious body of August Scott.

"How in blazes did you know that, Holmes," Lestrade said.

"Research and deduction, Inspector. The key was when I paid a visit to the morgue today and inquired as to who claimed the body of Philip Morton after he committed suicide. The name was Scott Morgan, the son who left for France some thirteen years ago with his mother. When I asked the attendant for a description, he described Mr. Scott. In his grief, Mr.

August Scott wrote his real name, Scott Morgan down."

Holmes bent down and removed the noose from Scott's hand. He handed it to Lestrade.

"I then went to Oxford," he continued," where Mr. Scott graduated and checked his academic records. It appears that in his sophomore year of study, a Mr. Scott Morgan changed his name to August T. Scott probably to escape the shame of his father's crimes. But he never lost his fondness for his father over the years. He was about eighteen when his father was incarcerated; but he had already had a love of poetry instilled in him by his father. When his father became ill and died, his filial love took hold and he swore revenge on those who took him away from him. The murders started a few weeks after his father's funeral. He obviously needed time to locate his targets and line up all the means of their deaths."

"But why the murders every other night?" I said.

"I answered that by checking out his schedule. He taught classes all evening every Monday, Wednesday and Friday nights making it impossible for him to get across town and carry out his schemes. That's why the crimes were carried out on Saturdays, Tuesdays, Thursdays, and here again on Saturday night. "

"And the poems. What them about?" Lestrade asked.

"Our friend down there is a man of letters," Holmes said.

"How can a highfalutin man of letters be a killer?" the Inspector said.

"Remember, a doctor was a serial killer, Lestrade," Holmes admonished. Lestrade lowered his head and stroked his chin while the Yarder put the Darby chain cuffs on the prone Scott.

"The man down there," Holmes said, "thought he was smarter than everyone else. The poems were probably in honor of his father. Reminiscent of the poems of his youth perhaps, or the suicide note. But if Scotland Yard couldn't make the connection between the original robbery case and the poem clues, then it was his little joke on the world."

"But he wasn't so smart after all," Lestrade piped in.

"On the contrary," said Holmes," he is very intelligent. He flaunted his supposed superiority from the very start of his murder scheme. He was toying with us when we called on him at Oxford."

"Professor Dardenbury was correct," I said. "He was a very sick man. And a large one."

"Yes, those rugby trophies behind his desk were well deserved, I'm sure," Holmes said.

"Rugby trophies. I missed those," I muttered. "It was strange how we met

Scott right in the beginning of our investigation. Do you think that your brother could have known that he was the killer?"

"I doubt that Mycroft would have kept the identity of a murderer from me in a case. It was a fortuitous accident. But I have no doubt that after you relate the particulars of the action to him that he will take credit for it," Holmes smiled and stepped aside as the Bobbie pulled the groggy Mr. Scott up off the floor and walked him to the door. By now, a police wagon had responded to the policeman's call and was waiting to take the prisoner away.

"Oh, Inspector, you might want to pick up Bart Eldridge and Snuffy Caniffer for the rash of burglaries in Pearson's Market. It's about time that affair is removed from the papers, wouldn't you say?"

The Chief Inspector stood there with his mouth agape doing his best imitation of a statue.

"I'll do that right away, Mr. Holmes," he stammered.

"These murders were indeed heinous, Holmes," I said.

"Yes, revenge is an ugly business. It scars the perpetrator as much as it does the victims."

"Now that this ghastly affair is over, I should choose a title for its composition," I said.

"How about the Rhyming Man?" Lestrade offered regaining his composure.

"Very clever," said I, "the Rhyming Man."

"More like what it led to, the rhymes of death," my friend offered.

"That's brilliant, Holmes. I think when I transcribe this adventure I'll call it the Rhymes of Death."

"Don't you think that's a little over dramatic, old friend?"

"A little exaggeration never hurts, Holmes."

"Am I going to be mentioned in it?" the Inspector asked. "I was very instrumental in solving the case since the very beginning."

"Especially if there is exaggeration, Lestrade. Especially if there is exaggeration," Holmes smiled.

THE END

THE STORY BEHIND THE STORY

Sherlock Holmes is always working with clues and bits and pieces that are left behind after a crime has been perpetrated. I wondered what it would be like for him to have the clues delivered to him prior to the crimes being committed and try to solve the who and the how the next murder would take place. I found it an intriguing premise. The usual characters are involved: Inspector Lestrade, Mycroft Holmes, the Baker Street Irregulars, and Shinwell Johnson. It was nice to visit them once more.

An old book of English nursery rhymes supplied key poems needed for the story. Interestingly enough, Sir Walter Scott had two poems placed in the story, thanks to The Norton Anthology of English Literature, my old college text.

One fun bit of research was delving into the turn of the century psychiatrists or alienists. It was the founding blocks for Freud and Jung. At times, I found a lot of myself in the writings.

The research for the story has revealed many interesting facts which I have jotted down for the further adventures of the world's first Consulting Detective. But that is a tale for another time.

DEDICATION

I am blessed to have Carl Wayne Ensminger as my own personal Victorian historian. From supplying me an 1897 Sears Roebuck catalogue to a Victorian toy catalogue to a map of 1894 London, he is also ready at a moment's notice to research the smallest fact for accuracy.

I would be remiss if I didn't thank my best friend and fellow author Michael A. Black. For over fifty years, his constant encouragement and friendship keeps me going when I begin to falter.

I dedicate this story to my mother, Elaine, who is a wonderful writer and fostered my love for the written word.

Lastly, everything I write is encouraged by the unconditional love from my lovely wife, Susan. She has been the light in every storm, guiding me home to the safety of her arms. I love you.

The Holmes & Watson Novels from Airship 27:

Printed in Great Britain
by Amazon

32563355R00106